VANISHED

By the Author

The House

Vanished

VANISHED

by
Eden Darry

2019

VANISHED
© 2019 By Eden Darry. All Rights Reserved.

ISBN 13: 978-1-63555-437-3

This Trade Paperback Original Is Published By
Bold Strokes Books, Inc.
P.O. Box 249
Valley Falls, NY 12185

First Edition: October 2019

Credits
Editor: Ruth Sternglantz
Production Design: Stacia Seaman
Cover Design by Tammy Seidick

Acknowledgments

Thank you to Ruth Sternglantz for her endless patience and excellent editing. I really landed on my feet with you. Also thank you to Sandy and Radclyffe for agreeing to publish me again.

For Catherine

PART I: THE LIGHT

Chapter One

L oveday Taylor wrestled the back door closed in a game of tug of war with the wind. It had certainly picked up since she'd come home, and weather reports were advising people to stay inside. Hurricane Hilda was about to blow into Southern England from the Atlantic after causing all sorts of damage, first in the Caribbean and then North America.

Loveday and other volunteers from town prepared all day for its arrival—a reluctant welcome wagon. In the afternoon they hoofed sandbags up to the Crane River, known to swell and breach its banks on occasion, sometimes flooding all the way up to the main road.

Loveday's back was sore and her hands chapped from lugging the rough, heavy bags. She would have liked a hot bath and a quiet evening in front of the fire with Claude, her ginger cat. He was the reason she'd opened the bloody door in the first place. He'd bolted through straight away—a pleasant change from his usual MO. Normally he'd stand at the door, sniff the air for a bit, and generally get on her last nerve before he strutted inside, completely ignored her, and headed for his food bowl.

Skinny, dirty, and with dried blood crusted on his torn, lumpy ears, Claude turned up on her doorstep one day and never left. Two years later he had the appearance—and carried the weight—of a healthy, if slightly overindulged, tomcat. Loveday adored him, and in his own stand-offish way, she thought he probably quite liked her too.

She shook some biscuits into his bowl, startled into pouring out near enough the whole box when lightning cracked overhead, followed by a peal of thunder that rattled the window in its frame. Loveday looked down to see Claude watching the storm. His intelligent orange eyes didn't flick to his overflowing bowl even once. He blinked, yawned, stretched, then went to his food, brushing against Loveday's leg on his way past.

Claude was pretty much unflappable, and that was good because Hilda looked like she meant business tonight. As if to prove it, a flurry of rain hurled itself violently at the window, and the wind picked up, howling and tearing through the trees outside. The kitchen lights flickered, dimmed, then went out.

❖

Ellery Jackson was in the veterinary clinic finishing up the last of her paperwork in her office when she was plunged into darkness. Rocky the Jack Russell started to cry and howl before the generator kicked in and the lights came back on. According to the staff, he hated the dark. Ellery knew just how he felt.

She'd sent her staff home early, just about the time the wind began to kick it up a notch and the sky turned a dark and ominous grey. Being alone here, no traffic whizzing past on the road outside—it was normally busy this time of the evening with the commuter traffic—left her feeling uncomfortable. Not that the town was especially lively, but they had a decent high street and a handful of restaurants. Being so close to a motorway meant that more and more people were moving here, attracted by the green landscape and cheap property prices.

The veterinary clinic had been converted from an old barn, and the high ceilings, open-plan layout, and myriad of windows amplified the emptiness. She could easily believe she was the only person left in the world. Except for Rocky the dog.

Ellery swivelled in her office chair and looked out the window. A fork of lightning lit up the night and rain hammered down. Usually she liked a good storm, but this one made her uneasy. Rocky was restless too, and maybe that was it. She had a way of picking up on what animals were feeling—a kind of vague interspecies telepathy, she thought with mild amusement. It had been with her since childhood. It was most likely what made her a good vet, and probably the reason she was eternally single. Ellery always found animals so much easier to deal with than people. Their needs were obvious to her, and they were free from the many layered and messy complexities of human beings.

Like any vet in a semi-rural town, Ellery dealt with a fairly even mixture of domestic pets, like cats and dogs and hamsters, and farm animals. The other day she'd helped an alpaca give birth. Admittedly, most of her farm animals were cows, pigs, sheep, and horses, but Dave Randell had a penchant for the slightly more exotic. Ellery managed to talk him out of adopting a flock of flamingos last year.

Ellery sighed and rubbed her eyes. It was getting late, and if she didn't leave soon, then she never would. Rocky had gone quiet again. She wouldn't leave him here alone for the whole night though. She planned to go home, have dinner, then come back and stay with him. The storm was supposed to be a big one, worse than most of the remnants that usually blew over from the Atlantic. She wouldn't let Rocky deal with it alone.

Ellery stood, stretched out her back, and groaned in pleasure as her spine popped. She'd sat for too long, and her office chair was hard as concrete. Sarah, the head veterinary nurse, kept telling Ellery to buy a new one, but most days she wasn't in it long enough to justify the expense.

She walked back to the cages where they kept the furry patients and smiled as Rocky stood on his back legs, tail wagging like mad, and began to scratch at the bars.

"Hey, boy, how's it going?" she asked softly, kneeling to stroke his head and tickle his chin. Rocky licked her hand and whined, as if to say *I've been better*. His owner—Jill Wood, who ran the local grocer's—brought him in, sobbing her eyes out, after he'd tangled with a wild pony in the forest. Nosy Rocky got a little too close, and the pony kicked out, bruised a couple of ribs, and broke his front leg.

Rocky was most of the way healed, apart from his broken leg which would stay in a cast for a few weeks yet. He would probably be allowed home in the next few days. All in all, Rocky was lucky. "No more making friends with wild ponies, eh, Rock?" Ellery smiled and gave him one last stroke. Rocky chuffed and lay back down in the corner, his intelligent eyes still on her. "I need to get my dinner. Promise I'll come back, though. Okay?" Rocky dropped his head onto his paws and closed his eyes.

Back out in reception, more lightning flashed, ripping the night in two, and Ellery thought it sounded a bit too close for comfort. Thunder rumbled and clapped so loud she thought it might crack the windows which ran along the front of the surgery. They shook and rattled but held firm.

Rain lashed down and the wind howled, kicking up the leaves outside and throwing them against the building. Ellery decided she had left it too late to go home after all. She mentally sorted through the contents of the staff-room fridge and figured it would be biscuits and an overripe banana for dinner. At least there was the generator to power the lights. Outside, the town was dark, and Ellery guessed everyone had lost their power already.

Loveday rummaged around in the kitchen drawer trying to find the torch. "Give me a hand, would you, Claude? I could really use your night vision." Claude ignored her and continued to crunch his biscuits. The loss of light didn't bother him at all.

Finally, she felt something hard and plastic and solid. She moved her hand along its shaft until she located the button. She clicked it on. It emitted a sickly beam of light, and Loveday chastised herself for not replacing the batteries ages ago. She'd kept forgetting about it, one of the mundane tasks she would do tomorrow, then tomorrow, until it slipped her mind altogether. Well, that would teach her, wouldn't it? Loveday sighed and went into the living room. She knew she had some tea lights around here somewhere—it was just a case of finding the bloody things with this crappy light.

After what seemed like an eternity, Loveday found them in a box on the shelf with a lighter—thank God—and proceeded to light several and place them around the living room. She kept back four or five because they were only small and wouldn't last very long. Another flash of lightning ripped the sky open. It was close. Loveday hoped everyone was safe inside. The tea lights weren't bright enough to read by, and the TV obviously wouldn't work, nor would the heating, which ran off the electric, and it would soon get cold. She decided to get a fire going in the hearth and try to doze in her chair.

She put as much wood as she dared on the fire—the last thing she wanted was to start a blaze—and dragged the sofa closer to better feel the heat. Loveday checked her phone and saw she didn't have much battery left. She turned it off to preserve as much as possible in case of an emergency. It wasn't as though anybody would try to get hold of her. She had no family left and hadn't been in the town long enough to form any friendships. She'd moved here three months ago and mostly kept to herself, easy enough when you were a writer.

This town was a big change from London but a necessary one. Loveday couldn't stay after everything that happened there. The wisps of memories made her feel like she couldn't breathe, like she was drowning in murky water. She quickly pushed them from her mind, before they properly formed, and concentrated on the flames, on the pop and hiss of the wood as it caught. Claude sauntered over to the fireplace and stretched out his long limbs. He yawned, then flopped down in front of the hearth and closed his eyes, oblivious to the storm raging outside.

CHAPTER TWO

Rosemary Decker stood at almost six feet tall. By the time she was thirteen she was already five eight and showed no sign of slowing down. Being so tall meant she often looked down on people, and that seemed just about right to Rosemary because her height was matched only by her prodigious brain.

Tonight she stood on a platform watching workers scurry around below her, making the final preparations for something she'd been waiting for a long time.

Today was a great day. Her life's work was about to be realized. Shortly, the superiority of her mind and all her planning was about to be tested against the might of nature and destiny. She was certain God's plan involved her survival, but tonight she'd find out for sure.

Tonight, the human race would cease to exist in its current form, and Rosemary planned to be at the head of a bright new dawn, one where the righteous would be rewarded and the sinners cast out forever, left to drown in a flood of their own immorality and depravity.

Rosemary regarded the great boat in front of her, which had taken every last penny she had and more besides. Donors from across the world had contributed to its building and they were all here tonight.

The boat filled the hangar. Her platform ran the length of it in fifty-two staggered parts with ladders and lifts and scaffolding rising up and all around, lending support to the majesty of her greatest accomplishment. She reached out and touched it sleek, cool body, ran her hand over the saviour of mankind. *Ark 2.* She smiled. Today was a great day.

Someone cleared their throat behind her and she turned. Claire or Chloe—Rosemary couldn't remember the woman's name—shuffled nervously, her eyes darting around. She was a mousy thing. Most of her sentences started with *sorry*, like some sort of nervous tic.

"What?" Rosemary asked.

"Sorry to bother you, Ms. Decker. Another four families have arrived. Jo said I should come upstairs and ask you where to put them."

Rosemary rolled her eyes. Did no one have any initiative? Must she do everything herself? "Put them with the others. If there's no room, find somewhere else. Anyone who wants to find their way back to God's light is welcome tonight."

Claire or Chloe nodded and hurried off.

It was the storm. People had been dribbling in all day, and once the rain started, the numbers had swelled. They now had about forty people in the hangar. Rosemary knew some of them would be the same people who had mocked her on Twitter and Facebook and in the newspapers. It didn't matter. She would forgive them because tonight, they were starting to believe. They'd come here, hadn't they? And they weren't laughing now.

❖

Ellery lay back on the stainless steel table, her arms behind her head serving as a pillow. She'd put a few blankets down and dragged out the old oil heater, positioning it on the floor near her feet. It was almost cozy.

She'd found some crackers and a partially shrivelled cucumber in the staff kitchen. With the overripe banana, it had been a pretty depressing dinner, but at least her stomach wasn't growling any more. Rocky whined as a fresh onslaught of rain and wind hammered against the windows loudly enough to almost drown him out. At the sight of the pathetic dog, cowering and crying in the corner of his cage, Ellery crumbled and let him out. She nestled him against her side beneath the blanket, and he was soon snoring softly. She wished sleep would come as easily to her. Instead she stared up at the skylight above her head and watched the storm.

Ellery had never wanted to be anything except a vet. When she was six or seven, her parents bought her a plastic doctor's bag for her birthday—she was surprised they'd even remembered, let alone bought a present. Mary and David Jackson always seemed more interested in drinking than in their only child.

Young Ellery Jackson carried the bag—bright red with a green cross printed on the front—everywhere, until the plastic cracked and the handle fell off. Inside was a yellow and white stethoscope. The buds wouldn't sit in her ears properly and kept popping out, but it didn't matter. In her bedroom, Ellery was Dr. Jackson, saviour of stuffed animals and occasionally of the family cat if she could get Trixie, their mangy tortoiseshell, to sit still long enough.

That little bag opened up a whole world of possibilities to Ellery. From the moment it was given to her—not wrapped in bright kiddie paper, but hey, you couldn't have everything and it was probably the first and only present she ever got from her parents—she was fixed on the idea of becoming a vet. The very thought of it seemed *right* somehow. All the sacrifices and all the work since had been worth it.

Ellery moved to the town three years ago. She'd grown up nearby and was familiar with the area. Although she'd studied in London, she always knew she would end up back in the countryside one day. And here she was, her own practice in a beautiful small town in the middle of nowhere. She didn't have any friends, and the staff at the surgery had given up trying to include her in their social outings. She was friendly enough to everyone but made sure she kept her distance. People had long since given up trying to breach her walls.

She didn't speak to her family any more either—not that she knew how to get in touch even if she did. They moved when she was eighteen and hadn't given her a forwarding address. But she was content. Maybe lonely at times—most of the time—but content.

There were times when she thought she should go out and meet people, make some friends. Sometimes she made a plan to do just that. Then it would come to it—accepting an offer to go out or whatever—and she just couldn't bring herself to go. What would she talk about? Who would be interested in a country vet with no friends and no social life? She'd bore people to tears. The thought of it made her chest tighten and sweat prickle her forehead. Ellery knew it was some kind of social anxiety, and it got worse the more she avoided new people, but she just didn't have the courage to do anything about it. She had the animals and that would have to be enough. It wasn't such a bad life.

Rocky yipped in his sleep and Ellery gently ran her hand along his flank to soothe him. He breathed deeply and started snoring again. Another burst of lightning lit up the sky. It illuminated the bare branches of the trees as they swayed and dipped, the wind pulling them this way and that. Ellery shivered. She couldn't put her finger on what it was about this storm that unnerved her, and it was frustrating. A worry she couldn't name gnawed at the back of her mind. She knew part of it was being alone with just Rocky for company in this big empty space. Part of it was the knowledge the generator could fail and plunge her into darkness at any moment. The dark had always terrified her beyond reason, and in her home she had about a dozen night lights plugged in around the place. True, she was embarrassed about the childhood terror which wouldn't leave her, but the embarrassment wasn't stronger than her fear of the dark. And it wasn't like anyone ever came over anyway. Her last girlfriend was four years ago and what a disaster that had been. Maddie was a vet Ellery met at a conference. Usually she attended the bits she had to, then skulked off back to her hotel room. But Maddie had made a beeline for her and wouldn't let her go. Ellery supposed she'd been flattered to be pursued so relentlessly.

It hadn't seemed to matter to Maddie that Ellery was so introverted. She'd even said she found it refreshing to find someone who listened when she talked. She said Ellery was like the ocean—deep and vast and fascinating—and Ellery liked that. It didn't last long, though. Maddie was an extrovert. She liked parties and bars and clubs—all the things Ellery hated—and Ellery's charmingly quiet and unassuming nature soon got boring for Maddie. And then infuriating. Then suddenly Ellery was just a puddle Maddie stepped in long enough to get the muck off her shoes before moving on to something better.

The storm picked up outside. The wind whipped around the surgery, shook the windows, and howled furiously. She couldn't shake the sense something was about to happen. A voice inside told her it was something bad. She recognized it as her intuition, the same voice that told her when something was wrong with one of her patients.

Ellery stared up at the skylight and willed morning to come quickly.

CHAPTER THREE

A t exactly two o'clock in the morning, a huge burst of light lit up the sky. At the other end of the village, Loveday woke. It felt like someone turned on a floodlight outside her house. At first she thought it might be another flash of lightning, but when it didn't go away, she got up to look.

❖

At the veterinary surgery, Ellery opened her eyes, blinking immediately into the brightness. Rocky went crazy and Ellery locked him in his cage to stop him damaging his broken leg further. She hurried to the front of the surgery to see what was going on.

❖

At her house, Loveday was surprised Claude joined her at the window. He growled low in his throat, then hissed at something she couldn't see. The hairs on the back of her neck stood up.

❖

Back at the vet's, Ellery squinted into the light which obliterated everything else, wondering if it would burn her retinas and make her blind.

❖

Loveday stared out her window. Looking into the light wasn't like looking at the sun at all—the strength of it probably should have blinded her, but she didn't need to squint or shield her eyes. The problem was she could see nothing beyond the brightness.

❖

A steady high-pitched whine—Ellery thought it sounded like a dentist's drill—started up. It got louder and louder until it was unbearable. Ellery felt it all the way to the fillings in her teeth and worried the pressure would work them loose. She put her fingers in her ears to try and block out some of it, but the sound seemed to be coming from *inside* her head. It didn't make sense.

❖

Loveday moaned as the awful screeching noise reverberated through her body. She felt pressure behind her eyeballs and thought they would burst if it carried on much longer.

The sound increased in both vibration and pitch until Loveday began to scream.

❖

Ellery screamed. The terrible noise was so powerful it felt like it was working its way into the muscle and sinew of her being and ripping her apart from inside out. As it increased, so did the intensity of the light, until in one final pulse, it exploded and Ellery knew no more.

❖

Loveday dropped to the floor, unconscious.

CHAPTER FOUR

Ellery opened her eyes. The tiles were cold under her back. She tested her arms and legs—wriggled the fingers and toes on each—relieved everything seemed to be in order. Her head ached. She sat up and gingerly felt the base of her skull, and her hand came away wet with blood. A little was smeared on the tiles but the wound didn't feel serious. She must have banged her head when she fell.

Outside, the sun was just beginning to peek from behind the hills. She looked at her watch and saw it was stopped on exactly two o'clock. Either she'd bashed it when she fell or that awful noise had interfered with the battery. Ellery sighed and stood. Muscles groaned and joints popped from her time on the ground, reminding her that she wasn't as young as she used to be.

She heard a bark from the back of the surgery. *Rocky.* She hurried to his cage. As soon as he saw her he began to yip, his tail thumped manically, and he frantically pawed at the bars. Ellery opened the door and he bolted out and into her arms. She held him close and let him lick her face. "I know, boy, I know. I was scared too." He trembled and whined, so she tucked his head under her chin and rocked him for a bit.

Without putting him down, Ellery went into her office and picked up her phone. She pushed the power button but the screen remained dark. She frowned and tried again. It had almost a full battery last night, so it shouldn't be flat already.

She put Rocky on the floor and left him to investigate the room while she sat at her desk and attempted to power up her computer. Again, the screen remained black and silent. *What the hell?* She remembered her watch, how it stopped working too, and decided that the strange goings on last night must have emitted some kind of pulse or wave that had affected anything electrical. It didn't seem very likely, but what other reason could there be? Not expecting much, she tried the office phone. That was dead too.

Frustrated, Ellery pushed back in her chair, stood, and turned to face the window. The sun was weak but rising. It must be fairly early in the morning still. She considered driving into town, then realized her car wouldn't start if everything electrical really had been destroyed by the storm. Didn't hurt to try, though.

Ellery glanced at Rocky who was busy sniffing under the door. She didn't have the heart to lock him back up in the cage. He should be okay to walk for a little while on the cast, and he was only small, so she could easily carry him the twenty-minute journey.

❖

Loveday woke up feeling pressure on her lips—something pushed down and mashed them into her teeth. For a second she panicked. Then she realized it was the same thing that happened every morning. The cat was pawing at her mouth again.

"Get off me, Claude." She gave him a gentle shove, and he hopped off her chest with a huff allowing her to breathe much more easily. She sat up and looked around.

She was on the lounge floor, facing the window. Loveday remembered the light and that awful noise and then…nothing at all. She must have fainted. Claude meowed and pawed her hand. He probably needed the bathroom. Usually Loveday let him out before she went to bed and back in in the morning for his breakfast. He didn't seem to be very pleased with the break in his routine.

Loveday reached out and ruffled his head. He tried to duck her hand but she got him anyway. She went into the kitchen. Through the window she saw that although there were a lot of branches and leaves strewn about the garden, there didn't appear to be much damage. She was surprised because Hilda had been fierce, and Loveday thought a fence would be down at the very least.

She let Claude out and propped the back door open. It was a mild morning and the sun was already most of the way up over the fields.

Loveday flicked the switch for the kettle. She needed coffee. She fetched her phone and tried to turn it on. The thing remained dead and she frowned. There should be some battery left because she remembered turning it all the way off last night. Strange.

Then she noticed the kettle had stayed silent. She flicked the switch a couple more times and decided the power must still be off, which was annoying because she needed coffee to kick-start every morning. Perhaps she'd walk down to the cafe and see if they had any power. Worst case, she'd buy a camping stove from Romans.

Claude was nowhere in sight, but his bowl was most of the way empty. She hadn't cleared up the spilt biscuits from last night, so he'd had a good feed and wouldn't need any breakfast.

Loveday set off down the lane, surprised at how quiet it was. The position of the sun told her it must be close to eight o'clock, so it was strange the town wasn't bustling. People's days started early around here. There were a good few farms in the area, and it was also a commuting town, so there should be at least a few cars passing through to join the motorway nearby. It was eerily quiet, without even the distant drone of traffic, or a radio from someone's house—the general noises of people getting ready for the day were absent.

She continued on and reached the cluster of shops that constituted their high street—a post office, a small supermarket, a café, and a handful of chain stores. Again, the place was empty. The shop windows were dark and nothing stirred behind them. *What on earth is going on?*

Living in London most of her life, and even here to a lesser degree, Loveday had never been alone. When she took long walks in the forest, she would see other people, or a plane would fly overhead. Even in the deepest silences, there had always been a sense humanity existed nearby. Not today. The birds called out to each other, but the presence—the *sense*—of life had vanished. Loveday felt entirely alone for the first time in thirty-two years. She'd spent the last few years wanting to be left alone, and now she was. And she didn't like it at all. She felt scared.

Chapter Five

Rosemary was pleasantly surprised to discover sixteen survivors from her group, The Children of the Ark. She had hoped for more but planned on less—sometimes sinners were hard to spot, and she wasn't naive enough to think they didn't lurk within her own ranks. Still, the number was adequate. There were bound to be others out there like her though she didn't have very long to find them. Eighteen days if her dreams were right. Though finding survivors would be secondary to finding the girl. Every moment she existed was a threat to Rosemary and the new world she planned to create. So far, her dreams hadn't revealed the location of the girl, but with every passing day she felt her connection to the child—she was certain the girl was still young—grow stronger.

Rosemary didn't come from a religious family. Both her parents were scientists, well respected in their fields, and couldn't understand how religion and science were able to coexist peacefully in her mind. Rosemary was equally perplexed about their views. How could they contemplate the vast and terrible beauty of the universe and not see God's hand in it?

Even though she was deeply religious and there was no doubt in her mind of God's existence, she was as surprised as the Virgin Mary was when He appeared to her nine years ago in a dream.

Rosemary had seen it all. The destruction of mankind and the end of civilization, all swept away in less than a few hours. She'd also been shown her own demise at the hands of a girl who would lead humanity on a course so far away from God's light, when she saw it Rosemary had screamed until her throat was raw and bloody. She hadn't been able to speak for a week due to the pain. Fortunately, she was blessed with foreknowledge and had a chance to save both herself and whatever was left of humanity.

This morning, those who survived were treating her as some kind of God. All morning she was forced to remind them of Exodus 20:3. *You shall have no other gods before me.*

Rosemary was not God. It was true she had been blessed with a vision, but there was only one God and her job was to serve Him and root out any evil if it still existed. To have any chance in this new world, she would need to begin with her own small group, and that meant putting into practice every dictate of the Bible. There would be no picking and choosing the parts that suited any more. It was all or nothing.

Over the last few months, she'd been very clear on social media, directing where survivors could come. It would probably be a few days yet before they saw anyone—possibly longer, depending on where in the country they were. They would come, though. Rosemary had been proven right and they would all come eventually. People would be scared. They'd be lost and confused and Rosemary would help them. She would show them the way of God, and teach them about what came next. About what God wanted from his children. It wasn't hard to understand. It was all there in the Bible. The very way they should be living was written down in black and white, and she would make sure the way was followed to the letter from now on.

❖

Ellery made slow progress down the lane and was tempted to pick Rocky up and carry him the rest of the way. He was having a great time after spending so long indoors, and she didn't have the heart to be a killjoy. Rocky tottered busily back and forth from one side of the road to the other, sniffing and peeing on pretty much everything he could find. Surely he had to run out soon?

As she'd expected, her car hadn't started. There hadn't even been a splutter. It was dead. Hopefully someone in town would know what was going on. No doubt there would be some sort of emergency plan in place—or she guessed there would be. Wasn't that how things worked? Governments, town councils had to have contingencies for things like this, didn't they? Ellery noticed there were no cars going by and the normally busy road was empty. Her intuition continued to warn her something was deeply wrong, despite every effort she made not to hear her inner voice.

The roads were silent because last night's storm caused some kind of wave or pulse that shorted everything electrical. This was the only explanation she was prepared to accept.

CHAPTER SIX

Terry Pratt woke up with the worst hangover of his forty-two years. He rubbed his face with both hands. They were big hands, rough hands, and he was proud of them. They defined who Terry Pratt was. Hands that had a done man's work their whole life. Pink scars criss-crossed his knuckles and the backs of his hands, where the hair was still black and coarse, unlike his head, which he'd finally shaved last year after a workmate told him he looked like Bozo the Clown.

The workmate lost two teeth, and Terry finally lost the tufts that sprouted around the sides.

They were hard hands—his wife Shirl could attest to that. Not that he battered her or anything. He wasn't a wife beater. Just sometimes, just now and again, when he'd had a few or she wouldn't fucking shut up about some thing or other. Like his dad always said, women weren't made like men, and they needed to be kept in line. Guided like children.

He started to shout for her to bring him a cup of tea, but the effort of even moving his head set off the bells of hell. How much did he drink last night? He couldn't remember. He'd been to the football and that bunch of useless, overpaid tossers lost, two–nil. He had a season ticket as well. What a waste of money. Wankers.

That was all it took to put him in one of his black moods. This headache and the memory of sitting in the freezing fucking cold—of course, they had to sit now. They'd got rid of the stands years ago. God forbid someone slipped and broke a nail. Shirl better have the kettle on and bacon in the pan when he finally managed to get up.

Of course when he got downstairs, Shirl was nowhere to be seen. He touched the kettle. Cold. Strange, because Shirl drank tea like water.

He couldn't remember seeing her without a cup on the go. He searched through the cabinet above the sink where she kept the medication, and shook two aspirin out of the bottle. He thought better of it and shook out two more. Terry dry swallowed them and flicked the kettle on. *Where the fuck was she?* Not work, because she'd given that up straight after they got married. His mum never worked, and he'd be damned if a wife of his would either.

He looked up at the wall clock which read two o'clock. It must have stopped because there was no way it was two—he'd not been *that* drunk. His body clock told him it was closer to ten. Shirley usually didn't go shopping until lunchtime, so where the fuck was she?

Terry clenched and unclenched his fists, the blackness settling even more securely around him like a comfy blanket. He went into the lounge to wait for her.

CHAPTER SEVEN

L oveday walked up the window of Paula's Cafe and looked in. The place was dark, with chairs piled on top of tables. No signs of life inside. She tried the small supermarket which was supposed to open at seven o'clock. Locked up and lights out.

Loveday refused to believe everyone had simply overslept. In her gut, in the place that recognized the truth of things, she knew no one was here. She was alone. Everywhere she looked, curtains stayed drawn, shops stayed closed, and apart from the birds, there wasn't a sound to be heard.

One person in town Loveday did know was her neighbour Libby Lee. She wouldn't call her a friend, but they'd had a few doorstep conversations and taken parcels in for each other. Loveday walked the short distance back to her street and knocked on Libby's front door. No answer. She went around the back and through the side passage which connected their houses. Libby's gate was open. Loveday looked through the back door window. It was dark inside like everywhere else, but she knocked anyway. She tried the door handle. Unlocked. She pushed it open and stepped inside. "Libby?" she called out. Still no answer.

Several dishes and a saucepan lay neatly on the draining board. They were dry. A mug full of tea sat on the worktop, and Loveday touched the side. Cold. She walked further into the house, feeling like an intruder, which she supposed she was. What else would you call someone who stepped into a house uninvited?

Loveday called out again, "Libby, it's Loveday. Are you here?" Her only answer was the groan of floorboards under her feet. In the lounge a few embers were dying in the fire, and a book lay tented over the arm of the sofa. The house felt empty.

She didn't want to go upstairs, but there was a chance Libby was sick and unable to call out to her. She put her foot on the first step and hesitated when it creaked loudly. Her heart began to beat faster, her mouth was dry, and for some reason she felt very afraid.

A familiar instinct poked her in the gut. She'd only felt this strongly once or twice in her life. This time it was telling her to get out of the house. Loveday trusted this instinct. She was too young to even remember the first time it had spoken to her, but her mother told her about it once, the only time. It was at the end, just before she died.

Loveday was two and they had been shopping in town. Her mother said she was always a good-natured child, happy and easy-going, so it was a shock when she refused to get on the bus. Her mother told her she made such a fuss, struggling and kicking and screaming, and her mother was so embarrassed by her behaviour they didn't get on. A few miles down the road, the same bus ploughed through a guard rail and plunged off a bridge after the driver suffered a massive stroke. Fifteen people were killed.

The second time the instinct warned her, she was fourteen on a school trip to France. Loveday and a group of girls snuck out of the hostel they were staying at and went to a local nightclub. They drank way too much—which probably wasn't a lot, but when you were fourteen and not used to alcohol, any amount was a lot—and met some local boys. The boys offered to take them to another club. By that age, Loveday was pretty sure she was gay, but the other girls weren't, and they wanted to go with the French boys. Again, instinct told Loveday not to go. She tried to warn her friends, but they wouldn't listen. She ended up walking back to the hostel alone. The second club caught fire. Two of the girls were killed, one in the fire and the other in hospital two days later. The girls who survived stopped being her friends. She didn't blame them. She didn't even blame them when they starting acting like she didn't exist. Except when she caught them staring at her with something like fear in their eyes. She became a social outcast, a ghost. She didn't have friends again until university.

And here was that instinct from old, telling her not to go upstairs. Telling her nothing good would come of it. She hesitated, one foot on the ground and one on the first step.

Above her, something moved.

It sounded as though it was trying to be quiet—the shuffle of slippered feet on wood—and it didn't want Loveday to know it was up there. She lifted her foot off the first step and it squealed again. Above her, something moved quickly across the floor, then stopped. Maybe it was listening to her listening to it.

She turned and ran. She thumbed the lock on the front door and wrenched it open, practically pulled it off its hinges.

She took off down the road and ran towards the shops.

❖

Eventually, Ellery and Rocky made it into town proper. She'd ended up carrying him the last fifteen minutes, worried about his broken leg. He hadn't objected and seemed to enjoy his higher than normal vantage point. Rocky was small and fairly light, but after a while even something his size became heavy when you had to carry it half a mile in your arms.

Ellery reached the shops and was surprised to discover nobody was about. Nobody except for a woman, sitting on a bench hunched over. She was wearing jeans, sweatshirt, and slip-on shoes. Her auburn hair was tied in a messy bun, the kind women sometimes put up before they washed their face. And she was crying.

As she got closer, Ellery saw it was Loveday Taylor, the novelist who owned Claude. She approached cautiously with Rocky still in her arms.

"Miss Taylor?"

Loveday Taylor looked up at the sound of her name, bright blue eyes red rimmed from crying. "Dr. Jackson?"

"Ellery, yes. What's wrong?" Ellery asked.

Loveday Taylor wiped her eyes on the backs of her sleeves and stood up. "Everyone is *gone*."

"Gone? What do you mean *gone*?"

"The whole town, I think. Vanished."

"That can't be. There's about three thousand people living here. They can't have just vanished."

Ellery didn't know Loveday Taylor very well, had only met her on a few occasions when she gave Claude his shots and once when he got in a fight and cut open his mouth. The few times she had spoken to her, Loveday Taylor seemed level-headed if not a bit reserved. What she was saying now was insane.

"Look around you, Dr. Jackson. Where are the cars? Where are the people?"

Ellery couldn't argue with her—the place was empty. But *gone*? "I think the light last night—"

"You saw it too?" There was relief in Loveday Taylor's eyes. She sat back down.

"Yes. And that awful noise. I think somehow it killed everything electrical. My car, my phone, and my computer—none of them are working." Ellery sat next to her on the bench.

"My phone too. And, just now...*Jesus*." She shivered, and her eyes welled with tears again. "Where *is* everyone?"

Ellery didn't know her, but she recognized fear, and Loveday Taylor looked scared. Ellery felt awkward. She wasn't good with emotional displays. Part of her wanted sit closer and take Loveday's hand, provide some sort of comfort. This might have something to do with the little crush she'd been nursing, but the other part won out, and instead she looked away, stared at the ground, and toed a loose pebble. "We can't be the only people in town. There must be others. Have you checked? Knocked on doors?" Ellery watched Loveday lean down and scratch Rocky behind the ears.

"I tried to. Just before you got here." Loveday's voice went watery. "Sorry."

"It's okay, Miss Taylor. Go on. This morning...what?"

"Please, call me Loveday. After I couldn't find anyone here, I went back home to see if my neighbour was in. Her door was unlocked so I went inside."

"Which neighbour?"

"Libby Lee. Do you know her?" Loveday asked.

"She owns the florist's?"

"Yes, that's her. Well, when I went inside, I thought the place was empty, like here. I started to go upstairs—you're going to think I'm crazier than you do already—but there was something up there."

"An intruder?" Ellery was confused.

"No, more like a...I don't know what it was." She threw up her hands. "I can't explain it very well. It was *bad*, though."

"It might have been Libby Lee. She might be hurt." Ellery stood, alarmed. "Where does she live?"

Loveday clutched Ellery's arm. "Please, trust me. You don't want to go in that house."

Ellery shook off Loveday's hand. "If she's hurt, I need to help her."

"It's not her."

"How do you know if you just left without checking?" Ellery didn't mean to sound so harsh, but Loveday must have spooked herself over nothing when there could be an injured person upstairs. Except, *was* it over nothing? Hadn't Ellery spent the night in almost superstitious dread of a storm that wasn't quite a storm?

Perhaps she was too harsh with Loveday. Something strange was going on in town. "I'm sorry. I didn't mean to be rude. I still need to check Libby Lee's house, though. You don't have to come with me. Just give me the address."

Loveday sighed. "I'll come with you. But I'll wait outside."

CHAPTER EIGHT

Loveday stood outside Libby Lee's cottage. Rocky snuffled the grass next to her and occasionally peed against the fences. She looked up at Libby's windows where the curtains were still drawn. Ellery agreed to open them once she was upstairs so Loveday could see she was okay.

She didn't want to be here, would not have come back if Ellery hadn't shamed her into it. But Ellery hadn't felt what she had inside that house. Some kind of dark intelligence. Its awareness of her felt cold and calculating, the way the lion was aware of the gazelle. It was waiting for her to go upstairs and…and what? *Maybe you're still just a coward, Loveday. Making up ghouls to excuse your selfish, childish behaviour.* No, not this time, she wasn't. This time wasn't like London. There really had been something upstairs. She sighed and worried her bottom lip with her teeth, praying Libby wasn't lying upstairs, hurt. Praying Ellery would open the bloody curtains soon so they could get out of here.

Loveday had met Ellery Jackson a few times at the vet's, and she always took good care of Claude. Loveday briefly wondered if Ellery was into other women—something about her told Loveday she might be. Ellery wore her thick dark hair short and had the most incredible grey eyes, like slate with green flecks around the irises. Loveday thought they were kind eyes, if a little guarded.

They were roughly the same age, and in another life, Loveday might have pursued the good-looking vet, but those days were behind her. New town, new start, new habits. Plus, Ellery was stand-offish. Always polite and professional, her face gave nothing away. Loveday watched her economical movements, precise and confident. She obviously kept herself under tight control. The old Loveday would have been drawn to the idea of making the uptight vet snap.

She sighed and looked up at the window again. Still no sign of Ellery. The last thing Loveday wanted to do was go back in that house, but could she just leave Ellery if the thing was still in there? *Why not? You did before.* Loveday shook off the voice that wouldn't let her forget about her ultimate cowardice. Knowing it was her conscience didn't give her any more control over it.

She almost cried out in relief when the curtains were drawn back and Ellery looked down and waved at her.

❖

Ellery almost smiled at the look of relief on Loveday's face and the way she returned Ellery's wave so enthusiastically. She still felt bad for snapping at her earlier and had an idea Loveday had only come back here because Ellery had pretty much called her a coward. She put it down to the stress of the situation. Usually even-tempered, she wasn't one for snapping at people.

She always approached everything in a logical and practical way. She reserved judgement until she had all the facts and waited until she had the facts before she made a decision—another reason she'd felt so uncomfortable last night during the storm. She wasn't ordinarily susceptible to flights of fancy or premonitions of impending doom.

Her last girlfriend told her she was eye-wateringly dull—well, shouted it—as she was walking out the door, walking out on Ellery. She'd told her she was like a tortoise, methodically plodding through life and boring everyone she came into contact with. Ellery knew most of those words were said to hurt her, but she recognized truth in them. She took her time and wouldn't allow anything to influence her decision-making process. Her dislike of the dark was the only irrational fear she allowed.

She stood in Libby Lee's bedroom, staring at the neatly made bed, pillows plumped and covers tucked. It was pleasant, homely, with refurbished pieces of old pine furniture. Ellery vaguely remembered Libby telling her about the furniture she'd bought from junk shops and did up. It was a nice room.

But there was no one here, other than Ellery. Not Libby Lee and

not the malevolent intruder Loveday told her about. All the same...
all the same, Ellery felt her heart beat faster than usual. Her normally
dry palms had begun to sweat and her skin prickled. She felt like she
was being watched. She opened the wardrobe, feeling foolish—no one
lurked in there. She crouched and peered under the bed. Empty except
for a couple of dust bunnies.

Ellery wanted to get out of there. She rubbed the back of her neck
compulsively—a nervous habit she'd gotten rid of at eighteen—and
forced herself to check the other bedroom across the landing. It was
empty too. Ellery was satisfied Libby Lee wasn't here and relieved she
could finally get out of the house. She resisted the urge to bolt down the
stairs and made herself take measured steps instead, one ear cocked for
the sound of someone behind her.

Outside again, Ellery took a deep breath and instantly felt better
for being out of the house. She approached Loveday who narrowed her
eyes and studied her.

"Are you okay?" Loveday asked.

"Yes, fine. Libby Lee isn't in there."

"I told you." Her eyes, though, betrayed her relief. "What about...
the other?"

"I was alone." Ellery glanced away, unable to lie to Loveday's
face.

"Right. Maybe I was just freaked out before. I don't know, this is
all so strange." Loveday sounded frustrated.

Ellery thought about patting Loveday's shoulder but changed
her mind. "I know how you feel. I think you're right about everyone
disappearing."

"You believe me now?" Loveday looked surprised.

"We should try more houses, but yes, it feels *empty*. People should
be up and about by now, and there's no one."

"What do you think happened to them?"

"That's the million-dollar question, isn't it? Where are they, and
why are we still here?" Ellery looked around the silent street. Nothing
moved. Curtains stayed closed.

"It feels like we're in a mausoleum," Loveday said quietly.

Ellery nodded in agreement. "Come on, let's check a few more
houses."

They each took one side of the street, knocking on doors and getting no answer. Ellery pushed open a couple that were unlocked and the houses were just as empty as Libby Lee's had been. It was clear the whole town experienced the power cut. There were melted candles and discarded torches in most places—Ellery was surprised there hadn't been any fires.

She glanced over her shoulder at Loveday who was reaching the end of her side of the road, Rocky limping along beside her. Ellery knocked and pushed the door. It swung open, offering a view of the hallway. She hesitated, then stepped inside. Like in all the others, Ellery called out and got no reply. By now, she didn't expect one.

In the kitchen, a saucepan sat on a small camping stove, baked beans congealed inside. Two slices of bread gone hard and lifting at the edges were on a plate beside it. Whoever had started to prepare this dinner was long gone.

Ellery checked the house phone, the computer in the study upstairs, and a laptop lying open on a bed. All dead. Not even a flicker of life. *Where is everyone?* It was becoming a mantra in her head. How was it possible all these people had just vanished? They hadn't searched the town proper, it was true, and there was the possibility people were still here, other than her and Loveday. If that was so, why hadn't they come out? Surely it was the first thing you'd do? The most logical. Ellery was becoming more and more certain Loveday was right. Everyone was gone.

Ellery started back down the stairs, but then she heard the scrape of a chair across the wood floor. It came from downstairs. Her skin prickled and panic rose. She was about to call out, when something stopped her. *You don't want it to answer you.* It didn't make sense, this irrational fear. Ellery was terrified and she had no idea why. *Don't you? Don't you know what's down there, Ellery? I think you might. I think you just might know. Maybe better than Loveday. It's the reason you're scared of the dark. It's the reason you keep the night lights burning. And it's waiting for you down there.*

Ellery bolted back upstairs. She ran into the front bedroom and thumbed the latch on the window. Her hands shook and her fingers slipped on the frame as she dragged the window up. She climbed out, her feet touched the porch roof below. Behind her, something came up the stairs.

All the way out the window now, she got on her knees, gripped the roof tiles, slid down, and hung off the edge, her legs dangling while she worked up the courage to let go. Her left hand caught on a nail, and it tore into her palm. The right didn't fare much better with the edge of a broken tile biting into it. Fortunately, Ellery was up to date with her tetanus shots.

She looked up and saw a shadowy face at the window. It was grinning at her.

How do I know it's grinning?

She let go.

CHAPTER NINE

When Terry woke up, the blessed headache was gone. The house was bloody freezing, though. He didn't have to call out to know Shirl wouldn't answer him. Briefly, he wondered if she'd left him. She'd done it once, near the beginning of their marriage. He probably would have let the soppy cow go, plenty more fish in the sea. But she'd taken Little Terry, his boy, with her.

He'd gone to her mum's house because where else would she go? Her brother Joe was a heartless bastard and wouldn't take her in. Terry had been all sweetness and light, told her he was sorry, it wouldn't happen again. He'd begged and promised and wheedled until she'd agreed to come home. Once they got back to the house, he'd taken Little Terry upstairs and put him in his crib. He stroked his hair, still amazed at how soft and silky it felt beneath his hard, rough hand. He watched Little Terry's eyes get heavy, and when the baby put his little thumb in his mouth, he thought absently that this thumb-sucking business was going to stop pronto as well. When the baby was asleep, he went back downstairs and laid out to Shirl what would happen if she ever tried to take his son away again. He spelled it out to her nice and clear.

So if she hadn't left him, where was she? It was only then he noticed the street outside was silent. He pushed aside the curtains. No signs of life. Their car was still in the drive as well, so she definitely hadn't gone far. Something didn't feel right. Everything felt somehow *off*. Terry picked up the house phone. There was no dial tone.

CHAPTER TEN

L oveday watched the strange display from across the road. She held on to Rocky's collar when he would have run to Ellery. He strained forward, strong for such a small dog, barking and yipping, desperate to get to her.

When Loveday saw Ellery drop to the ground and lie unmoving, she released Rocky, who took off at warp speed despite his cast, and sprinted after him.

"Ellery?" Loveday dropped to her knees beside her, touched her shoulder. Rocky started madly licking her face and Loveday held his collar again, pulled him backward.

Ellery sat up rubbing her shoulder, and Loveday noticed her hands were bleeding. "I'm okay. Let's get out of here." Ellery glanced up at the bedroom window and Loveday wondered at the look of fear on her up to now stoic face. "Quick."

"You've cut your hands."

"That's the least of our problems. Come on. My place isn't far."

"Mine's closer," Loveday pointed out, helping Ellery to her feet.

"No, I don't want to stay on this street. Let's go."

Loveday followed Ellery, Rocky limping along beside them. She noticed he was struggling to walk and scooped him up and into her arms. Grateful, the little dog licked her face and made her feel better.

Loveday wasn't really a dog person, but she had to admit Rocky was cute.

Ellery opened the door to a tidy cottage at the south end of town. She led Loveday into the lounge and cleared a stack of books off the sofa. "Please, have a seat. I'm going to clean up my hands."

"Wouldn't it be easier if I did it? They both look painful."

Ellery seemed to consider for a moment and Loveday guessed she didn't accept help very often. She nodded. "Okay, thanks. I'll get the first aid kit. Make yourself comfortable."

Loveday looked around the room. A bookcase in the far corner held a number of titles she was familiar with. Lesbian titles. *Knew it.* She was surprised to see a few of her own books lurked among the work of better authors. *Interesting.*

Various charcoal drawings of animals lay in a pile on the coffee table. She picked them up and looked through. They were good.

Behind her, Ellery cleared her throat. "Um, here it is. Shall we sit at the table?" Ellery nodded to a dining table at the other end of the room, also stacked with piles of books.

"You're an artist," Loveday said.

Ellery blushed. "Not really. It's more of a hobby."

"They're good."

"Thank you."

Loveday sorted through the first aid box, tearing open a sachet of antibacterial wipes. "Give me your hands."

Ellery had nice hands. Long, strong fingers like a pianist's, the nails neatly trimmed. The cuts weren't too deep. "Want to tell me what happened?" She didn't look up from her task, gently dabbing at Ellery's bloody palms and along the creases where blood crusted. She checked that no debris was caught in them. The last thing Ellery needed was an infection.

Ellery sighed. "I suppose you wouldn't believe me if I said that's how I usually exit houses?"

Loveday glanced up, surprised to see a sheepish grin on Ellery's face. The capable vet didn't strike her as someone who looked that way often. She laughed. "Is it?"

"No. I think whatever you heard in Libby Lee's house was also in the house I climbed out of. It was downstairs. I thought…"

"You thought what?" Loveday asked, peeling the backing off a plaster to put on Ellery's palm.

"Going back out the front door was a bad idea with *it* down there."

Loveday did look at her then, understanding passing between them. It wasn't something you could easily vocalize. Neither knew the other well enough to just come out and say *there was some kind of bogeyman in that house and it terrified me.*

"I think you're all squared away. You were rubbing your shoulder earlier—shall I—"

"It's fine." Ellery blushed furiously and Loveday wondered about that. Did she think Loveday was going to ask her to take her jumper off? And even if she did, they were both adults, so what was the problem?

"I'm not wearing a bra," Ellery said. "I mean, I took it off last night to sleep and didn't get around to putting it back on."

"Oh." Loveday's cheeks heated. "I see. Well, as long as it's okay."

"It's fine. Just a bit sore," Ellery said quickly.

Loveday nodded and stood, trying not to think about a topless Ellery. "I'll throw this stuff in the bin."

"No, it's fine, I'll do it." Ellery began gathering up the detritus. "Would you like tea or coffee? I have a camping stove in the cupboard."

"*Oh my God*, yes, please! Coffee if you have it?" Loveday couldn't believe her luck.

"Sure, no problem." Ellery laughed.

❖

Ellery busied herself in the kitchen. She boiled the kettle and spooned coffee into the coffee press. There was some bread in the cupboard and cheese in the fridge. They looked okay. She sniffed them. They smelled okay too.

She laid out some ham on a plate for Rocky, and he wolfed it down in a couple of bites, sniffing and licking the plate and the floor around it in case he'd missed anything.

Ellery thought about their options. They had no way to communicate with the outside world. Every device she owned required electricity or electrical components to work. The town was quite clearly empty of people, so that left them with a couple of possibilities. Find an old vehicle and try to drive to the next town or city—perhaps the government had set up some kind of emergency shelter for anyone who hadn't disappeared. Or stay here, wait it out, and see if anyone came to them. After the incident earlier, Ellery wasn't keen on the idea of staying.

Of course, it had completely slipped her mind to ask whether Loveday had family. She shook her head. Or if Loveday even wanted to stay with her. Loveday might have other plans that didn't involve her at all. Ellery knew if she had any family or even friends left, looking for them would be the first thing she'd do.

Would that be so bad? If Loveday wanted to go her own way? Ellery wondered if it might be a relief in a way. She'd spent so long alone, and now there was another person to think about. To care for. For someone who avoided people like the plague, why did Ellery feel so comfortable around Loveday? It couldn't just be the attraction. Ellery had been attracted to people before and never wanted to be around them in the way she wanted to be around Loveday.

Perhaps it was the situation they found themselves in. That was probably it. There wasn't any other logical explanation she could think of.

The kettle began to whistle. She poured water into the coffee press. She'd recognized Loveday the first time she came into the surgery with her cat. She'd read all Loveday's books. She hadn't admitted to being a fan, that would have been embarrassing, but Loveday had been alone in her lounge for a while now and had probably seen Ellery had her books.

Loveday's author's photo didn't do her justice. Ellery had been mortified when Loveday'd been about to suggest looking at her shoulder. The thought of getting topless in front of her had filled Ellery with equal parts arousal and embarrassment. She would need to grab a bra from upstairs. Just in case.

She put the sandwiches together quickly, grabbed some mustard and mayonnaise, arranged it all on a tray, and went into the lounge.

Loveday was browsing her bookcase again and turned at the sound of Ellery coming in.

"Here we go." She unloaded everything onto the coffee table. She saw Loveday's eyes light up at the sight of the coffee.

"That smells delicious. I'm so happy you have a camping stove."

They sat down and began to eat.

"I was thinking," Ellery said, "maybe we should get out of town. Go somewhere bigger and see if there's any people. That is, unless you have family you want to try and find."

Loveday shook her head. "No, no family."

Ellery didn't ask any questions—the challenging look in

Loveday's eyes told her not to. "Who knows, the disappearances might be a localized thing."

"You think it's just here that everybody's disappeared?" Loveday groaned at her first sip of coffee.

"No. If that was the case, someone would have come by now. And there's still no sound of traffic from the main road. I don't think it's just here. But in a larger town, there might be more people. An emergency shelter. Something." Ellery bit in to a sandwich, realizing just now how hungry she was.

"We'll have to look for an old car. One from before the advent of on-board computers. Do you know of any?"

"I thought about that. I suppose we'll have to have a walkabout and see."

Rocky jumped on the sofa and lay down between them, his eyes tracking their movements, probably hoping for bits of dropped sandwich.

"It sounds like the best plan. I can't think of what else to do. God, this is so strange," Loveday said.

"I know. It feels…surreal. How can everyone just disappear like that? Without any trace."

"I don't know. Yesterday I was thinking about what colour to paint my bathroom. Now, we're talking about finding out whether we're the last two people on Earth. It's insane." Loveday shook her head and bit in to the sandwich. She made a face. "No butter?"

"Oh. I don't usually put butter in sandwiches."

"Then you're no longer in charge of sandwich making. Coffee, maybe. Sandwiches? No."

CHAPTER ELEVEN

Terry thought it was about mid-afternoon by the time he left the house. He'd tried the TV, his mobile phone and Shirl's—he also found her purse with all her cards and her house keys, so he knew she hadn't walked out on him—and the computer upstairs. All of them were dead. He tried unplugging the TV and computer and plugging them back in, like Little Terry showed him. He got the volt tester out of his toolbox, and even that didn't turn on.

Terry finally decided to head out and see if everyone else was having the same trouble. He'd go down the pub, he thought. Have a pint and see what was what. He stepped outside and double locked the front door like always. The street was still empty and strangely quiet. It took Terry a moment to realize there were no planes flying overhead, and that was odd because they lived directly under the flight path. He got to the end of his street and turned onto the main road. A few cars sat abandoned in their lanes. One had smashed straight into a brick wall, the front end crumpled.

Terry went over and looked inside. No one. He straightened and looked about. Something fluttered in his belly, and at first he didn't recognize it. It had been years—since his dad died, really—since he'd felt anything like it. So at first he didn't understand the feeling swirling in his gut. He looked up at the empty skies and over to the houses which lined the road like sentries, their windows black. He felt the absence of life, *really* felt it. He scrubbed his big hands over his face again, felt the back of his neck prickle with the sensation of being watched.

He spun around in the direction he'd felt eyes on him, but there was no one. Goosebumps rose on his skin and Terry finally realized he was afraid. And on the heels of that, *Little Terry*. His son. Terry started to run.

❖

Loveday walked up the road carrying a coat hanger. Ellery walked up ahead on the opposite side of the road with a hammer and flathead screwdriver. The whole situation would have been comical if it wasn't so weird. Two thirty-something women looking for a car to break in to. Two women who were confirmed loners throwing in their lot with each other. They were virtual strangers, yet Loveday felt a connection with Ellery she couldn't explain. Being with her felt right even when everything else about today felt completely wrong. Maybe it was just the attraction between them, but Loveday didn't think so.

Well, no point mulling it over now when they had cars to steal. "What about this one?" she called out, stopping by a beaten-up red hatchback.

"No," Ellery called. "The immobilizers on those are buggers."

They walked on, Loveday not entirely sure what she was looking for and also wondering how Ellery knew about hot-wiring cars. Appearances could be deceptive.

Ellery stopped by a battered blue estate car and called Loveday over. "I'm going to try this one. Can I have the hanger, please?"

Loveday watched as Ellery bent the hooked end further, then pushed it down between the window and the seal. It wasn't long before the lock popped up.

"Do I even want to know where you learned that?"

Ellery turned to look at her and grinned. "Misspent youth."

"Clearly."

"I was in foster care for a while, made some interesting friends and learnt some skills." She opened the door and got in.

Loveday watched as Ellery gently hammered the screwdriver into the ignition. "Pray this works because I'm not much good at *actual* hot-wiring." Ellery turned the screwdriver like a key.

Nothing.

Shit.

"Now what?" Loveday asked.

Ellery didn't answer. She sat for a moment with her brow furrowed, then felt around under the steering column. The bonnet popped open. She got out and walked around to the front.

Loveday leaned against the car, her back to the window, and felt dejected. She was hoping this would work. The alternative had them walking God knew how many miles to a city that might also be empty of people.

"Loveday?" Ellery's voice was quiet. It sounded strange.

"Everything okay?"

Ellery looked around the side of the open bonnet at her. "I don't know what to make of this. I...come and see."

Loveday walked around to the front and stared down at the engine. It was a twisted hunk of scorched metal.

DAUGHTERS OF LILITH WALK was spray-painted on the underside of the bonnet in red, and underneath it SAVE THE GIRL. Some of the paint dripped down so the letters looked like they were bleeding. Or crying.

"I don't understand. Who did this?" Her voice sounded odd to her own ears and she realized what had been strange about Ellery's voice when she'd called her over. They were both trying not to scream.

Loveday shivered, the hairs on her neck stood up, and she felt eyes on her. "I think we should go back to your house," she said.

Ellery's eyes bored into hers. "You feel it too?"

"Yes. Someone's watching us. That thing from before."

The air turned colder and a gust of wind kicked up autumn leaves and sent them skittering down the silent street.

"Come on." Ellery held her hand and led her away. They walked silently, both aware something marked their progress. Its gaze felt cold, alien. Loveday forced herself not to break into a run. Ellery squeezed her hand, as though she knew she might, and whispered, "I want to run away too. I don't think we should. I think it would be the wrong thing to do."

Loveday knew exactly what she meant. Her feeling reminded her of Claude, how he might track a bird or a butterfly across the garden. The faster it moved, the more interested he became.

Chapter Twelve

L oveday watched Ellery start a fire in the hearth. Her fine-boned
hands moved with confidence, as though she'd done this a
thousand times before. Why on earth was it turning her on so much?
Loveday looked away in the hope it might calm the fluttering feeling
in her stomach.

The afternoon had taken on a chill that signalled winter was
coming. They'd been lucky so far—the weather remained mild for
autumn.

"Should we try another car?" Loveday asked.

"Do you think there's any point? I don't." Ellery paused in her
task and sighed. "I think they'll all be exactly like that one."

"Why would it…they…whatever—why would it want us to walk?
And who's Lilith? What girl?"

Ellery stood and walked over to the bookcase. She looked through
the titles, obviously found what she was looking for, and pulled out—

"Is that a Bible?" Loveday asked.

"Not really. It's sort of a study on the Bible. I don't know about
saving any girl, but this might explain Lilith."

"You're religious?" Loveday was surprised.

"Yes, I am. But that's not how I know about this. I like to read
about all sorts of things, and the writing on the car bonnet jogged my
memory."

"Daughters of Lilith? She's in the Bible, or her daughters are?"

"Lilith was supposed to be Adam's first wife in the Garden of
Eden. She refused to submit to Adam, saying they were made at the
same time, so they were equal. She left him."

"Good for her. Do you think this is all some kind of biblical prophecy?" Loveday shifted on the sofa. Three things you should never talk about with friends: money, politics, and religion. Were they even friends? Not if Ellery turned out to be some Bible bashing fruitcake, they wouldn't be. As someone from the LGBT community, Loveday had a strained relationship with God. And by strained she meant non-existent. She didn't bother God and He didn't bother her. That was the way she liked it.

"No!" Ellery laughed. "Don't worry, Loveday. I'm not a religious nut or one of those weirdos...What are they called? Children of the Ark? The Lilith thing might not be anything to do with them. Whatever wrote the message, the thing that's been stalking us, might be. I don't know, this whole thing is beyond my realm of understanding. I'm logical, practical." Loveday watched her pace the small room. "I have no explanation for any of this, except to say it wants us to leave town— on foot."

"I think you're right. Where does it want us to go? And why do we have to walk there?" Loveday brightened. "Hey, maybe we could find bicycles."

"I think if we decide to use bicycles, they'll be fucked as well. Maybe this is all some biblical nightmare. Maybe the River Crane will part for us on the way out of town."

Loveday giggled. It wasn't funny, really, but it was either laugh or scream. Ellery looked like she could go either way as well.

"I'm glad one of us finds it funny," Ellery griped, except she didn't look annoyed. Ellery smiled and shook her head. "Do you know what I mean, though?"

Loveday sighed. "Yes. Blinding light, everyone's gone. Technology destroyed, have to travel on foot. Judgement Day or something. Maybe those nutters from Children of the Ark were right after all."

Ellery grimaced. "God, I hope not. That woman, Rosemary Decker, scares the shit out of me. It looks like she was right, as well. Hasn't she been predicting this for a few years?"

Loveday nodded. "Looks like she's had the last laugh."

"I hope not. Her version of events involves people like me being put to death."

"She's definitely an Old Testament throwback." Loveday thought about Rosemary Decker, wild-eyed and vengeful, and about the little nugget Ellery revealed about her sexuality. Not that Loveday was interested. She couldn't be.

Ellery spoke and interrupted her thoughts. "Tomorrow, I suppose we get some supplies together and—oh, what about Claude?"

Loveday had already thought about him. "I think he'll come with us. With cats you can never be sure, but he's followed me to the local shop a few times."

"We aren't going to the local shop," Ellery said gently.

"I know. On foot, I couldn't carry him all that way. He won't go on a lead." Loveday's heart broke at the thought of leaving Claude behind. Of course, he was a cat, so his chances of survival were high, but he was her best friend. *You make a habit out of leaving your friends behind, don't you?* She was sick of that voice, whether it told the truth or not. And could she? Could she leave Claude behind to fend for himself?

"If he won't follow us…I don't know if I can leave him, Ellery."

"It's okay. I understand."

Loveday felt an awkward pat on her shoulder and almost smiled. Bless her for trying.

"I can go on my own and see if there's anyone left. Or we can stay here together."

"No, you should go."

"But that thing. Watching us…"

Ellery didn't have to say it, Loveday knew. She also knew—she couldn't explain how—it wanted them to leave town. She didn't know why, or what would happen if she didn't. She supposed they might find out tomorrow.

"Let's wait and see what happens. It may follow us, after all."

CHAPTER THIRTEEN

Terry thumped on his son's front door. He stood back and shouted his name into the silence. He bent down to the plastic rock the lad kept behind his recycling boxes and turned it over. He fumbled with the spare key, his fingers greasy with sweat and shaking, finally pulling it off the magnet that held it in place.

He got the key in the front door, and at first it wouldn't turn. He tried again, nearly snapped it off, then remembered you had to hold the handle up before the key would turn.

Inside, the house was silent. He could hear the drip, drip, drip of the tap in the kitchen. In the hall, his son's work boots and the beaten-up trainers he always wore were lined up next to his girlfriend's shoes and the tiny shoes of their little boy, also called Terry, which got confusing at Christmas.

Dread settled in Terry's belly to keep company with the fear.

"Please, not my boy. Please, not my boy," he found himself whispering over and over as he climbed the stairs. Little Terry's bedroom was empty, the bed sheets rumpled but cold, their inhabitants long gone. In his grandson's room, the child-sized bed was empty. Above it, a *Thomas the Tank Engine* wall sticker stared down at him. He had helped Little Terry decorate this room. He and Shirl had both been worried when their son had told them he'd got his girlfriend pregnant. Terry was ashamed to admit he'd urged the lad to convince her to get an abortion. Little Terry wouldn't hear of it, and it wasn't as if he and Shirl had been much older when she got pregnant.

He'd given them a loan so they could buy this house—not much, a two-up two-down—but he and Little Terry had spent weekends working on it to bring it up to scratch. They were some of the best months of his life. Spending time with his son, listening to the football on the radio, talking about how shit their club was and who they needed to buy and how they should play to get back up the table. Both agreed the manager was a wanker.

Terry found his legs couldn't support his weight and he slid down the wall onto the floor. For the first time since Little Terry was born, he started to cry.

He wasn't sure how long he stayed like that. At some point he'd curled into a ball like a little baby. Eventually, the tears dried up. A horrible emptiness settled in his belly, pushing out the fear from before. If Little Terry was gone, then he didn't care about anything.

He stood up, wobbled a bit, then straightened. He would go to the pub. He would drink himself to death if it was possible. If not, he would think of some other way to kill himself.

❖

Ellery walked Loveday back to her cottage. They'd left Rocky at her place in front of the fire. The plan was to get Claude into his carrier and take him back to Ellery's. In the morning, they'd gather any supplies they needed and head out, probably to Southampton because it was the closest, but they'd hit other towns on the way and see if there were any survivors.

The sky had begun to darken, and Ellery was reluctant to be outside when night came fully. She sensed those cold alien eyes on her all the time now, except when she and Loveday were in her cottage. She knew it wanted them out of town and felt her own sense of urgency grow with every hour they stayed, like a clock was set to a countdown in her mind, and she didn't want to be here when it reached zero.

Claude was waiting for them on the garden wall when they got to Loveday's cottage. He stood, stretched, and meowed loudly when he saw them.

Ellery watched Loveday stroke his long back, scratch his ears, and kiss his head. She hoped he would follow them tomorrow. Loveday opened the door. "I'll find his carrier. We can feed him once we're back at yours."

Ellery nodded. Since their discussion about Claude, Loveday had been quiet. Ellery thought she probably knew the risk of staying here too. They both seemed to be aware of the thing that watched them and had an uncanny understanding of its intentions.

The thought made Ellery nervous. She wasn't a stranger to knowing things she couldn't explain or understand. By even by her standards this was weird.

But that wasn't the only thing that was weird. Her connection with Loveday unsettled her too. They were virtual strangers and yet they had an easiness between them as though they'd been lovers for years. *No. Do not go there.* They were not and never would be lovers. Ever. They were sort of friends. They had a connection, it was true, but they would only ever be friends.

Loveday looked on as Ellery smiled at Claude who wrapped himself around her legs, rubbing his big face against her calf. "Sorry, friend, I don't have access to your food. And you're going to have to wait a bit longer anyway."

As if he understood, the cat huffed and shot upstairs, no doubt to search out dinner.

❖

Back at Ellery's cottage, night had come. They cooked beans on the camping stove—Ellery was reminded of the deserted kitchen earlier in the day, and almost couldn't bring herself to eat them—and sat in front of the fire in the lounge.

Claude hadn't proved to be much of a problem. He got into his pet carrier fairly easily. She and Loveday took turns hoofing him back, and Ellery realized it would be difficult to take him in a carrier. He was the same size as the dog and too heavy to carry.

He was wary of Rocky once they got him home and kept an eye on the dog from his position on the back of the sofa, behind Loveday's head. Ellery though he would get used to him soon enough, if he would follow them out of town.

Loveday put down her bowl, and Ellery watched her stare at the flames. Their reflection flickered in her eyes, and her chest rose and fell gently as she breathed. Ellery quickly looked away. The last thing she wanted was to get caught ogling Loveday's boobs. Not that she'd been doing that, not at all, but it would *look* like she had if Loveday caught her. And they were pretty great boobs.

"What are you thinking about?" Ellery surprised herself. She never asked people questions like that. It invited too much familiarity.

Loveday looked over and smiled sadly. "It's strange. I moved here to avoid people. But I miss them now they're all gone."

"I know what you mean." And she did. Ellery wanted to ask why she wanted to avoid people but sensed Loveday wouldn't welcome the intrusion. She was kind but closed off. Like Ellery.

"You know, I never even asked if you'd lost family or friends in this. How selfish am I?"

"I didn't. And you aren't." Ellery smiled. "I'm a loner too."

"What about your family?" Loveday asked gently.

"I haven't seen them for years. Besides, they're alcoholics—have been since I was a kid. If the storm didn't get them, sclerosis of the liver probably did, ages ago." Ellery didn't ever talk about her parents. Especially not with strangers. Why was she telling Loveday?

"I'm sorry. Is that why you were in foster care?"

"Yes. When Granny Ivy was alive, things were okay. She made sure I had clean clothes, food. That the bills were paid. After she died, all that stopped. The worst was when they didn't pay the electric bill. We'd be stuck in darkness for weeks." Ellery shivered at the memory. Walking through the cold house and up the stairs to her bedroom in the pitch dark. Waiting for something to reach between the banisters and grab her ankle.

"That's horrible. I'm sorry."

Feeling embarrassed because she'd revealed too much, Ellery leaned forward and gathered up the empty bowls. Loveday put her hand on Ellery's arm. "Leave those. I'll clear up."

"It's fine." Ellery's throat was dry, her skin warm where Loveday touched her. *When did this happen?* Not that she hadn't been attracted when she'd met her—before, if you counted staring at her author's photo.

"You cooked. I'll clear," Loveday insisted.

Ellery was grateful Loveday let the subject of her parents drop without question.

"I heated beans."

Loveday grinned, squeezed her arm. "Don't split hairs. Plus, you added Worcestershire sauce to them. It's almost cooking."

Ellery laughed. "I'm glad you're so easy to please."

"Oh, really?" Loveday raised an eyebrow and Ellery felt her face flush.

"Not like that. You know what I mean."

"I do. Relax, Ellery. It's okay." She smiled and gathered the dishes.

The kitchen was freezing cold. Loveday shivered and pulled her sweater tighter around her body. *Get these washed and then get back in the lounge.* She also wanted to go back because Ellery was there and it felt safer somehow—strength in numbers and all that. Since returning to Ellery's cottage, the sensation of being watched had gone away. Loveday didn't doubt the thing was still out there, but for now its watchful eye was closed.

Loveday turned on the tap to rinse the bowls. How much longer would luxuries like running water last? Not long if everyone had truly disappeared. Machinery broke down, pumps failed, pistons stopped... pistoning. She guessed it wouldn't take long at all. They'd be back to living in caves in no time. And medicine? Doctors? All of that would be things of the past. If you broke your leg or got an infection, you were your own. It didn't bear thinking about. Loveday prayed they weren't the only survivors, that there was some sort of emergency shelter somewhere with the remnants of society huddled inside. In the next few days they—or perhaps just Ellery—would find out.

Loveday held a bowl under the tap to rinse off the soapy water and looked out the window. At first, she wasn't sure what she was seeing. In the dark, it could just be a trick of the light. When she realized what it was, she screamed. The bowl dropped out of her hands and smashed to pieces in the sink.

CHAPTER FOURTEEN

Terry belched and poured himself another whiskey. He'd almost finished the bottle and didn't even feel tipsy. Fuck.

The pub had been locked and empty, like all the other shops and restaurants on the high street. Usually, it was four or five people deep on the pavements, and double-decker buses, cars, vans, lorries clogging the roads as they inched along. Horns blared, peopled shouted, sirens wailed as the ambulances from the local hospital roared past. Today, silence ruled. Like in the main road, there were cars and a couple of buses stopped in the street. Several had mounted the kerb, and one had knocked over a rubbish bin. Its litter blew along the streets on the back of a gentle breeze.

Terry had looked through the pub window and seen it was empty. He used the sandwich board that hadn't been brought in last night— advertising pints of lager for two ninety-nine, shots for a pound—and smashed the glass in the door. He unbolted the top and bottom and let himself in. He didn't even bother to call out this time because the sound of glass breaking would have brought someone downstairs if there had been anyone left.

Buried in his grief, Terry didn't care where everyone was, why they had disappeared, or why he was left behind. All he was interested in was getting blitzed. The sooner the better.

He drew himself a lager off the tap and swallowed it down in a few mouthfuls. It was warm but he didn't give a fuck. He got himself another and settled down behind the bar with a bottle of whiskey.

Terry knew he was being watched, had felt it as he ran to his son's house and now, as he sat in the pub, trying unsuccessfully to get drunk. Whatever it was, it could have him. He didn't care. Above him, a floorboard creaked, like someone was up there. Now that was strange. Another board creaked, this one by the stairs behind the bar. It led up to the landlord's flat. Terry put down his glass and leaned back on his stool. He cracked his knuckles.

The sensation of being watched grew stronger. The back of his neck itched and his heart began to beat faster. He felt adrenaline surge and his senses sharpen in a way they hadn't since he'd been a very young boy and heard the front door open, signalling his old man was home.

The stairs creaked again—someone was coming down. Terry waited.

❖

At the sound of her scream, Ellery came running. Loveday couldn't take her eyes from the window, at what was outside. She felt Ellery clutch her shoulder and turn her around. She looked into calm, kind eyes and forced herself to relax. She knew Ellery wasn't tactile, but she couldn't help herself. Loveday leaned into Ellery's arms, wrapped herself around Ellery's warm body, and willed her breathing to even out.

She buried her face in Ellery and breathed her in. She was overwhelmed by a feeling of safety, of being home. She pushed it down with brutal force as quickly as it came up, but it wouldn't go away completely. She didn't want it to. It felt too good.

She was surprised when Ellery pulled her in and held her tightly, the awkwardness she'd displayed earlier gone. Loveday tucked her head under Ellery's chin.

"Can you tell me what happened?"

Loveday wanted to cry at the gentleness in Ellery's voice.

She nodded, leaned back, but didn't leave the circle of Ellery's arms. "It was out there. While I was washing up."

Ellery turned slightly to look out the window. Loveday watched her squint. "I can't see anything."

"It's gone now. It was only there for a moment."

Ellery's mouth opened but Loveday cut her off, saying hotly, "I didn't imagine it, before you ask. I'm not some hysterical moron."

"No, I wasn't going to question you. After everything that's happened today, I believe you, Loveday. I'd be an idiot not to. I was going to say, we should draw the blinds. So it can't see inside. In case it comes back."

Loveday nodded. Well. She hadn't expected this response from calm, logical Ellery. "Okay, sorry. I didn't mean to bite your head off."

Ellery grinned at her briefly. "Don't worry about it. What was it doing out there? What did it look like?"

"It was too dark to see it properly. Tall and thin—I think it had a hunchback. Or at least, it stooped. It was standing towards the end of the garden. I suppose I felt, more than saw it. Does that make any sense?"

"Yes. It's been the same all day. Not seeing it, but feeling it. What does it want?"

"It wants us out of town."

"*Why?*" Ellery sounded as frustrated as she felt.

"That's the million-dollar question isn't it?" Loveday echoed her words from earlier.

Ellery lowered the blinds, looking out one last time. "Maybe I should—"

"Don't say it. Don't even *think* it. Don't you watch scary films? People who go outside to *investigate*"—she made air quotes—"end up dead. Neither of us is going out there. We're going to stay in here, and when morning comes, we're getting the fuck out of Dodge. If Claude's up for it, of course."

"Yes, boss." Ellery gave a dorky little salute and smiled. Neither of them wanted to think about what would happen if Claude had other ideas. Loveday didn't think she could leave him behind. But staying would mean death—she knew that somehow. There had to be a way to take him with them, even if it meant dragging him in his carrier.

CHAPTER FIFTEEN

*E*llery *stood high on a hill with a huge sprawling city spread out below her.* To her left was Loveday, and to her right was a young girl she'd never seen before. The girl was no more than sixteen with short, spiky hair and a multitude of hoops rimming her ear. Before she could speak, the girl turned to them.

"This is it, Ellery and Loveday. The end and also the beginning."

Ellery thought she had a sweet voice, light and musical. "Who are you? What do you mean?" Ellery asked.

"I've had many names but this time you can call me Dani. It's the rebalancing, you see. Time for the world to make itself again."

"I don't understand. What's a rebalancing?" Loveday asked.

Above them, clouds darkened and rain began to fall, soft at first, then hard. The wind came up.

"We don't have very much time, so you must listen. Find me. Find me before Rosemary Decker does, or there can't be a rebalancing. The world will end and there will be no beginning. You must head north."

"Stop talking in bloody riddles!" Ellery shouted to be heard above the wind.

"Ellery, Ellery, look." Loveday held out her arm and pointed. Below, a great wave appeared, rushing towards the city.

"No!" Ellery cried. "It'll kill us all. We have to run." She grabbed Loveday's hand and began to pull her backward. To the girl she shouted, "Come with us. We have to go. Now."

The wave rose higher, almost as high as the hill they stood on. Ellery watched in horror as it came down like a giant vengeful hand and smashed through the city, obliterating everything in its path. *Beside her Loveday screamed.*

❖

Ellery woke. She sat up and blinked slowly as the room came into focus. From the back of the sofa, Claude looked up at her, flexed his claws into the material, sighed deeply, and went back to sleep. Loveday lay stretched out on the opposite sofa, Rocky curled by her side and snoring softly, his plastered leg pointing straight out.

The dream remained vivid, which was strange because on the rare occasions she dreamed, she had no clear memory of them when she woke up, just snatches of hazy images. She could still feel the bitter wind whip her face and hear the loud roar of the wave. She shivered. The logical part of her mind frantically searched for answers. For some way to explain what had happened and put it all into a neat little box. It wasn't that simple, though. Something was going on in the town. The dream *did* mean something, and time was running out.

Then there was the girl. Ellery had no way of knowing where she was or how to even begin to find her. Was she even real? Maybe this was all a dream and Ellery had lost her mind.

She glanced across at Loveday who still lay sleeping with one arm thrown over her eyes. She was beautiful. Ellery sighed and lay back down. She pulled the blanket around her. She didn't think she'd sleep again, but within minutes she was gone. This time, she didn't dream.

When she woke again, it was to the smell of fresh coffee. Loveday must have opened the curtains because sunlight came streaming through the window. It was a hard sun, bright and cold. A winter sun. At least it wasn't raining. If they left today like they'd planned, it would be better to do it in sunshine. It might even be quite pleasant; they could kid themselves they were out for a hike.

Ellery was about to go in search of the coffee when Loveday came back in the lounge, balancing two plates and two mugs in her arms. She smiled when she saw Ellery, and Ellery's heart fluttered a little.

"Morning, sleepyhead. Here." She handed Ellery a plate and put the coffee down on the table.

"This looks good." It was beans with cheese melted over the top. Loveday shrugged. "It's not cordon bleu, but it should fill a hole."

Ellery tucked in, ignoring the pleading eyes of Rocky who had padded in with Loveday. He seemed to have taken quite a shine to her, and Ellery was slightly put out by it, if she was honest. "How did you sleep?" She sat back on the sofa to block Rocky's sight line to her.

"Okay, I suppose." Loveday put down her spoon and looked at Ellery. "Why do you ask?"

"I had a dream last night."

Loveday nodded, as if she had suspected as much. "City being smashed to bits and a girl we have to save called Dani?"

"You too?" Ellery put down her bowl, appetite gone.

Loveday nodded at it. "You should eat that. There'll be a lot of walking today."

Ellery picked the bowl back up, swirled the spoon through the beans and cheese, turning it gloopy. "Is it for real, do you think? Is something like that even possible? A shared dream and everyone vanished, gone who knows where, and a mission to save a girl we've never met and have no idea where she is."

Loveday shrugged. "I can't even begin to try and make sense of it. I feel...I feel like it *is* real though. Do you know what I mean?"

"What do you think *it* is? I mean, if it's the thing that's been watching us, do we want to do what it says?"

"I don't know. In the dream...it didn't feel bad. Like the writing on the car bonnet did."

"It could be a trap," Ellery said.

Loveday nodded, tapping the spoon against the side of the bowl. "What's the alternative? That dream, it didn't feel like a dream. I know it sounds crazy, but I think we should head north. Find the girl. It feels... *right* somehow. Right in a way heading further south doesn't. Does that make any sense at all?"

"Yes. Yes, it does. So we head north."

"And find the girl. If Claude will follow."

"If Claude will follow. Any ideas where in the north we should head to? I mean, it's a fairly big place."

"Nope. Maybe we'll be filled in on tonight's instalment of *Fucked Up Dreams from the Apocalypse.*"

Ellery laughed. "Good game-show-host voice."

"Thanks. For now, I think we just head north. What's the plan this morning?"

Ellery finished off her beans and took a sip of coffee. It tasted good. "Romans first."

"The camping shop?"

"Yes. Then the supermarket for some food to take with us. I'd like to get going soon." Ellery gathered up the empty bowls and mugs.

"Me too. That countdown in my head is getting louder."

Ellery nodded. "Me too. Can we try to get Claude to follow us? Like a test run?"

Loveday nodded. Neither of them was holding out much hope.

"There's one other thing I've been thinking about," Ellery said.

"Go on."

"Where are all the pets?"

"What do you mean?" Loveday asked.

"I treat pretty much all the animals around here, and there are quite a few. When we went knocking on doors yesterday, we should have seen cats and dogs. There weren't any in the houses we visited."

"Do you think they've vanished too?" Loveday asked.

Ellery shrugged. "Why not? I mean, if the people have, why not their pets too?"

"Claude and Rocky are still here," Loveday said.

"And us."

"Yes. And us."

"Don't you find that strange?" Ellery asked.

Loveday threw up her hands. "I mean, I find the whole thing strange. And I earn a living writing made-up stories."

Ellery had to laugh at that. It made her feel a little better.

❖

Loveday smashed the window. Just like before, she was surprised when no alarm went off, though of course there was no electricity to power a system. Nor did the police come careening around the corner to arrest her. Like most people, Loveday didn't steal as a general rule. And she most certainly didn't break into shops. But all morning, that's what they'd been doing, and she would have been lying if she said part of her didn't get a thrill from it.

She also got a kick out of taking whatever she wanted off the shelves. From Romans: a winter coat, a fleece jacket, walking boots, waterproof trousers, gloves, a hat, socks, a sleeping bag, a tent. The gear would have added up to hundreds of pounds in the real world, but she just walked out the smashed doorway with it all in her arms.

At the supermarket they took mostly packet soups, dried instant pasta meals, and anything that wouldn't weigh too much. Loveday supposed they would be able to pick up more supplies from other deserted towns, unless there was some kind of law-and-order in existence somewhere. Although she doubted it. They would have come by now.

Their last stop was a bookshop. Ellery wanted a map. It was on the tip of Loveday's tongue to tell her they could use the GPS on their phones. She didn't feel as sad as she expected to when she realized she would probably never use a smartphone again.

She watched Ellery browse the Maps/Ordinance Surveys section. Glancing around at all the books on shelves *did* make her sad. Would people even remember writers like Dickens and Hemingway? Stephen King? Or would these books sit here for generations to come, going mouldy and stale and unreadable? And it wouldn't be just books. Hundreds of years of literature, plays, films, music, medicine, and science would disappear. All that knowledge, gone forever.

Ellery looked as though she was finishing up, a stack of maps under her arm. Loveday hoped she knew how to read them because left to Loveday, they'd end up heading east or something. She wasn't a good map reader.

Rocky sniffed around the base of one table displaying some half-price paperback books, *Reduced to clear!* and cocked his leg. She noticed her own novel sitting there and almost let Rocky go about his business. She sighed. She couldn't. "Rocky, no." The dog looked at her guiltily, then shuffled off.

She almost smiled as Ellery walked past the table and snagged her reduced-to-clear book. "Haven't read this one." She winked and carried on walking. Loveday was tempted to crack a joke, something like, *You owe me two ninety-nine*, then decided it was a sweet gesture and would be ruined by a joke. Instead, she let the way it made her feel settle inside her. The feeling was warm and made her smile. She should be terrified but she wasn't. She was scared of the thing watching them, and she was scared about what would happen to them, but Ellery somehow managed to make everything seem better.

Part of her felt like she was in one of her own novels. None of this was quite real. She supposed that was normal. How could anyone process all of this? But she wrote romance, so why did she feel like one of the characters in her books? Before she could dwell on this more, she saw Ellery had left the shop and begun walking up the road. Loveday felt a rush of fear at being left alone. She hurried to catch up.

As they started to head back up to Ellery's place, Loveday saw her stop, freeze. "What's the matter?" Loveday looked around, trying to see if the thing from yesterday was about.

"I've had an idea. Wait here." Ellery handed her the stack of leaflets and dropped her other pilfered items at Loveday's feet.

Loveday was curious. But when she saw which shop Ellery went into, she was shocked. *I did not see this coming.*

CHAPTER SIXTEEN

Terry almost laughed out loud when the spiky head of a teenager poked around the corner. On the heels of that came sharp relief. Those nasty cold eyes were still on him, but part of Terry was waiting for some creature or other to stick its head round, not Dani the landlord's daughter.

"All right, love?" Terry asked, surprised at the slur in his voice. He didn't feel close to drunk.

"Mr. Pratt?" Dani stepped around the corner, big eyes darting about. "What are you doing in here?"

"Well, Dani, princess, it seems like everyone's disappeared, including my boy Terry. I thought I'd come down here and see if I could drink myself to death." To his horror, Terry felt his eyes well up, his throat thicken and tighten. He heard his father's voice: *Don't snivel, you little queer.* It didn't matter though; Terry couldn't stop himself. He started bawling like a fucking baby.

He was dimly aware of the girl standing there, probably dumbfounded. Probably wasn't used to seeing a man like Terry weeping. Then he sensed movement. Dani had walked around to his side. "It's okay, Mr. Pratt. My mum and dad are gone as well."

Terry felt Dani's arm come around his shoulders and squeeze him gently. That sort of brought him to his senses again. He used his sleeve to wipe his eyes and the snot that had dribbled onto his lips and reached for the bottle, shaking the girl off. She stumbled backward.

"You want one?" He offered the bottle to Dani, taking in her smooth young face. He let his eyes slide down. In the last few years she'd started to fill out. Her hips had rounded and she'd grown a decent pair of tits.

"I'm sixteen, Mr. Pratt."

Terry shrugged. "So? Everyone's gone, love. If ever there was a time for a drink, it's now. Don't you think?"

Dani licked her lips, her eyes darting to the bottle. She nodded. "Okay. But not whiskey. I had it once and it made me sick."

"Fine. Get what you want. I don't suppose your old man will mind."

Dani went back around behind the bar. Terry thought she'd be prettier without that horrible short hair, and her ears looked like pin cushions. She poured herself a pint. Terry burst out laughing.

"What are you, a dyke?" He'd had his suspicions about the girl for a while. Would watch her walk around behind the bar, restocking the crisps and bottles. Something in the way she moved and took up space like a bloke. Confident. She didn't speak much and looked bored when the other blokes chatted her up.

Terry saw her flinch. Her eyes slid away from him, and she looked hurt. Disappointed. And like maybe she'd heard it before.

"No," was all she said.

Terry sighed. It wasn't much fun kicking a dog that was already broken. "Pour me another lager while you're back there." He pushed his empty pint glass across.

PART II: THE JOURNEY

Chapter Seventeen

Loveday laughed again. She didn't think she'd ever get used to the sight of Ellery pushing Rocky and Claude in a double pram.

Ellery scowled at her. "If you keep laughing at me, I'll make you push them."

"Oh no. Not when you're doing such a good job. You look like a proud mummy." Loveday giggled. Ellery looked like she was trying not to smile, but failing.

When Ellery had first disappeared into the Little Tots shop, Loveday was shocked. The idea of Ellery being pregnant hadn't crossed her mind. Why would it?

She hadn't taken long in there, and when she came back out pushing the navy blue pram, Loveday's first thought was *twins, OMG*. Ellery practically fell apart with laughter when Loveday asked her if she was pregnant.

"Yep, and all I needed was this pram. Come off it, Loveday." She shook her head and chuckled. "It's for the pets. If I was pregnant, this really would be a biblical situation."

It was a great idea. With Rocky's dodgy leg and Claude's possible reluctance to follow them—especially after walking for long periods of time—the pram was genius.

Loveday looked over at Rocky who napped in one carry cot, then at Claude who lay in the other, watching the world go by, sun shield pushed down so it wouldn't obstruct his view. She shook her head in admiration at Ellery's resourcefulness.

Her anxiety had receded as well, since they had been on the road and away from those watching eyes. She thought Ellery felt the same.

She'd seemed less stressed since they'd left town. Even the pets looked happy to be on the road—to her great relief, Claude happily jumped into the pram, then looked at them as if to say, *Come on, let's go.*

Loveday was glad Ellery had insisted they only take essentials with them. Her pack was already heavy and her shoulder muscles ached. She could tell the small of her back would be tight and painful by tonight.

Ellery, on the other hand, looked as fresh as when they'd first set off. Loveday knew for a fact she'd loaded more stuff into her own pack, a fact Loveday felt equal parts guilt and gratefulness for. She supposed it was another life lesson for her—stay in shape because you never know when the apocalypse is coming. She imagined it as a tagline for one of those fancy, shiny gyms which had popped up all over London and which she'd successfully avoided joining. She didn't feel guilty about it either—there was more to life than working out.

"What are you grinning at? Can't still be me pushing the pets," Ellery asked good-naturedly.

"No. Although it is still funny. I was just thinking that my pack is heavy, and I wish I'd done a bit more exercise to prepare for the end of the world."

Ellery looked confused but smiled anyway. She shook her head. "You find the damnedest things funny, Loveday."

"I know. It's important to laugh in the face of disaster, though."

"I guess. Listen, once we hit the motorway, we'll have a break and eat some lunch."

"Sounds lovely. You know, my grandparents used to have picnics by the side of the motorway when they were first married. I don't suppose it was as busy back then—otherwise that would be awful."

❖

Ellery imagined the motorway looked very similar to how it had back in Loveday's grandparents' day. If you ignored the abandoned cars dotted about, that was. Some seemed to have just stopped in their lanes, while others had crashed either into each other or the guard rail running through the centre.

Ellery checked inside a few of the cars. Empty. Not even a drop of blood in the ones that crashed. The people must have disappeared before impact, she guessed. And where did they disappear *to*? Were they driving along one minute, thinking about getting home in time to bath the kids, or before their favourite show started on TV? Was it quick? Or did they have time to be afraid?

Ellery jumped when Loveday touched her shoulder. "You should come and have something to eat," she said softly, squeezing briefly. The points where her fingers touched Ellery's shoulder sent pleasant ripples down into her belly. She was developing a full-blown crush on Loveday Taylor.

Ellery had packed sandwiches—with butter this time—and they sat in a sun patch to eat. Loveday filled a bowl with water for the pets and shook out some biscuits. Ellery laughed when they found each other's tastier.

She watched Loveday lean back on her elbows and turn her face up to the sun. She could almost imagine they were on a normal picnic. She itched to reach over and brush away the strands of hair which had fallen across Loveday's face. Instead, she lay down in the grass warmed by the sun and closed her eyes.

It only seemed like minutes later when she felt a soft warm hand on her forehead, brushing away her hair. "Hey," Loveday said gently. "You fell asleep."

Ellery opened her eyes and found herself staring directly into Loveday's. Loveday had bent her face so close that Ellery could feel her breath tickle her nose. They stared at each other for a moment, and Ellery knew all she would have to do was lift her head a little, maybe a foot, and their lips would meet. Loveday seemed to realize the same thing because her eyes widened and dropped to Ellery's lips, and her mouth opened slightly in surprise. She stroked Ellery's forehead once, twice, then quickly moved away.

Ellery sat up, brushed grass from her arms and legs, and stood, continuing to brush off bits from her jeans. She stretched her arms and her sore back and shouldered her pack again.

"I'll push them for a while," Loveday said, her back to Ellery as she fiddled with the straps on her own pack.

"I don't mind."

"You've been pushing them all morning. And I *know* your pack is heavier than mine. Don't be a martyr," Loveday snapped, turning to face her, all the warmth gone from her eyes.

Ellery nodded. It seemed easier that way. The last thing she wanted was an argument with Loveday, and Ellery had an idea she was pushing for one. She knew it had something to do with their non-kiss a moment before. She couldn't work out why Loveday was angry about it. Nothing happened.

Loveday looked like she was about to say something else, then changed her mind, tapping one of the carry cots which Claude obediently jumped into. He didn't look like he wanted to argue with Loveday either.

They walked on into the afternoon, stopping again for a snack and some water next to a disused services station. They had barely spoken since the lunchtime incident; Loveday slowed her pace so she walked a little behind Ellery. Ellery sensed she didn't want her to wait and pushed on, giving Loveday her space.

The distance Loveday put between them—both physical and emotional—confused her. It seemed like a big overreaction to such a non-event. If Ellery hadn't known differently, she might have assumed Loveday was uncomfortable with the idea of a woman being attracted to her. Ellery knew she dated women from her blogs and some of her books, so it couldn't be that.

Ellery was sure the almost-kiss was mutual, but maybe that had been more wishful thinking. She briefly closed her eyes, face heating in shame. Perhaps she had read the whole situation wrong. Maybe Loveday sensed Ellery wanted to kiss her and felt uncomfortable. Loveday *was* attracted to women, but not *her*. Now she was probably worried Ellery would leave her if she rejected her advances. That was why she hung back, that was why she was so cold.

Ellery was angry with herself for putting Loveday in this position. It just proved she was right to stay away from other people. She was hopeless in their company, misreading cues and situations. She'd never felt more like an alien than she did now. From now on, she'd keep it polite but formal—like before everyone disappeared. She'd get over her childish crush on Loveday. What had she been thinking anyway? Why in the world would a woman like Loveday go for someone like her? It was a relief she'd come to her senses before she'd done something really stupid.

Chapter Eighteen

L oveday concentrated on putting one foot in front of the other. Her back ached and there were matching bright spots of pain on each heel where her boots rubbed. She squinted up into the sky and saw the sun had begun its descent. Good. That meant they would stop soon.

She watched Ellery trudging along in front of her. Poor Ellery. Loveday felt horrible for the way she was treating her, but she couldn't seem to help it. The almost kiss had terrified her. When she'd looked down into trusting, sleepy eyes, a bolt of arousal shot through her, stronger than anything she'd felt before. She knew that all she would have to do was bend down and capture those perfect lips with hers and...

Loveday shook her head, like Claude sometimes did, and cast off the memory, not to mention the horny feeling that was back again. She sighed. Ellery was probably confused and wondering what she'd done wrong. Loveday knew they'd need to talk about it. This was the sort of thing that festered and grew into an issue. Something they could ill afford when it seemed they were the last two people left on earth.

She wasn't looking forward to it though. What would she even say? *So, Ellery, sorry for being a bitch earlier, but I'm really attracted to you. And I can't be.* There was no way. She'd promised herself she wouldn't again. She didn't deserve it, for one thing. For another, Loveday needed Ellery—in survival terms, they were all each other had. As she knew from past experiences, sex always complicated things. And things were already complicated enough.

She looked up to see Ellery had stopped and turned to face her. "Sorry, Ellery, what did you say? I was miles away."

"I said we should stop here for the night. There's a copse of trees over there that should give us decent enough shelter. Is that okay? Are you ready to call it a day?"

Loveday wanted to cry with relief. She wanted to get down on her knees and kiss Ellery's boots in thanks. "Sure. If you've had enough of walking," she said instead.

She followed Ellery down to the cluster of trees, thick enough to hide them from the view of the motorway—not that they'd seen anyone all day. The pram bumped over the uneven ground, and she nearly tipped the pets out at one point. Ellery left her to it, while she searched through her pack, taking out the camping stove and kettle.

"What can I do?" she asked when she finally reached Ellery.

"Do you know how to put up the tent?" Ellery didn't look up from her task of sorting out Rocky's and Claude's dinners.

"It's a pop-up, right? Can't be that hard."

"Don't put it directly under the trees. And kick away any stones and twigs."

Loveday got the tent from where they'd stored it under the pram. She went a little way from the trees where they would still be out of sight of the motorway. The tent didn't take long to pitch, and Ellery walked over as she was adjusting the guide lines on the final pegs.

"Are you ready for a cup of coffee?"

"Definitely. I've been thinking about it for the last two hours." That was a lie. She'd been thinking about it since lunchtime.

Ellery grinned. "Only two hours? I've been thinking about it since this morning."

They walked back in silence. The tension from earlier had eased a bit, and Loveday wondered if bringing up the almost kiss was a good idea. It might make things awkward again.

Loveday sat down while Ellery made coffee. Bless her, she'd even bought the coffee press. She eased off her boots, sighed with relief, then steeled herself to peel off her socks. She could feel where they stuck to her heels. Where they'd blistered, burst, and bled.

She pulled at them gently, gingerly. With a quick flick, she ripped away one sock and bit her lip against the sudden, sharp pain. The stinging intensified when air hit the raw skin of her heel. She squeezed her eyes shut and did the same with the other foot.

"Loveday!"

She opened her eyes. Ellery was on her knees. She looked torn between wanting to come over and wanting to stay where she was. That was Loveday's fault, her uncertainty.

"It's okay. Just blisters."

"Why didn't you say anything? We could have stopped," Ellery said, more softly this time. She shuffled over on her knees and took one of Loveday's feet gently in her hands. She hissed through her teeth. "This is nasty. You should have said something."

"I've had worse. I spent most of my twenties in cripplingly high heels." Loveday attempted a smile that came out more like a grimace.

"All the same, if you damage your feet, you won't be able to carry on. Not to mention infections." Ellery's brow creased with worry, and Loveday wanted to smooth it with her fingers. She had such soft skin. Loveday was also aware of her foot still being held in Ellery's hand. Not wanting to be a bitch again, she gently moved it out of Ellery's reach.

"I'll be fine. If you pass me the first aid kit, I'll clean it up."

"No. I'll do it."

"Excuse me?" Loveday bristled at Ellery's commanding tone. She wasn't fond of being ordered around.

"I may be more used to treating animals, but I'm still a doctor. It'll be better if I do it. I'll bandage it properly to prevent it becoming infected. You've rubbed off all the skin."

"Fine." Loveday couldn't argue with her. Now, more than ever, it was important to take care of themselves. It wasn't as if she could just pop down to the doctor's for some antibiotics.

She lay down and rolled onto her stomach as Ellery instructed. The feel of Ellery's hands on her calves and feet tingled all the way up to her crotch. She wanted Ellery to stop, and she wanted her to carry on. She wished she didn't like the feel of her gentle fingers as they cleaned and wiped and softly stroked the top of her foot while she washed out each heel. Loveday didn't think Ellery was even fully aware she was stroking her. Her touch was meant to soothe rather than excite, but to Loveday it did both. By the time Ellery finished, she was horny as hell.

CHAPTER NINETEEN

*T*erry was in The Palace, one of those tacky discos with the glitter balls and sticky floors where all the glasses still had lipstick on them. They'd knocked it down in ninety-five and put up flats. It had always been a pit, but it was open until two, and if you hadn't pulled that night, it was a dead cert to at least get a hand job around the back.

He thought he was dreaming, but was certain of it when he clocked Shirl standing at the bar. She looked the same as she had at sixteen when he'd met her, only nineteen himself. Shirl had never been what you'd call a looker, but she had the best pair of tits he'd ever laid eyes on. If this was the night they'd met, she'd let him buy her a drink and feel her tits up round the back of the club, but when he went to put his hand up her skirt she'd pull away and smile shyly. He'd think about doing her anyway, up against the wall, whether she wanted it or not—What self-respecting girl went round the back of the club with a strange bloke anyway? One that was asking for it, that's who—but her mates had come clacking round the corner in their too high heels, painted faces that made them look like clowns. He'd take her number even though he had no intention of calling her, but then he'd start thinking about those tits and how they'd felt in his hands. He'd take her out a few times, and somewhere between the third and fourth date he'd knock her up.

His dad would find out when she turned up at the house crying her eyes out because Terry wouldn't do right by her. Then Terry Senior would knock ten bells of shit out of him—Terry outweighed his dad by about fifty pounds by then but wouldn't raise a hand to stop him—and drive them down to the registry office. Shirl with her belly starting to round out and Terry with a black eye and split lip. There were no wedding pictures.

Terry looked at Shirl in this weird dream and had an idea he wouldn't buy her a drink this time. Or feel up her tits, as great as they were. She smiled at him shyly and looked away. His legs moved of their own accord, and he was heading straight for the bar and straight for Shirl.

His mouth moved of its own accord, and he was asking to buy her a drink and asking what she wanted. Shirl always drank vodka and Coke but tonight she wanted a Son of Adam Head North, whatever the fuck that was.

In the next moment he was out the back of the club and his hands were full of Shirl's tits, and her hand was on his cock, rubbing it through his trousers. Her mouth tasted sweet and was sloppy on his, until she broke away. "Son of Adam, head north," she said, and he almost smacked her one right there.

"What the fuck are you talking about, you silly bitch?" He moved forward, trapping her body against the wall, and tried to push his hand up her skirt. She wriggled out from under his weight, stronger than he ever remembered her being.

"Son of Adam, head north," she said again.

"I'm warning you, Shirley," he said in his warning voice, using her whole name so she would know she'd better pack in whatever she was doing that was pissing him off.

"Son of Adam—"

He hit her across the mouth. Her lip split open and blood trickled onto her chin. "I warned you, Shirl. Didn't I warn you?"

"Son of Adam, head north." She said it again and he couldn't fucking believe it.

Before he could stop himself, he hit her again and again and again. Again with his fist closed and her head was bobbing back and forward like a nodding dog as he struck her blow after blow after blow. He'd never beat her like this in real life, although sometimes he thought about it. When that black mood came knocking and settled around him like a heavy cloak and all he wanted to do was hurt something.

In the dream he couldn't stop himself, and he beat her to the ground. Certain he'd killed her—what woman could survive that sort of beating?—he stood over Shirl, breathing heavily. His fists were sore from where he'd split his knuckles open and already swelling.

Shirl opened her eyes, looked up at him. "Son of Adam, head north." It didn't quite come out like that because she was speaking around a mouthful of broken teeth and most likely a broken jaw, but he knew what she meant.

He laid into her again.

❖

Terry woke up, his head pounding from the booze. He'd been drinking for two days solid now. Dani had puked her guts up the first day and the second morning, but she seemed to be holding it better now. She'd stopped drinking pints the first night, saying she couldn't stand the smell of it. She wouldn't touch the whiskey still but seemed to be getting on all right with screwdrivers.

She was like a little mother hen, shuffling about in the kitchen making sandwiches. Left to Terry, they would have starved to death because he really didn't give a shit any more. Every time he thought about his son Little Terry, his heart felt like it was tearing in two. He ate the food Dani brought him some of the time, and sometimes he threw it at her.

He winced. He remembered last night. He'd given the girl a smack, hadn't he? It was hazy—being drunk for two days would do that to you—but he did vaguely recall winding up and unloading on her. Maybe that's what the weird dream with Shirl had been about. He hoped he hadn't done that sort of damage to Dani. Not that there was anyone about to arrest him for it, but still, it wouldn't have been right.

Just then, the girl shuffled in, limping a bit, and Terry realized just now he was wedged between the bottom of the table and a chair, the foul smelling carpet—God only knew when it had last been cleaned—beneath him.

He crawled out and sat in the chair, holding his head between his hands. He looked up when Dani put a cup of tea down in front of him. "Cheers. What time is it?"

"I'm not sure. Definitely after four, I reckon. Sky's getting darker."

He looked up at the girl's face, one eye swollen shut and going purple, her lip split in the middle. Not as bad as he was expecting, which was good. Little Terry and Shirl had gotten worse when the black mood came down.

"Sorry about that, love," he said, nodding at the damaged eye.

"Okay." Dani kept a wary distance.

"Didn't knock you about too bad, did I?" he asked, taking a sip of the tea.

"No, Mr. Pratt."

"Saw you limping."

"Just my side from when I fell against the table." She angled her head to the table which had tipped onto its side near the bar.

"All right, good." The girl wasn't a whiner. Terry respected her a bit more for it.

"Mr. Pratt?"

Terry looked up. The girl sat down opposite him at the table, ran her fingers over it, and started to pick at something long dried.

"What?"

"I had a funny dream last night. It might be the booze, but... well..."

"Spit it out, Dani."

"I was at the football, one team was called Son of Adam and the other was called Head North, and I—"

Terry slammed his fist on the table and the mug of tea tipped over. Dani pulled her hand back quickly and half stood, ready to bolt.

"I don't want to fucking hear it," Terry said.

He wasn't sure why Dani's dream had made him suddenly angry. It probably had something to do with his own dream. That fluttery feeling of fear was back, and Terry didn't like it one little bit. It made him feel like he had lost control.

"You bring up anything about Son of Adam or fucking head north and I'll cave your bloody head in. Got it?"

Dani nodded. She stood warily and backed away from Terry like he was a rabid dog. In a way, he supposed he was. All the booze. Little Terry. Everyone gone. It was too much. He went back to the bar to pour himself another drink.

CHAPTER TWENTY

Ellery leaned back and watched Loveday prepare the soup for their dinner. She was worried about her heels and annoyed she hadn't said something earlier. Loveday could be so stubborn. Ellery hadn't known her for long, but she could already tell that Loveday hated to admit any kind of weakness. Not that it was even a weakness, but Loveday would see it as such. She was infuriating. And it was dangerous. They were on their own now. It wasn't like they could just pop into a doctor. Infections could kill them now.

Loveday was going to drive her mad. They'd take it easier tomorrow, have a few more breaks.

Ellery looked at her map, marking off with a finger where they were. She'd been keeping an eye on the motorway signs and they'd made decent progress today. She thought it would be another couple of days before they joined up with the A36, which would take them north. Now that they were moving, the sense of running out of time had lessened slightly. She still felt the need to keep going, but it was better now they were out of town and on the move.

The constant feeling of being watched had also gone away, and she was relived. She just hoped it would stay that way. Ellery wasn't looking forward to spending the night out in the open, but they didn't really have any other choice.

She looked up as Loveday brought over a bowl of soup and took it gratefully. "Thanks."

Loveday smiled and went back to her side of the camping stove. She was still quiet, though the awkwardness between them seemed to have gone. Ellery decided it was easier to let it be. She was surprised when Loveday spoke.

"How long have you lived in town?" she asked.

"I grew up nearby, and after I finished studying, I moved there to open my practice. So about eight years now. When did you move there?" Ellery put her empty bowl down and leaned back on her elbows.

"Only seven months ago."

"Where are you from originally?"

Loveday got up and began tidying. Ellery sensed she'd overstepped again and cursed herself for her poor social skills. "Sorry, I didn't mean to pry."

Loveday sighed. "You didn't. It's a normal question to ask somebody."

"But you don't want to talk about it, and that's okay. We're all entitled to our privacy." Ellery stood up and brushed the grass off her trousers. "I'm going to take a walk up to the road. I won't be long."

Ellery was annoyed with herself. Up until earlier, they'd been getting on well, and a tentative friendship seemed to be forming between them. Now, Loveday was defensive and remote, and Ellery couldn't help feeling responsible. She shouldn't have nearly kissed her. On the other hand, Loveday's sensitive spots seemed close to the surface and easy to trip over. She was secretive and remote, and Ellery understood that because she was the same, but she thought Loveday might be even more closed off than her.

Ellery looked across at the road and studied the occasional car that had either crashed or rolled to a stop. What was happening? Where was everybody? It occurred to Ellery that apart from the birds, she hadn't seen any animals either. Had they vanished too? The thought of it made Ellery feel sick. So far today they'd found no signs of life at all. Was it really possible that she and Loveday were the last two people left? She hoped not, because the way things were going, Loveday wouldn't be talking to her at all soon. Ellery wished she'd gone out more with the practice staff. At least she could have brushed up a bit on her social skills.

CHAPTER TWENTY-ONE

Loveday washed the bowls with some of the bottled water they'd brought and packed them away in her rucksack again. Both Claude and Rocky were fast asleep in their pram, and Loveday had to laugh at the sight of them all tucked up.

She could just about make out the top of Ellery's head where she stood near the road. Loveday felt guilty, knowing she was the reason Ellery was over there. It would serve her right if Ellery took off in the night and left her to it. She couldn't blame her. She'd probably leave her too.

Asking someone where they were from wasn't a nosy question, and yet she'd reacted like Ellery asked her how many sexual partners she'd had. And that was the other problem, wasn't it? Loveday was attracted to Ellery and she could feel it getting stronger. And it wasn't just sex—it was worse than that. Loveday actually liked her. Ellery was funny and sweet and kind and a great catch.

The problem was, Loveday wasn't. She was selfish and cowardly, and she didn't trust herself not to hurt her. Plus, it seemed like they were the only two people who'd survived the weird storm, and they needed each other. Loveday couldn't shag her and do a runner—well, she could, but that would be suicide.

Loveday sighed and looked back at the tent, which drew her attention to another problem. It was going to be hell sharing that small tent tonight. Looking at it, there was no way they couldn't not touch each other. Loveday just hoped she wouldn't do anything stupid in her sleep. She was a snuggler and naturally gravitated towards anyone she shared a bed with. In her other life it hadn't been an issue because she usually only shared a bed with someone she was sleeping with.

Tonight, she was sharing a bed with sweet, sexy Ellery. Life was such a bitch sometimes. How easy would it be to roll towards Ellery in the night? To kiss her. Would Ellery kiss her back? Loveday imagined trailing her fingers over the soft skin of Ellery's cheek. Over her lips and down her neck. Shit. She shouldn't be thinking like this. It was dangerous and no good could come of it. Loveday needed to get a grip, and fast. Before she fucked everything up and found herself alone in a world where everyone had disappeared.

❖

Loveday opened her eyes. She was lying on her side with one arm draped over Ellery's middle, though mercifully she'd kept half a foot of space between their bodies.

She quickly rolled in the other direction and came face-to-face with Rocky, who was sitting up and staring at her expectantly. "Hey, boy," she whispered and stroked his head. "Do you need the toilet?"

Rocky cocked his head to one side and chuffed. She wasn't sure what that meant. Loveday didn't have any experience with dogs. Cats had always been her pet of choice, though after the short amount of time she'd spent with Rocky, she was beginning to think she might have missed out.

"Come on, I'll take you." Loveday got up as quietly as she could and slipped out of the tent. She pulled on her boots and winced as her heels caught on the backs of them. Rocky waited patiently for her to do her laces, then followed her into the copse of trees.

She aimed her torch near the ground and watched as he sauntered off a ways and began to sniff the grass, pawing here and there. "For someone who spends a lot of time with their nose up Claude's backside, you certainly are fussy about where you take a shit," Loveday said.

Rocky ignored her and continued with his routine. Loveday sighed and glanced around. She'd never been afraid of the dark, but it just now occurred to her how dark it was. Even with the torch she couldn't see more than six feet in front of her.

Off to the left, a twig snapped and Loveday jumped. She spun the torch wildly in the direction of the noise and braced herself to see the same figure who had been in Ellery's back garden. Relieved to find she was still alone, Loveday shone the torch back on Rocky, who was staring hard in the same direction, his ears pricked.

"Oh, bloody hell," Loveday whispered. She was back to being completely freaked out now she knew Rocky heard the noise as well and it wasn't just her imagination. "Rocky, come on." She urged the little dog who was still staring intently into the darkness.

Loveday didn't want to leave him, but she also didn't want to be stuck out here in the open if someone—that person from Ellery's garden—was out here with her. The tent wouldn't offer any protection either, but at least Ellery was in there. Out here, she was alone.

Without warning, Rocky took off further into the copse. "Rocky, no!" Loveday called, but he paid her no mind. She took several steps towards him, then stopped. She took a deep breath. Should she go after him and possibly to her death? Or back to the relative safety of the tent? *Back to the tent, back to the tent,* a little voice whispered. It was the same cowardly voice that had led her to this point in her life. The voice that had ruled her for too long.

Surely he couldn't get too far with that cast on his leg? Loveday took a deep breath, squared her shoulders, and walked deeper into the copse.

CHAPTER TWENTY-TWO

Ellery woke up. She knew before she opened her eyes she was alone in the tent. The steady sound of Loveday's breathing which Ellery found comforting was absent. She sat up and saw the tent flap was open. Ellery pulled it to the side and peered out into the darkness. The torch by the exit was gone and without it, she could see nothing.

It was funny how even in the countryside you got used to a certain amount of light pollution. The small glow from a distant house or headlights from the road. Now, since everyone disappeared, there was nothing.

Ellery poked her head out of the tent (it was as much as she was willing to do in the total blackness) and called out to Loveday. She waited a moment, listening for any reply.

She's probably gone to answer the call of nature. But there was an uneasiness inside she couldn't place. Claude lay curled by Loveday's pillow and blinked slowly at her as if to say, *chill out, everything's fine.* Everything didn't *feel* fine though. *Maybe she's gone. Maybe she left me.* Things had been strained between them since the incident that afternoon. Perhaps Loveday decided it would be easier to go. No, she wouldn't leave Claude, Ellery was sure of that.

Without a watch, it was difficult to mark time. It seemed like ages since Ellery had woken up but in reality it was probably only a couple of minutes. She thought about going out to look for Loveday but quickly squashed the idea. She couldn't even get up at night in her home for a pee without a night light. There was no way she could face going out into the pitch black.

Coward.

So what if she was? It wasn't like things were exactly normal right now. Who could blame her for staying in the tent?

Such a coward.

Ellery ignored the voice and moved back to her sleeping spot. What if Loveday was in trouble? No, Ellery would have heard her cry out or Rocky bark. She most likely went to the toilet and Ellery had a distorted perception of time. They'd be back any minute.

What if they're not?

Well, then she'd cross that bridge when she came to it. For now, she'd be better waiting here. She couldn't do much good crashing about in the dark.

There's another torch in Loveday's bag.

If they weren't back soon, maybe she'd get it and go outside.

What if it's too late by then?

Ellery made a fist and hit the ground. Why was she such a coward? Why couldn't she just go outside and look for them?

Surely she should have grown out of a stupid childhood fear by now?

Before she could talk herself out of it, Ellery lunged for Loveday's bag, startling Claude who looked up and narrowed his eyes at her. "Sorry, but I need to do this quick before I bottle it," she told him.

Ellery dug about in the bag until she felt cold plastic in her hand. She pulled out the torch and switched it on, satisfied it was working.

Gingerly, Ellery pulled back the flap of the tent and leaned halfway out. She could feel the blood rushing in her ears and her heart was beating like she'd just been on a run.

She shone the torch in the direction of the copse, hoping not to light Loveday up while she was in a compromising position. Ellery almost smiled at that.

"Loveday," she called again. Still no reply.

Ellery took a deep breath and came most of the way out of the tent. She could just about make out the first few trees before the darkness seemed to suck the rest in out of sight.

"Come on," she told herself, "you can do this." Ellery wiped away the sweat which beaded on her forehead—strange, because it wasn't warm—and took several steps towards the copse of trees.

Her heart threatened to beat itself out of her chest, and the torch shook in her hand so much she thought she might drop it. *And be plunged into total darkness. Great.*

As she was about to head in, something lithe and quick darted out of the trees and ran straight towards her. Ellery screamed.

❖

Terry could hear banging in the kitchen, like pots and pans falling to the floor. What the bloody hell was Shirley up to? If he didn't feel so sick he'd get up and hit her with damn things.

Terry discovered his lips were stuck to his teeth and his mouth tasted like sandpaper. Must have been quite a night if he was feeling this way. A brass band had taken up residence right at the front of his head. Fuck, even the roots of his teeth ached. How much did he have to drink?

It hit him all at once then. Shirley, little Terry, and his grandson all gone. Just him left behind. Terry groaned and struggled to sit up.

That was right. He was in the pub. With that girl—what was her name? Dani. Yeah, Dani. Probably a lesbian, but she didn't whine and she stayed out of Terry's way.

Terry didn't know what day it was. All he knew was that his attempts to drink himself to death had so far failed. Although if the girl kept up the banging, someone was going to be dying, and soon.

"Will you shut the fuck up!" Terry roared and immediately regretted it. His eyeballs tried to jump out of his head, and he started heaving. Before he could stop himself, Terry had puked all over his own lap and across the pub table. Tendrils of long, ropey spit hung from his lips as he panted and gulped and tried to calm his gut down.

Finally in control of himself, Terry heaved himself up from the table and promptly fell to the ground. He blacked out.

❖

Terry looked down. A huge boat squatted before him like something out of a sci-fi film, a stark white against the grey churning sea and the darkening sky. He stood at the edge of a cliff, buffeted by a bitter wind.

Beside him was his son. Terry knew it was a dream because Little Terry wasn't more than eight years old. He was wearing his school football kit but didn't look cold. When he first got it, he wanted to wear it to bed.

Little Terry nodded towards the boat. "They're waiting for me, Dad. I need to get on board now."

Terry gripped his son's hand tighter, as something swelled and ached in his throat. "No, son. You need to stay with me. Please don't go."

"It's okay, Dad. You can come too." Little Terry looked up at him and smiled. His two front teeth were missing and Terry remembered the day he knocked them out when he fell off his new bike. He hadn't cried.

"I can't, son. I didn't disappear, so I can't come with you."

Little Terry grinned. "But you can. Rosemary said you can. Rosemary Decker. All you have to do is one thing. One tiny little thing and you can be with me forever."

Terry felt a spark of hope catch inside him. It was stupid. This was a dream. Just a stupid fucking dream that didn't mean anything except he'd drunk himself into oblivion again.

Even so, he found himself asking, "What? What do I have to do, son?"

"Bring the girl Dani with you. Rosemary wants her."

"What for?"

Little Terry's face darkened and he stepped away. "She's a bitch, Dad. She's not to be trusted. She's going to ruin everything."

"She's just a girl."

Little Terry shook his head. There was something in his eyes. Something Terry hadn't seen before, something sly and secretive.

A horn sounded. It came from the boat.

"That's me. I have to go."

"Wait! Son, don't go. Stay here with me. Forget about that fucking boat."

Little Terry shook his head and that look was still in his eyes. Terry's hands became fists and he itched to knock it out of his son.

"I can't, Dad. It's been decided. It's the rebalancing."

"What the fuck are you on about?" Terry lunged for him, reached for his shirt, but Little Terry moved easily out of his reach. He didn't look scared.

The horn blared again and Terry swore it sounded impatient.

"I have to go, Dad. If you ever want to see me again, head north. Bring the girl. It's the only way."

Terry lunged for him again. The blackness rose inside him like a tidal wave, threatening to obliterate everything. "Don't you dare. Don't you dare get on that fucking boat. I forbid it. I fucking forbid it, you little bastard!"

Little Terry continued to elude him. Every time Terry reached for him, his son moved further away, further towards the edge of the cliff, until he stepped back, then disappeared over the side.

Terry screamed and dived for him. He brushed Little Terry's shirt with his fingertips, and then his son was gone. Agony ripped through Terry, threatened to tear him apart. Not his son. Not his boy who he loved more than anything on earth.

Terry looked towards the boat. The huge hulking thing was moving away. It cut through the water like it was softened butter and picked up speed. Terry rolled onto his back and looked up to the sky. The girl, Dani. She was the key to getting his son back. *Head north.* Wasn't that what Little Terry had said? *Head north and find Rosemary Decker.*

❖

When he came to, Dani was leaning over him and wiping at his face with a flannel or something similar.

"What are you doing?" he croaked out. Terry noticed the girl's eye looked a bit better. It was still swollen and raw looking, but it did look better. "How long was I out?"

"You've been in and out for a few days. You wake up, start drinking, and then pass out again. I stopped getting you booze this morning—not that there's much left. I was worried you would die."

The girl's concerned face almost made Terry laugh. Afraid he might die? Didn't the little twit know he was trying to kill himself?

Terry pushed the flannel away and struggled into a sitting position. He waited while the urge to puke again passed and the world righted itself. He stared up at the girl who looked concerned. "Why do you care what happens to me? I haven't exactly been nice to you."

Dani shrugged and glanced away. "I didn't want to be left alone."

Terry didn't know what to say to that. He supposed he could see the girl's point, but he felt sorry for her if Terry was the only thing standing between her and being completely alone in the world.

It was then he noticed the backpack resting neatly by the bar. He nodded at it. "Going somewhere?"

Dani followed his gaze, then regarded Terry warily. "It's those dreams. I can't take it any more. It's gotten so I can't even sleep for more than an hour. Every time I do, I dream about heading north, and then I wake up. I decided I might as well do what it wants."

Terry nodded. Dani did look tired. Apart from the bruise there were dark circles under her eyes, and she was pale. Did she have the same dream as him? He doubted it. She wouldn't be so keen to head north if that was the case. "These dreams. What happens in them?"

Dani looked uncomfortable. Shifty. She shrugged. "I don't remember them very well. There's a storm. A…a flood. And then someone tells me to head north."

"That's all?" There was more. She wouldn't tell him. It didn't matter, though. She wanted to go north and that was where Little Terry was. He wouldn't have to drag her there.

"Mr. Pratt? Do you have the dreams?" Dani asked.

"No, love. I haven't had any dreams."

Dani sighed. "I wish you would come with me, Mr. Pratt. I know your wife and your son are gone, but I'd like to have someone to go with. Just in case it really is only us left."

Terry looked at the girl again. She wasn't old, not much younger than Little Terry when he disappeared.

There was a good chance these dreams meant nothing. If Dani wasn't having them too, Terry would put them down to the booze. He'd drunk enough to sink a ship, and a few strange dreams would be getting off light. But what if they did mean something? What if there was a chance he could get his son back?

It would be at the expense of this girl, but who was she? No one, really. No one important. Little Terry was his son, his flesh and blood. If this woman, Rosemary Decker, was going to kill her, he'd make sure it was quick. If he was going to lead Dani to her death, it was the least he could do.

"Okay, love. Yeah, I'll go with you. Just let me clean up first."

Dani smiled with obvious relief. "Thank you, Mr. Pratt."

Terry nodded. "Give me an hour to sort myself out. I have to see if I can get off this fucking floor."

CHAPTER TWENTY-THREE

Loveday raced out of the copse and straight into Ellery, knocking her flat and landing on top of her. The torch hit the ground, cracked, and skittered away, plunging them into darkness. She heard Ellery grunt, then lie still. Ellery's breath was warm against her ear.

"Is everything okay?" Ellery's voice was muffled and her lips whispered against Loveday's neck where her face was mashed.

"I'm so sorry." Loveday struggled upright, kneeing Ellery in the crotch as she did so. Ellery *oof*ed. "God, sorry about that too. I'm fine. Rocky ran off into the trees and I followed him. Then I spooked myself."

Loveday held out a hand to help Ellery up. She could barely make her out in the darkness. Even living in the countryside, she didn't think she'd ever been in such utter darkness. She was grateful when Ellery clicked on their remaining torch.

"Are you sure that was all it was? Are you sure it wasn't—"

"It wasn't. I'm sure." Loveday cut her off before she could mention the thing that stalked them in the village. She knew it was irrational, but she didn't want Ellery to say it out loud in case it brought the thing to them. "I'm pretty sure it was a rat or something I disturbed. That's probably what Rocky chased after to begin with."

As if he'd heard his name, Rocky came trotting out of the trees and chuffed good-naturedly at them before heading back into the tent.

Loveday laughed. "Like he hasn't a care in the world. I really am sorry I frightened you." She couldn't make out Ellery properly but thought she saw her shrug.

"Don't worry about it. You're safe and that's all that matters.

We'd better head back inside the tent. We've a long walk ahead of us tomorrow."

Inside the tent, Claude barely acknowledged them as he reclined on Ellery's recently vacated sleeping bag. Loveday watched as she gently moved him, climbed inside, and lay down.

"Ellery?"

"Yeah?"

Loveday sighed. "I'm sorry. About before."

She heard Ellery shift, roll towards her. "Don't worry about it. It's dark out there and you got spooked."

"No, not that. I mean, I am sorry about that too, but it's not what I'm talking about."

"Okay." Loveday smiled at the confusion in Ellery's voice. "What are you sorry for, then?"

"I was a total bitch earlier. I'm sorry."

"It's not your fault. Look, Loveday, I want you to know I would never do anything to…to, you know, make you uncomfortable on purpose."

Loveday heard her blow out a breath and felt horrible all over again. "You didn't do anything wrong. It was me who nearly kissed you."

"Oh. Well—"

"I shouldn't have. It was a mistake. What I mean is I won't do it again. I like you, Ellery, but not like that." It was a lie. A total lie, but she needed to nip this in the bud. Stop it before it even started. It was better for them both.

"I understand." Ellery's voice was small, hurt. "Let's get some sleep. It's a long day tomorrow."

"Okay. Ellery?"

"Yes, Loveday?" A hint of amusement in Ellery's voice now.

"Are we okay?"

"Of course we're okay. We're more than okay. We're good. Now go to sleep before I throttle you."

Loveday laughed. "Right, then. Night."

"Night."

Chapter Twenty-Four

They had been trickling in since the early morning—Rosemary's flock, as she was beginning to think of them. Bedraggled and hollow-eyed, they shuffled into the hangar.

Rosemary watched them from her position on one of the platforms, and her insides warmed. These were her children now and she had a responsibility to them, to help them find their way to God's light. Her followers had set up partitions on the far side of the hangar to make dormitories. One for women and children and one for men.

Rosemary frowned as she observed a young man and young woman share a kiss. She turned to Chloe or Claire. "Those two"—she pointed at the couple who were now cuddling—"are they married?"

Chloe-Claire consulted her clipboard. Each person was required to register their details when they came in. "No. They are a couple, though."

Rosemary just knew they were sleeping with each other. She wouldn't allow sin to go unchallenged here. "I'll hold a service in the chapel this evening. Make sure everyone is there. It's time to lay down the rules. Make sure there's a copy of the Bible for everyone. It will help them to fully understand how things are going to be from now on. God willing, our new world will look nothing like the old one."

Rosemary didn't wait for Chloe-Claire to reply. It was time for her daily inspection of the *Ark 2*. Only God knew how long they would need to be on it, and everything should be just right. She climbed down the ladder to her left. There were ladders on each platform, each eventually leading to the ground. Rosemary wasn't keen on them, but a lift had proved impractical. She would never admit it, but the ladders scared her. When she'd made the mistake once of looking down, her foot slipped, and for a second she saw herself falling, crashing over the edge of the platform below, and tumbling to her death. Lying broken on the hangar floor.

Rosemary shook thoughts of her own mortality away and continued her descent.

❖

Ellery breathed in the smoky air, then looked at her map again. She traced the A road they were on with her finger. For the past two days, the smell of burning had gotten steadily worse, and she was afraid there was a fire somewhere to the west of them. A big one.

They couldn't see any smoke yet, but there was a very real danger she would lead them into the path of it. Ellery doubted the fire brigade had survived, and so even a small fire would rage out of control if left unchecked.

They still hadn't seen any animals. Ellery worried that if they were still alive, the fire would kill hundreds of them if it raged unchecked. And what about those still trapped in houses or cages in gardens? It didn't bear thinking about. It made her feel sick. And useless. She'd become a vet because she loved animals. She should be checking the homes that now stood empty to see if any pets were inside, but there wasn't time. And the time they did have was running out. She could feel it.

They could start heading east, towards London, which would add two days at least to the journey but should take them far enough out of the path of the fire. She hoped. There was really no way of knowing. Ellery took a deep breath and looked at the map again.

Loveday leaned into her from behind and looked over her shoulder. Ellery closed her eyes briefly and tried not to notice Loveday's breast as it pushed against her.

"Well? Figured it out yet, Bear Grylls?" Loveday poked her to let her know she was teasing.

"I think if we head east we should link up with the M25. It'll take us to the outskirts of London and then to the M1. We can head north again from there." Ellery stepped away from Loveday on the pretence of putting her map away. Truthfully, she found it difficult to be so close to Loveday and keep her feelings in check.

Loveday had been totally clear on what she didn't want from Ellery and, since the first day when they'd almost kissed, had given no indication she returned Ellery's feelings. She bent down to stuff the map in the front pocket of her pack. She closed her eyes and muffled a groan when Loveday trailed her hand over her shoulders.

"Ellery? Are you okay?"

"Sure. Why?"

"I don't know. You've been really quiet these last few days. Is there something you aren't telling me?"

Ellery opened her eyes wide in alarm.

"The fire," Loveday continued. "Are you more worried than you're letting on?"

Ellery sighed with relief. "I am worried about it. They can spread quickly, and I'm concerned we won't get out of its path in time if the wind changes direction." She stood and lifted her pack onto her back, tightened the straps.

"You can share this stuff with me, you know. If you're worried or scared or whatever. I'm not some fragile little doll you need to protect."

Shit, Loveday looked annoyed. "No, I—"

"I know I'm not exactly a survival expert, but I am an adult. Okay?"

"Okay. I didn't mean to upset you," Ellery said.

"You didn't upset me. You pissed me off."

"Oh. Right. I don't mean to treat you like a doll. I'm just not used to sharing my concerns. That's all." Ellery looked at the ground. Conversations like this made her feel awkward. She didn't have a lot of practice at them and was always worried she'd say the wrong thing and bugger everything up. Also, confrontation made her insides churn. When she was still at university and renting, her neighbour kept parking his car in front of her drive. Rather than speak to him about it, she'd moved house.

She heard Loveday sigh, and there was that hand again, gentle on her shoulder. "Just, share stuff with me next time. Who knows, I might even be able to help." Loveday squeezed her shoulder and Ellery looked up and smiled.

"Yeah. Okay. Well, one concern I have is water. We need to find some more soon. If I remember correctly, there should be one of those huge out-of-town supermarkets around here somewhere."

Ellery had driven past it a number of times going back and forth from London. It was a superstore that sold clothes, electricals, and pretty much everything else you could think of. They were positioned just outside of towns, and there'd been a lot of opposition to them at first. They undercut local businesses in towns and killed off high streets. Shops in business for years found themselves closing down, unable to compete. Ellery hated them, but now, finally, they might prove useful.

She estimated it would take them half an hour's walk to get there. She wanted to push on for another few hours afterwards if Loveday was up for it. Assuming the role of leader wasn't something she was entirely comfortable with. Sure, at work it was fine—it was her business after all. Outside of work she was used to fading into the background, and the fact that Loveday had easily handed over the reins terrified and honoured her in equal parts. Especially as Loveday didn't seem the type to willingly let someone else tell her what to do. Ellery was determined to do everything possible to earn the trust Loveday put in her. And part of that meant keeping her growing attraction to herself.

In the distance, grey clouds started to roll in, promising rain. They'd been lucky with the weather so far, but it was October, after all, and the rain would come more frequently. Temperatures were bound to drop as the days got shorter. Ellery remembered the dream from a few nights ago and shivered.

Well, no point pondering. Better to get on and stay on the move.

CHAPTER TWENTY-FIVE

L ike a lot of people in the modern world, Terry wasn't used to walking long distances. The first couple of days, they'd barely managed twelve miles. Only the thought of his son forced him onwards.

He stank. He was constantly sweating. His feet ached, and his back screamed with every step. By the end of each day he fell quickly into an exhausted sleep, and thank God there were no more dreams.

Dani, by comparison, was like a puppy. Boundless energy. He'd come close to belting her a couple of times, but the guilt of knowing what he was leading her to stopped him. Also, watching her young arse bounce around as she walked in front of him helped some. He was a man, after all, and even though she was sixteen, she was pretty much a woman—same age as Shirl when he'd knocked her up.

They stopped for a minute by the side of the motorway. They were following the M4, hoping to link up with the M1. When Terry'd realized none of the cars were working—fuck knew what happened to the engines, but someone had done a number on them—he almost backed out. It was stupid anyway, going on this journey because a dream told him to. Little Terry was gone to Christ knew where with everyone else. Even so, what if? What if he could see his son again? Wasn't that worth taking the chance?

Terry mopped his forehead, tried to ignore the stench from his underarms as it wafted up and engulfed him. He couldn't blame Dani for wanting to walk upwind of him.

"Do you want to stop for the night, Mr. Pratt?" Dani asked.

"How long have we been walking now?" All the fucking clocks and watches had stopped working as well.

Dani shrugged. "A few hours, maybe. Over there looks like a good spot." She pointed to a grass verge across the way.

They'd picked up a couple of tents and some bits and pieces for the journey. Not much of a camper, Terry left most of the set-up to Dani—not that she had much of a bloody clue. He'd put a few cans in her backpack and sat now sipping from one while she put up their tents. He was running low and would need to restock soon.

Suddenly, Dani looked up, head cocked to the side. The metal pole she held thunked on the ground. Terry turned his head in the direction she was looking. Nothing there. Bunch of useless cars crashed into each other and against the central reservation. Then he felt it. Those creepy fucking eyes. Watching them.

Terry stood and tried to see where the bugger might be hiding. He cracked his knuckles and bounced on his toes. On the opposite side of the road were a small line of trees—a windbreak of sorts. Scraggly and small, they weren't dense enough to hide a grown man, but his eyesight wasn't what it had been. He squinted, strained his eyes. There. Between two of the healthier looking trees, something moved. A wave of coldness swept over him. It was watching them. Had probably been following them since they left the pub.

Without looking at Dani, he said, "Stay here."

"But Mr. Pratt, it's not—"

"Stay here." The irony of being worried about her safety wasn't lost on Terry. If that nasty little peeper was over there, Terry was going to beat the shit out of him.

CHAPTER TWENTY-SIX

Loveday watched Ellery over the rim of her mug. She smiled slightly at Ellery's furrowed brow and the way she rubbed her earlobe which was pinched between her two fingers. Loveday thought she was exactly the kind of hero she would put in one of her books. Not that she would be writing one any time soon. Maybe never again. The thought hurt her heart. It hurt even more when she thought about writing a book using pen and paper. Because that was how it would be from now on.

Ellery had been studying the map spread across her lap like it held all the secrets of the world. When they woke up this morning the faint smell of burning laced the air, and Ellery thought a fire might have caught somewhere to the west of them. Although they weren't heading exactly west, they were going in that direction to pick up some motorway or other that Loveday had forgotten the name of, because, honestly, boring.

"Has the map spoken to you yet?"

Ellery looked up and grinned. Loveday's breath caught in her throat. Ellery had a really good smile.

"I think if we head east, it'll be safer. We can pick up the M25—"

Loveday held up her hand. "There's no point naming them, Ellery. We've been through this. I won't remember."

"But you drive. You must have been on motorways."

Loveday threw her coffee dregs out on the ground. "I followed a sat nav. You know, the little blue line? That's it."

She squeezed Ellery's shoulder as she walked past to rinse and repack her mug. And what was that all about? She'd taken to touching Ellery all the time—a shoulder squeeze here and a brush on the arm there—and since when was she so touchy-feely?

"It'll take an extra couple of days, but I think it's worth it." Ellery's voice followed her.

"If you think it's for best, we should do it."

And that was another thing. Loveday was staunchly independent, always had been. Frustratingly so, she'd been told by various girlfriends. Yet here she was, following Ellery's lead without question, and she was fine with it.

Maybe because Ellery wasn't dictatorial—in fact, she was the opposite. She was thoughtful and measured her words, and Loveday could see the wheels turning behind her lovely eyes as she gave every decision proper thought.

Perhaps that was it. Loveday trusted her because despite her awkwardness she had a quiet confidence, a sureness about her. Yeah, nothing to do with the fact Loveday wanted to kiss her senseless, and a lot more besides. But that couldn't happen. For a multitude of reasons, including the fact Loveday wouldn't be able to creep out of her bed in the morning and disappear.

"Everything okay?"

Loveday jumped. She hadn't been aware of Ellery coming to stand behind her as she repacked her mug.

"Sorry, in my own world. I'm fine, though."

"You sighed."

"Did I?" Had she?

"I know an extra couple of days walking isn't ideal but—"

"I trust you, Ellery. If you think it's for the best, then it's what we'll do."

Loveday stood and turned. She hadn't realized Ellery was so close, and now they were inches from each other, almost the same height, lips lined up.

She watched as Ellery's eyes widened, flicked down and back up again.

Ellery stepped back, almost stumbled, and looked away.

"We should get going. Make a start," Ellery said.

Loveday sighed again and picked up her pack. It was just

attraction, nothing more. It was normal and it would pass. Eventually. All she needed to do was ride it out.

In better news she was getting more used to the weight of her pack and hoped when they next stopped to restock their supplies she'd be able to carry more.

Even after a few days, she felt stronger and she liked it. She would probably never be a frequenter of the gym—well, no one would—but she was enjoying the way her body had started to feel. She felt capable.

Ellery was already on the move with the pets snuggled in the pushchair. It still gave Loveday a laugh every time.

"I can't believe this still tickles you," Ellery called over her shoulder, slowing down so Loveday could catch up to her.

"What can I say? I'm a child." Loveday came alongside her in time to see Ellery shake her head and smile. She liked to make Ellery smile, Loveday was starting to realize. She frowned. That wasn't a good sign.

"Where are you from? Originally?" The question popped out of Loveday's mouth before she could stop it. Wanting to know about Ellery wasn't a good sign either.

"About eight miles from town. I went to London to train, then came back."

"Didn't like London?"

Ellery shrugged. "It was okay. Bit too loud, bit too…anonymous?"

"You like knowing your neighbours?"

"Sort of. I'm not social at all, but I like being on a first-name basis. The practice staff are always—*were* always—trying to get me to go out with them."

"Why didn't you?" Loveday knew it was dangerous to be so interested, but she wanted to know Ellery. What made her smile and what made her laugh? What her favourite food was and what side of the bed she slept on. Nothing good could come of it, and she sensed the danger in becoming too familiar, in caring too much. But she couldn't stop herself.

"Why didn't I go out with the practice staff?" Ellery's voice was contemplative. "I suppose I'm not very good with people. I never have been. I seem to say the wrong thing or miss social cues that everyone else picks up. It seemed easier to just avoid it."

Loveday ached for her. Before everything that happened, Loveday had enjoyed going out and had been part of a large friendship group—the kind that was easy to have in London. Someone was always available for drinks or dinner or to see a film.

"That surprises me."

Ellery looked at her and frowned. "Really?"

"Really. To me you seem…I don't know. Confident. Eloquent."

Ellery's eyebrow rose so high it was nearly lost in her hair. She'd stopped walking. "Are you serious?"

"I am serious."

Ellery frowned, opened her mouth to say something, then closed it again. She looked genuinely stumped. "Well, thank you. That means a lot."

"You're welcome."

Ellery nodded and they started walking again.

After a while Ellery asked, "What about you?"

"Me?" The question startled Loveday. They'd spent the last half hour walking in companionable silence. No traffic, no planes, no people. If Loveday didn't think about all that had happened, she might have quite enjoyed it. She'd been relaxed. Almost happy.

"Where are you from? Originally?" Ellery asked.

"Oh. London. Born and raised."

"Wow. A real live Londoner." Ellery opened her eyes wide and gave a fake little gasp.

Loveday didn't mind the gentle teasing. She rolled her eyes. "Yep. I came to the countryside on a mercy mission. To bring some excitement to you bumpkins."

"Hey, we had a Chinese restaurant open last month." Ellery winked and Loveday's belly fluttered in response. Shit. Ignore it, didn't mean anything.

"I take it back, then. I had no idea."

The truth was, they lived—used to live—a ten-minute drive from a large town, and being so close to the motorway meant the town was a fairly busy place.

They lapsed back into easy silence.

It wasn't long before they came upon a small village. It was typical for the area. Pub, church, local shop, and a bunch of houses tightly clustered that spread out the further along the road you went.

"We should see if there's anyone here," Ellery said.

"I don't think there is. It feels empty."

Just like when she'd stepped out of her own house a few mornings ago, this place was still and lifeless. There was nothing to indicate anyone was around, and at this time of the day, there should be people about. Instead, there was that same absence of life. A stillness. A breeze ruffled the leaves of trees and birds sang. A sign squeaked on its hinges somewhere to the left of them, but the place was dead.

"It does feel empty. But all the same, we should check," Ellery said.

"What about that thing. What if it's in one of the houses?"

"I can't feel it. I don't think it's watching us today. I haven't felt it since we left. Have you?"

"No." She hadn't. Ellery was right. Since they left town, whatever watched them seemed to have gone away. That didn't mean it couldn't come back, though.

Ellery touched her shoulder gently. "You can stay here with the pets if you like. I'll knock on a few doors. It shouldn't take long."

Loveday shook her head. "It'll be quicker if I help. We can take different sides of the road, like before."

They split up and made their way down the street. Rocky hopped out of the pushchair and followed Loveday. She felt better for having him beside her, hobbling along. Claude decided to stay put and have a snooze. She didn't blame him. She'd get in there with him if she could.

Loveday made her way down the street, unsurprised when no one answered her knocking. She half-heartedly pushed on a few doors, but none of them opened, and she was relieved. She felt bad for feeling that way, but she was a coward after all. Not like Ellery who knocked hard on each door—and more than once—and seemed hopeful someone would answer her.

She glanced over at Ellery who was still a way behind her. She was stopping to look through windows. Guilt settled in Loveday's belly, hot and heavy. Why did she have to be such a coward? So selfish all the time?

She reached the end of the street and waited.

She watched Ellery knock on a door painted bright red. Loveday got the sudden urge to tell her to stop. Her mouth filled with saliva and she was afraid. Relieved when there was no answer, fear surged again when she saw Ellery step over a small pile of bricks and go to the front window, knock again, then try to open it.

Before she could shout at her to stop, to run away, the front door swung open with a bang. A man stood holding a knife. Loveday called out to warn Ellery who still had her back turned.

Rocky took off towards him at the speed of light, barking. Without much thought, Loveday ran towards the house. Straight at the man with the knife.

CHAPTER TWENTY-SEVEN

Rosemary stood on a makeshift platform in front of thirty-four people. She was surprised so many had arrived so quickly, with more drifting in every day.

They'd set up this area for group meetings and religious services. Rosemary was pleasantly surprised to find people were so keen on them.

But tragedy tended to bring people back to God, and the truth of the message she preached reached these lost souls in their hearts. She was conducting services every day and had married two people yesterday—not that she was ordained. She considered the fact she was God's representative on earth to be authority enough.

At first, the idea of being God's chosen representative seemed blasphemous. As the days ticked on and more people flocked to her message—no, His message—she'd begun to see the truth. He'd sent her here for a reason. To lead His people out of despair. Out of darkness and into light. Into His grace.

She faced her flock now. Eager faces turned up to her.

"Let us pray."

Heads lowered obediently.

"Dear Lord, thank you for bringing us together. Thank you for sparing our lives so that we could find our way back to you and live forever in your truth. Lord, we renounce our former ways and ask for forgiveness for the sins we committed. Adultery and fornication have no place in this new world. Homosexuality and intermarriage have no—"

"Excuse me."

A murmur went up around the room as everyone turned to look at the woman who'd interrupted Rosemary. She was pretty and young. The kind of woman who'd carefully constructed her physical appearance for sin. She was everything that was wrong with the world.

"Are you serious? You're going to take the Bible literally?"

Rosemary gave her most patient smile. "Yes. We follow the Bible in its most literal sense. No marriage between the races, no practicing of homosexuality, no adultery, and no sex before marriage." She said it calmly but rage boiled inside her. Who was this woman to question her?

"Well, that's ridiculous," the woman said, then sat down.

Somewhere a chair leg scraped against the floor. Someone coughed. The room held its breath. Rosemary could feel it. Everything hung in the balance. This was a test for her. If she let the woman get away with disrespecting her, she would have no hope of leading the survivors to salvation. Of realizing her destiny.

"Do you call yourself a Christian?" Rosemary addressed the woman.

"Yes. Do you?" The woman stood again and Rosemary saw only defiance in her eyes. She was not afraid. She didn't look like the other survivors, beaten down and shell-shocked. She was a fox in the henhouse.

"I think that's obvious." Rosemary scoffed and shook her head. She looked around the room, smiled at them as if to say, *Who is this stupid woman?* Some smiled back and some looked nervous.

"That surprises me. I mean, it shouldn't, I've seen what you've been saying all over social media before this…this vanishing. I'd hoped you might be different now that it's actually happened. Even so, since I've been here, I've seen nothing but bigotry and ignorance. Listening to you speak, I can see why. You fuel these people's hatred and prey on their distress. I'd rather go out on my own than stay here and listen to your vile, twisted version of my faith."

Her faith? As though Rosemary was excluded from it. As though Rosemary wasn't the guiding force behind its resurgence. As if Rosemary wasn't the one who had brought the survivors here and welcomed them in. Fed them, sheltered them.

"*Bring forth him that hath cursed without the camp; and let all that heard him lay their hands upon his head, and let all the congregation stone him.*" How handy Leviticus was. She nodded at the two men standing near the back with their arms crossed. Easy to miss but necessary in this new world.

They moved quickly and took hold of the woman. Another murmur from the congregation.

"What are you doing?" the woman asked. She tried to pull away, but the men tightened their grip. "Get off me. You can't do this."

Indignation. Disbelief from a woman who had up to now lived her life saying what she wanted, doing what she wanted, and living how she wanted without thought or care. No concern with how her selfish existence affected others. No consequences, no real faith—despite what she said—only a certainty she should have what she wanted and be able to say what she wanted because she was all that mattered. Her needs and wants overrode everyone else's. Well, not today. Not anymore.

"You can't do this," she said again. She struggled as she was dragged out.

Rosemary turned to watch the congregation. She looked for anyone who might stand up to defend the woman or try to help her. No one did. Some looked shocked and others looked pleased. She made a note of the ones who looked pleased because they might be useful later.

Rosemary continued with her sermon. She'd deal with the woman later.

❖

It was Loveday's scream that made Ellery turn away from the window and towards the man with the knife. She held up her hands to show she was no threat.

He was young, early twenties maybe, and his eyes held a strange light. He thrust the knife out in front of him. Not really an attempt to stab her but to keep her away.

"Are you one of them?" His voice was uneven, scared.

"No." Ellery didn't know who he meant but she knew she shouldn't be one of them.

"Why should I believe you?" He used the arm he held the knife in to wipe his nose on his sleeve.

"I'm like you," Ellery replied. "My friend and I are just passing through. That's all. We're just passing through." She kept her voice calm.

Out of the corner of her eye, Ellery saw Loveday approach and stand near the house's gate. Rocky was in her arms and had stopped barking.

"To where? North?" He thrust the knife at her again and Rocky growled. "That dog. Is it yours? I need a dog like that."

Ellery chanced a look at Loveday and tried to smile reassuringly.

"We're just passing through, and we're going to go now," she said again. He was blocking her exit from the front garden, but she could probably climb over the hedge and on to the street if she had to.

"North?" he asked again.

"Yes."

"You've been dreaming too?"

"Yes. We've been dreaming too. What's your name?"

"I can't sleep for those fucking dreams. And that thing. Watching me all the time." He made a strange whimpering noise.

"How can you dream if you don't sleep?" Loveday asked.

Ellery silently cursed as his attention left Ellery and zeroed in on Loveday.

"They come when I'm awake, you stupid bitch." He took a step towards her and Rocky began to bark.

"My name is Ellery. What's your name?" Ellery asked. She hoped he would turn his attention back to her.

"Shut that dog up."

It didn't work. He moved closer to Loveday and she stepped backward, onto the road. This gave Ellery a chance to get away from the window and back on the path, not trapped now. She realized that had been Loveday's plan.

Rocky continued to bark, struggling to get out of Loveday's arms. The man took a half-hearted swipe at him. "Shut that fucking dog up."

"You're scaring him," Ellery said.

The man swung partially back around, not sure which of them to focus his attention on.

"We just want to be on our way. Go back in your house and leave us alone," Loveday said.

He seemed to consider it for a moment, and his hand dropped slightly. Then Rocky broke free of Loveday's grasp, and all hell broke loose.

C HAPTER T WENTY-E IGHT

T erry looked around. The grass where he'd seen that peeping little bastard was flattened. It had definitely been here. But it was gone now. The trees were small and sickly looking and left nowhere for anyone to hide. Beyond them lay fields. Terry supposed they'd go fallow now and choke with weeds. The smell of damp rotten vegetation was thick in his nose.

From the corner of his eye he saw a dark shape move. It came from behind one of the trees, and Terry couldn't understand how anything could hide behind them. Certainly not a man. And there was someone here because the grass was flat and because Terry could feel it watching him. Cold eyes. It'd been there in London. The morning it happened, and then later in the pub. It'd gone away for a while, once they started walking, but now it was back and Terry was fucking sick of it.

"Come out. Come out, you sneaky little shit. Fight me like a man," Terry shouted. Overhead, birds took flight, but nothing else moved.

Footsteps came up fast behind him. Terry tried to turn but he was too slow. He made out a shape—like a man but not a man—something hard cracked against his head, and the lights went out.

Rocky jumped from Loveday's arms and charged straight at the man with the knife. Even without his cast, Rocky would have been no match for him. Rocky lunged and the man kicked out, missing Rocky by inches, and Loveday was grateful he hadn't used the knife. Rocky went for him again, tried to bite his ankles.

Without warning the man lurched forward, his knees buckled, and he dropped to the ground. Behind him Ellery stood, holding a brick. Her face was a mask of shock. She looked at Loveday, looked at the brick. Her face briefly contorted and she dropped it.

The man lay inert, the knife a few feet from his hand. Rocky had stopped barking, thank God.

"Come on. We should leave." Loveday got hold of Rocky by his collar and picked up the knife. Ellery still hadn't moved.

"Ellery. Before he wakes up."

"What if I killed him? I should check." Loveday watched as Ellery started to kneel.

"No. Ellery, we need to leave. *Now.*" It was no use. Ellery ignored her. She reached out and held her fingers to his neck.

"He's alive." She looked up with a relief that nearly broke Loveday's heart. Ellery was such a gentle soul.

"Then we need to go."

"But—"

"No. Ellery, he came at us with a knife. He's dangerous, and we need to leave."

Ellery looked up at Loveday with such pain in her eyes it took Loveday's breath away. "I can't just leave him to die."

"Why not? It's exactly what he would have done to us." Loveday couldn't keep the coldness out of her voice.

Ellery flinched. "I'm not him. We're not him."

"What do you suggest? Stay with him until he wakes up and tries to stab us again?"

"No. I—"

"The world has changed, Ellery. Whether we like it or not, it's changed, and we need to look out for ourselves. No one is going to help us. There's no police to report him to. No courts to punish him if he hurts us."

"I don't want to live in a world like that," Ellery said quietly.

The man groaned, and Loveday was gripped by the knowledge they needed to get away from him. Fast. They wouldn't get lucky again. She knew in the way she had. A certain knowledge.

"Grow up."

Ellery flinched.

"Don't be a fucking martyr all your life. He's going to wake up and kill you. You aren't a hero, Ellery. This isn't a bloody film. God isn't going to protect you. He's not going to save you." Loveday took a deep breath and prepared to deal the fatal blow. "If he wakes up and stabs me or Rocky it'll be your fault."

Ellery flinched again, and Loveday tried to ignore the ache in her chest. She didn't want to hurt Ellery, but she had no choice.

"Okay." Ellery stood on shaky legs and stepped over the man who groaned again. "But this is wrong."

Ellery walked past her, and Loveday wondered how much damage she had done.

❖

Terry thought he was dreaming. A figure stood over him. A man but not a man. The winter sun was bright behind him and left his face in shadow. Terry squinted. The man who wasn't a man had a long face, longer than a human's should be, and suddenly Terry stopped trying to make it out. He didn't want to see any more. He didn't want to know.

"I can't move." Terry's voice was hoarse, the way it usually sounded after he'd been on a bender.

The man who wasn't a man shifted away from the sun, and Terry slammed his eyes shut like a child who thinks they'll keep the bogeyman away if they just don't look at it.

"Just do what you're going to do. Get it over with." Terry's fingers dug into the soft earth. He braced himself.

He heard footsteps. He thought it crouched down, and he felt its breath on his cheek. It smelled like Plasticine.

What was it doing? Sniffing him. The fucking thing was *sniffing* him. Would it eat him? Tear his throat out like an animal? Would it be quick or slow and drawn out into long minutes of agony? How would it feel to be eaten alive? Terry felt his bowels go watery. "Please," he begged, "please, just do it quick."

"Terry." It said his name in a funny way, like it was testing it out, moving the word around its mouth. Tasting it. "Terry." It was a flat, cold voice. And Terry Pratt who was scared of no man began to cry.

"Terry. If you want to see your son, do not look for me again. Trust that I will always be around. Watching you. Marking your progress.

Take the girl to Rosemary Decker, or I will tear your intestines out of your arsehole with my teeth."

"Who are you?"

Terry heard it shift again, finally, mercifully away from him. "I am the Bringer of Chaos. I am older than all things."

The devil. That's what it really meant. That thing was the devil, and what did it make Terry if he was doing its work? What did that mean for the girl? Was his son even there? With this Rosemary Decker? The first thing you learned about the devil was he lied.

Terry heard it move away. He refused to look, certain if he did he'd go mad. He knew instinctively not to look at it. Was it definitely gone, though? What if he opened his eyes and it was there, right in front of his face, staring at him?

The devil lied.

Would Terry be taking the girl to her death for nothing? His head throbbed from the blow. This was all too much. Too much. Terry lay on the ground, stared up at the sky, and wondered what to do. It was only now, as the birds began to sing again, he noticed they had been silent before.

CHAPTER TWENTY-NINE

Loveday put Ellery's pasta down beside her on the grass, and Ellery mumbled her thanks. They hadn't spoken at all since the incident with the man, and Ellery didn't know how to bridge the chasm that had opened between them.

Also, she was conflicted. On one hand, she knew Loveday acted out of concern for them both, but she had used Ellery's sense of responsibility for them all against her. Had made her do something she was ethically and morally opposed to—leaving someone to die. It was true the likelihood of him coming around while she helped him and trying to stab her all over again had been high. He was unwell—that much was clear. What was less clear was whether his instability had come about as a reaction to everyone vanishing or the dreams.

Loveday had done what she thought was right. Ellery couldn't blame her for it even though part of her wanted to. Maybe this was the result of ignoring the dreams and not heading north. It drove people mad.

And what about her? She'd hit someone over the head, could have killed him, but in the moment she hadn't cared. What did that say about her own nature?

Ellery looked at the pasta next to her. Limp, pale noodles and anemic peas floated in a watery, tasteless broth. Her stomach turned over.

And what about the girl? They were still no clearer on who she was or where she was.

What if they didn't find her?

"It'll get cold, and it's horrible when it's cold," Loveday said.

Ellery looked up and gave Loveday a weak smile. She picked up her mess tin and poked at the congealed crap inside. They would need to find somewhere to restock soon. With the extra food for the pets, they weren't able to bring too much for themselves.

"I'm not mad at you," Ellery said. She watched Loveday pause with her spoon halfway to her mouth, put it back down.

"I'm sorry anyway," Loveday said.

Ellery nodded. "You were right, I think. I would have been taking a chance trying to help him."

"I know I was right. He would have hurt you."

"Maybe. But it wasn't worth the risk."

"Definitely," Loveday said.

"You can't know that." Okay, so maybe Ellery was a bit mad.

"I can."

"How?"

Loveday sighed loudly and plonked her mess tin on the grass. "I just do."

Ellery shook her head. "Not good enough."

"Excuse me?"

Ellery put down her own mess tin and went to sit by Loveday. "You're so...secretive. And that's fine. Unless it involves me and you made me do something I would never—"

Loveday jumped up like she'd been burned. "I didn't make you do anything."

"Fine. You manipulated me, then."

As quickly as she'd fired up, Loveday deflated. "Yeah. That's true."

"Why?"

"If I tell you, you'll think I'm mad."

"Are you going to tell me aliens made you do it?"

Loveday huffed out a laugh and sat back down. "No. But something equally strange."

"I'm all ears."

"I suppose you could say I'm sort of psychic. I know how that sounds, but it's true."

Ellery stayed quiet and waited for Loveday to continue.

"I've had it since I was little. One time I stopped my mum from taking us on a bus that crashed. Another time, when I was a teenager, a club caught fire. Today I knew that man was going to hurt you. Maybe even kill you, and I had to get you away. Do you think I'm crazy? I know how I sound."

Ellery thought for a moment. Did she think Loveday was crazy? Her only experience of psychics was in horror films or at funfairs. Women with headscarves and big hooped earrings. Not attractive women who were perfectly normal in every other way.

It was funny how quickly she was changing. A couple of weeks ago, she would have nodded and backed away slowly from Loveday, convinced she was at best on a wind up, and at worst, unhinged. A lot had changed. Her mind was slowly opening. Ellery's ex would be shocked.

"No. I believe you," Ellery said.

Loveday let out a breath Ellery hadn't realized she was holding. She imagined this was stressful for Loveday. Even in the short time she'd known her, she understood vulnerability was hard for her—well, it was hard for everyone, but it seemed especially hard for Loveday. Ellery had the sense she'd been let down badly in the past.

Ellery handled Loveday like one of the injured animals. From refusing to admit her feet were blistered and raw to trying to carry her fair share of the equipment even though Ellery found it easier, Loveday could not admit weakness—or what she thought was weakness—and she would do anything, it seemed, to avoid it.

Telling Ellery she was psychic must have been excruciating.

"There's something else, isn't there?" Ellery didn't know for sure, but she had a feeling.

"No. That's it." Loveday's gaze slid away.

"You're a terrible liar." Ellery grinned.

"I don't think I can tell you." Loveday looked so unsure, and Ellery wanted to hug her.

"What are you afraid of?"

"That you'll think less of me. I just don't think I can."

"I think it'll make you feel better."

Loveday shook her head and looked away. "I like you, Ellery, and I want you to think well of me. And not just because I'd be useless out here on my own. I'm scared if I tell you, you'll think I'm a terrible person and weak and just fucking awful, and I couldn't bear it." The words rushed out of her like air out of a balloon, and now she sat there, facing Ellery like she was waiting for some sort of judgement. Judgement Ellery would never pass down. But Loveday didn't know that.

Ellery had her own fair share of moments of weakness. She'd made bad decisions—she'd hidden away from the world most of her life, hoping to get on unnoticed and under the radar. Sometimes she'd stayed quiet when she should have spoken out and backed down when she should have fought her corner—or someone else's.

"I can't imagine anything you tell me will make me think less of you. I don't think you'd do anything bad."

Loveday snorted. "You can't possibly know that about me."

"Yes, I can. Today, you could have run and left me to it, but you didn't. You tried to draw him away from me."

"Self-preservation. I need you alive."

"Bullshit." Loveday's words stung, though Ellery saw them for what they were. An effort to divert and deflect. To move away from the thing Loveday didn't want to talk about. She wasn't so different from some of the animals Ellery treated, lashing out in fear and pain.

"You don't know me, Ellery."

"I think I do. I think you've revealed yourself quite without meaning to."

Loveday's head snapped back as if she'd been slapped. This was the worst thing, Ellery knew, she could say to her because it was the worst thing she herself could imagine someone saying to her. She took a deep breath and ploughed on.

"Want to know my greatest shame? The thing I hate about myself and I'm terrified of anyone finding out?"

Loveday nodded.

"My parents are raging alcoholics who think so little of me they moved without giving me their address. I have no idea where they are, and they don't care. What's so wrong with me that even my own parents don't want to know me?"

"There's nothing wrong with you. Nothing at all," Loveday said in a small voice.

"It's why I hide myself away. Why I've spent my life hugging the walls and trying not to be seen. There must be something wrong with me."

"I killed my girlfriend," Loveday whispered.

CHAPTER THIRTY

R osemary heard the screams before she walked through the door.
They echoed around the hangar, and she was sure people could
hear them from the makeshift mess hall. That wasn't necessarily a bad
thing, but Rosemary hated drama, and this woman was proving to be
very dramatic.

When she'd ordered the troublemaker removed from her sermon,
the guards automatically brought her here. They were using this room
to store food, but it was the only area in the hangar with a door that
locked from the outside. The troublemaker had found something, a tin
by the sound of it, and was alternating between screaming at the top of
her lungs and battering the door with the tin.

This would not do. Even now, the woman remained unafraid. Even
though she'd been dragged out of the service and effectively locked up,
she still didn't grasp the reality of her situation.

The world had ended, and a new one was about to begin, but still
this stupid woman thought she had rights and recourse in the way of
the old world, the old Britain. Rosemary sighed. She was getting a
headache.

Rosemary approached the locked door, currently guarded by the
same two men who'd dragged the woman out. They'd been with her
since the beginning, and she was glad they'd survived the vanishing.
They were loyal and believed the same things as her.

"Open the door," she commanded.

"I'm not sure that's a good idea, Miss Decker. She's been pretty
violent," one of the men said.

Rosemary looked at him with all the authority of her position. "Open it. Now."

The man's gaze slid away, and he used his key to unlock the door. "Be ready for her if she continues to be unreasonable," Rosemary said.

Rosemary pushed open the door, saw the woman was backed against the far wall with what looked like a catering tin of baked beans in her hands. Her arms shook from the weight.

"You can't do this," the woman said. There was still too much strength in her voice for Rosemary's liking.

"The problem, as I see it, isn't that I can't do this, because clearly I already have. The problem is that you won't accept it. Even though it's happening. Even though you're currently cowering in the corner of a cupboard with a tin of beans as your only defence. And it *is* your only defence. Did it not escape your notice that no one came to your aid earlier? That no one told me I couldn't, or I shouldn't do it?"

The woman lowered the tin of beans, nestling it against her stomach, but still kept hold. "This is still a free country." Her voice was less angry but still defiant.

"No. No, it isn't. All the old laws and ways are gone now. Swept away. Or at least they will be soon. This is a new beginning. A new world shaped in God's image and as He intended it to be. Honestly, can you look in your heart and say you were truly happy with the old way? That it worked? Food banks being used by nurses. Children being fed by teachers because their parents couldn't afford to do it themselves. Knife crime, rape, murder out of control. The rich getting richer? They stood on our shoulders to reach what they thought they deserved and didn't feel us groaning under their weight. What did you really have?"

"The right to marry who I wanted. The right to a fucking lawyer if I got arrested," the woman said, pointedly. "The right to say what I wanted without being locked up."

"Small things," Rosemary said.

"What?"

"Small things that mean nothing."

"Freedom means everything. The right to choose."

"The right to work every day for less money than you would have earned thirty years ago? The right to live in abominable sin while everyone around you pats your shoulder and tells you it's fine? We moved so far away from God we were never going to find our way back. Until this happened. Everything has changed. Take my hand and come with me into a bright new world."

The beans dropped to the ground with a bang and rolled a few feet away. "You are not the answer," the woman said.

"No, I'm the messenger. God is the answer."

"You're mad."

"Come with me," Rosemary said. "Please. Please come with me." She held out her arms to the woman.

"No. Never. Let me go, you mad old bag."

"I can't."

The woman dropped to the ground, picked up the tin of beans, then launched herself at Rosemary. She was fast. Faster than Rosemary thought she would be. But still, not fast enough.

Rosemary stood her ground. Waited for the woman to raise the tin above her head. She slipped the knife out of her sleeve so the handle was in her palm. It was sharp, that knife. And it cut through the woman like butter.

The tin of beans crashed to the ground. Rosemary wondered if it would be salvageable. They couldn't afford to waste food like that.

The woman followed the beans to the floor. On her knees in front of Rosemary, bent forward, hands clutched at her stomach, and watching blood and God only knew what else run through her fingers. She looked at Rosemary, disbelief in her eyes, as though she couldn't quite understand how it had come to this.

Rosemary leaned down, not too close. "I'm sorry. I tried to tell you. You wouldn't listen." And she meant it.

She straightened and walked out of the room. The two men had probably seen everything and looked almost as shocked as the woman. "I had no choice. She attacked me. You saw it."

Rosemary didn't wait for either man to respond. She tucked the knife away again and walked quickly back into the main part of the hangar. She didn't like to be away from the *Ark 2* for very long.

CHAPTER THIRTY-ONE

The girl's eyes widened, and Terry thought he must look like shit. His head throbbed, and he could feel the dried blood tight and tacky on his face.

At least she'd set up the camp while he was gone. She'd started a small fire and got some food going.

"I fell," he said, pre-empting any questions from her. "And I don't want to talk about it." That had usually been enough to shut Shirl up.

"Do you want a plaster and some anti—"

"I said, I don't want to talk about it." His voice was loud in the silence. Birds who had begun to roost for the night squawked and beat their wings, took panicked flight. Terry kicked the closest thing to him which happened to be a pile of sticks Dani must have gathered. They scattered and rolled away.

He looked around him for something else to take out his anger on. The only thing likely to give satisfaction was Dani, but she was already backing away further into the field, and he knew he wouldn't outrun her. As quickly as it flared, his temper banked. But it wasn't gone, and Terry knew it would likely spark again at the slightest provocation.

Terry sat down and held up his hands to show he wasn't angry any more. Dani stayed where she was. Smart girl.

"I'm sorry, love. I fell. My head hurts and I'm tired."

Dani nodded and edged closer but not close enough to be within reach. She'd learned from the last time he lashed out at her. "Do you want a beer, Mr. Pratt? The food should be ready soon."

"Thanks, love. That would be nice."

He watched her bend over and reach inside the tent. Something low down stirred, and he felt shame and excitement at the sight of her.

By the time she came back out and handed him the beer, Terry was leaning back on his elbows and watching the sky darken to a deep red-blue. *Red sky at night, shepherd's delight.* Meant it would be a lovely day tomorrow.

"Did you have a boyfriend, love? Before all this." Terry sipped from his beer and watched her carefully. She didn't look up from poking the fire.

"No, Mr. Pratt."

"You'd be pretty if you grew your hair. Got rid of all that metal in your face."

"I like the way I look," she said, and there was a hardness in her voice.

"Must put the boys off, though."

"I'm not interested in what boys think, Mr. Pratt."

"So you are a dy—lesbian."

Dani sighed as if he was boring her. She probably rolled her eyes but he couldn't tell because her face was hidden. Staring down at the fire.

Terry's rage lit again and he threw the bottle at her. Missed by a mile.

"Stop *doing* that." She looked up at him, anger in her eyes. Defiance. "Or I'll leave. We both know you've got no chance of catching me."

You fat git was left unsaid.

"Hey now, don't you speak to me like that, young lady—"

"No, Mr. Pratt. *You* listen to *me*. I thought I needed you. That I was safer with you along, but I'm not. I realized this afternoon that I don't need you at all. You need me, though. I don't know why yet, but you do."

Terry sat up. His fists clenched, his face heated. His stomach churned and roiled. Not used to being spoken to like that, he didn't know what to say. His mouth bobbed open, then closed. She was right. If he wanted to see his son again, he *did* need her. He wanted to smash the little bitch's face in. Crush her with the force of his rage. Instead, he took a deep breath. Exhaled. "I didn't mean anything by it, love. Sorry if I upset you. You shouldn't be so sensitive. Let's eat and say no more about it."

He leaned back on his elbows again and pretended to look at the sky. All the time the anger lapped at the shore inside him, and his mind worked, ticked over, weighed up his options.

It hadn't occurred to him the girl might have a backbone. That she might recognize the situation for what it was and realize she was the one with the upper hand. He would need to think on it because if she didn't need him, if she wasn't scared of him, she might not stay.

❖

Loveday took a deep breath. She didn't want to tell this story—she preferred to tell the ones she made up. She'd kept it to herself for so long. The shame of her greatest cowardice. But Ellery was looking at her with such compassion and understanding. Even when she'd said the words, Ellery's face hadn't changed—she didn't take them literally. She'd understood it wasn't what Loveday meant.

"I had a girlfriend four years ago. Grace. We met through friends." Loveday's words were halting. She felt around them with her tongue, which was thick and heavy in her mouth.

"It's okay, Loveday," Ellery said.

"She was fun and exciting and things moved quickly. We moved in together, far too soon. We hardly knew each other. Grace was troubled. Angry, sometimes. She'd go into these rages."

"Did she hit you?" Ellery asked.

"No." She hadn't ever hit Loveday, but the anger and vitriol in her words worked just as well as a slap. "We stayed together for two years. I should have left earlier, but when she was in a good mood she was amazing. You just wanted to be around her."

Ellery nodded. Loveday studied her but found no pity in her eyes, and she was relieved. "One evening, she kicked off. Worse than I'd seen her. She started trashing the flat. Screaming nonsense. I ran. It was the last time I ever saw her."

"What happened?"

Loveday breathed deep and closed her eyes. "The flat burned down. I don't know if she started it or something caught when she threw it in a rage. Either way she didn't or couldn't get out."

"How is that your fault?"

"Because it was like earlier. I knew something was going to happen. Something bad."

"You knew she'd die?"

"*No.*"

"Then what?"

"I felt...dread. I knew something would happen. But I wasn't sure if it was a response to the situation I'd just run from, so I ignored the feeling. I left her to it. Left her to die." Loveday's throat was tight. Too tight. Her eyes stung but stayed dry. After Grace died, she'd done nothing but cry. Maybe there were no tears left.

"After that, I decided to move. Get away from my old life and be on my own." Over the years with Grace, her heart had hardened with every cruel word and outburst. When Grace died, she finally sealed it up, like a manhole cover being pulled across a sewer. Done with it all.

"I'm so sorry, Loveday. I'm sorry someone you loved treated you that way. And I'm sorry you blame yourself for something that wasn't your fault. Mostly, though, I'm sorry you've allowed it to rule your life for so long."

Loveday's head shot up at that. How fucking dare she. "You don't know anything about me." Her voice was cold.

"That's true. But I know this."

"You're a fine one to talk. Your parents are arseholes who don't care about you, so you cut yourself off from everyone else and live a half life in the middle of nowhere."

She saw Ellery flinch and felt bad, but she couldn't stop it. This was her defence mechanism. Cruel words. And she had a knack for finding her mark every time. Not so different from Grace.

She watched Ellery stand up. Waited for her to walk away and leave her. It's what she wanted, after all, and it always worked before.

Loveday was confused when Ellery came and sat down beside her, pulled her into her arms. She struggled and then was still. She tucked her head under Ellery's chin and allowed herself to be held. It felt good.

"I'm sorry. I shouldn't have said that. You're right that I don't know you. But what happened with your girlfriend wasn't your fault. You have to believe that."

In Ellery's arms, she wondered if maybe she could. She'd told her the worst thing about herself, her biggest shame, and Ellery hadn't run away. Loveday closed her eyes and leaned in to Ellery's warm body.

"I'm sorry too," she mumbled against her neck.

"Okay. We're both sorry. I'm probably sorrier, though."

Loveday laughed and poked Ellery's side. "Shut up. You're ruining the moment."

Ellery squeezed her tighter and kissed the top of her head. "Sorry."

Sometime later they climbed into the tent and by unspoken agreement got into the same sleeping bag. The pets flanked them on either side and it was nice. Loveday couldn't remember the last time anyone held her just to give comfort. She wondered if anyone ever held Ellery that way. She wanted to ask but didn't want to cause any more pain than she already had. Instead she shifted, so Ellery's head was under her chin. She pulled her tight against her body and stroked her hair. It was softer than it looked. It was nice. They fell asleep that way.

Chapter Thirty-Two

*L**oveday stood high on the edge of a cliff.* The same one as before. Ellery was next to her. The sea was calm and blue and blended with the sky above. A mild breeze drifted in off the water.

"Back here again," Ellery said.

"Looks like it. At least the weather's better."

Loveday turned, and the girl, Dani, walked towards them. She raised her hand in greeting and smiled.

"You're on the way and that's good, but you need to hurry."

"Hurry to where?" Loveday asked. "We don't even know where you are. Where we should go."

"You're heading in the right direction, but you need to move faster. I don't have much time."

"Before what? How can we help you if you won't make sense." Ellery sounded frustrated. "Can't you just tell us where we should go and why?"

"I told you before. This is the end—"

"Yes. You've said. But what does it mean?"

"It's not information you need yet. Keep heading north, and hurry. That's all you need to know. My time is running out. He's going to kill me."

Dani said it simply, but it sent chills up Loveday's spine. As if in sympathy, the sky darkened and the wind picked up. The waves began to crash and foam. A storm was coming.

"Who's going to kill you? Can't you get away from him?" Loveday shouted to be heard above the screaming wind.

Dani shook her head. "I don't know what I don't know."

"What the fuck does that even mean?" Ellery shouted. *"Make sense! Speak fucking sense!"*

❖

Ellery sat up. Her throat burned, and she realized she was still screaming. A hand on her back rubbed small circles. Loveday.

"It's just the dream, Ellery. It's just the dream." Loveday's voice cut through her panic and she was quiet.

Claude had moved to the far corner of the tent, and Rocky barked in sympathy with her. "Shush, shush," she told him and held out her hand. He came enthusiastically and licked her palm and fingers. She pulled him onto her lap and nuzzled his neck.

Loveday was still rubbing her back, her hand warm and welcome.

"Sorry," Ellery croaked.

"Don't worry about it."

Ellery scrubbed her eyes roughly and lay back down. Loveday rested beside her, and Rocky stretched along the length of her.

Claude wasn't convinced and lay down where he was with his paws tucked under him.

"How many miles do you think you can do tomorrow?" Ellery asked.

"I don't know. How many do we need to do?"

Ellery didn't know. The dreams were infuriating in their vagueness. Why couldn't whoever it was just say, *Head here to this point*? Why was it all so fucking convoluted?

"I suppose we can just pick up the pace. We still need to stop and restock our supplies."

Ellery felt Loveday curl into her. She rubbed her arm down Ellery's shoulder and let it rest on her chest, over her heart. It helped.

"We'll get there," Loveday said. "We'll find her. Dani said we were on the right track, so let's pick up the pace like you said. It's all we can do."

"Is it enough, though? Supposedly the fate of humanity is on our shoulders. What if our best isn't enough?"

"It has to be because there's nothing else, Ellery."

And that was the crux of it. She and Loveday were Dani's only hope of survival. It was ironic, really. Two loners with more baggage than Heathrow Airport were responsible for the survival of the human race. You couldn't write this stuff. Well, maybe Loveday could.

When Ellery next woke up, Loveday was sprawled across her. Loveday's hair was in her nose and her mouth and mostly covered her eyes. She brushed it away and slid out from under her. Loveday rolled onto her side with a grunt. Ellery smiled.

Outside the day was bright and cold. She walked a little way into the trees with Rocky so he could do his business. Claude preferred privacy and would come back in his own time.

Ellery's eyes felt grainy and itchy and she rubbed them, then yawned, satisfied when her jaw cracked. She supposed she should put the coffee on to settle Loveday's grumps when she woke up.

She sorted through their supplies. Through the packets of pasta, cat food, soup. It wouldn't last them more than a couple of days. Fortunately, following the motorways meant lots of opportunities to restock, but she'd rather not do it too much. Case in point was the man with the knife. It was unlikely they'd run into many more people like him—she hoped—but Ellery was aware they were two women on their own and needed to be careful.

Plus, what had Dani said last night? *He's going to kill me.* That meant she was either travelling to or in a place with a man and he was dangerous. Great.

"Why the big sigh?" Loveday brushed her hand over Ellery's shoulders as she walked past, and it felt nicer than was probably safe. After last night, had Ellery opened the door for even more casual touching? She hoped not because it was going to drive her mad.

She smiled at Loveday who was pouring out coffee. "Just thinking about the dream and what we need to restock and how much quicker we need to walk."

"Bloody hell, Ellery, one thing at a time. And preferably not at all until I've had my coffee."

"You asked."

"Be shush," said Loveday as she sipped from her cup and winked at Ellery over the rim.

Ellery's heart did an annoying little patter before she managed to squash it. She needed to get a grip.

They sat in silence, drank their coffee, and thought their own thoughts. Rocky sniffed around them, probably hoping for a scrap of something. Claude swanned off back to the tent. He liked to sleep pretty much all day.

Ellery leaned back on her elbows and turned her face to the weak sun. Still, weak sun was better than no sun.

"How did you learn to break into cars?" Loveday's question broke through her daydreaming.

"One of the times I was in foster care. There was a boy who took a shine to me."

"Oh, really?"

Ellery laughed and opened one eye to see Loveday grinning at her and wiggling her eyebrows like a dork. "Not like that. He was about five years older. He used to take me out with him and get me to help him nick out of cars. I was good at it."

"Are you pulling my leg?" Loveday asked.

"No. Why? Don't I look like a master criminal?"

Loveday snorted and Ellery laughed and sat up. "You look like a vet."

Ellery was nonplussed. "What does that even mean?"

Loveday shrugged. "Not a car thief."

"I wasn't a car thief. I stole stuff *out* of them. Usually sunglasses. CDs. Sat navs. I feel horrible about it now."

"How old were you?"

"About eleven," Ellery said. She stood and stretched. "And only old cars with manual locks you can pop with a hanger."

"So a pretty crap thief, then," Loveday teased.

"I didn't devote much time to it. To be fair, I was back with my parents inside a month or so. If I'd had longer, who knows, I could have been Pablo Escobar."

"He was a drug smuggler."

"Yeah, well, I can't think of any famous car thieves. Come on, we should get going."

Loveday grunted and stood up. Ellery started taking down the tent.

CHAPTER THIRTY-THREE

Since the incident with the woman, people were wary of Rosemary. Chloe-Claire had told her several people left the hangar overnight. It didn't matter. Let the non-believers look out for themselves. She didn't need them here, and more were still coming in all the time. God's army was growing every day.

She continued to hold daily services and there hadn't been a peep out of anyone. The room was so full, people were crowding in at the back to listen. They would have to expand the area soon. She was thinking about offering an additional service in the evening as well. The *Ark 2* was completed, so other than daily inspections she had more free time. She wanted to get a school set up as well. Rosemary noticed a number of children arriving, and they needed an education. The correct education. Not the nonsense they were taught before, but a religious education. Everything they needed to know was written in the Bible.

"Miss Decker." Chloe-Claire again. "Sorry, but we have a small problem."

Rosemary sighed. Did she have to handle everything herself. "What is it?"

"There are some people who want to come in."

"And?"

"Well, they aren't Christians."

"What are they?"

"They said Sikh. One of their party is ill. They want to rest here for a couple of days until he's better. They knew about you from the internet. They don't want to stay."

Rosemary smiled but there was nothing friendly about it. When she was younger she'd tried to make her smile into something friendly. Had practiced in the mirror until her jaw ached. It didn't work. She still unnerved people. She learned to stop caring.

"Exodus 34:14. *For you shall worship no other God, for the Lord, whose name is Jealous is a jealous God,*" Rosemary said.

"Right, then. So that's a no?" Chloe-Claire asked.

Rosemary sighed. "That's a no."

Loveday sat down with a bump, the weight of her pack pulling her down quicker than she would have liked. They'd made it to the superstore in good time, and just looking at it was freaking her out. It loomed over them, a hulking white and blue construction with rows of windows like blank, empty eyes. The reflection of the sun made it impossible to see inside. In the car park, vehicles were dotted about, abandoned. One had rolled right up to the doors of the superstore and planted itself like a belligerent bouncer, blocking the entrance.

If they needed a reminder everyone had vanished, this was a good place to be.

"Do you want to go in or stay out here with the pets?" Ellery's voice pulled her out of her thoughts.

"Stay here."

"Okay. I'm going to get some more water and pasta meals. Is there anything you need?"

"No, I'm good." Loveday felt bad about sending Ellery in on her own, but the place was creepy. Also, someone needed to stay outside with the pets—at least that's what she told herself.

So far, Ellery had shouldered the burden of their journey while Loveday tagged along. It wasn't a position she was used to being in, but she trusted Ellery. It was strange. Loveday didn't trust anyone. True, she was attracted to Ellery, but it was more than that. Despite her awkwardness, she had a quiet confidence, an innate goodness about her. It was evident in the way she paid so much care to the pets. The way she always thought about Loveday before she thought about herself. Even when that man in the town had attacked them, Ellery still couldn't bear the thought of leaving him there injured. Loveday had never met anyone quite like her.

Loveday realized she was staring, and poor Ellery's cheeks were bright red. She wondered what expression had been on her face. She smiled. "Hurry up, I'd rather not set up camp near here tonight."

Ellery nodded. "I know what you mean. It's got a weird vibe. I think because it's so empty."

Loveday looked around her. She didn't like it here. That old familiar feeling was back. Something in her gut telling her they should leave. But they did need water and some more meals. And there was a chance her feeling was more to do with the creepy emptiness than anything else.

Ellery turned to go and Loveday reached for her arm. "Be careful, okay? Careful and quick."

Ellery nodded and walked away. Loveday watched her go. The sun disappeared behind clouds. Loveday looked up. It was going to rain.

❖

Ellery hadn't wanted to let on to Loveday how freaked out she was about going into the superstore alone. She climbed over the car blocking the entrance and hurried in before she lost her nerve.

It was just an empty supermarket. If you didn't look at the flowers rotting inside cellophane on the plant display. Or focus too long on trolleys abandoned in the aisles. She'd grab the things they needed and they'd be on their way. Even though the electric was off, the windows let in a lot of light which made it easier to see, though the back of the store was gloomy.

Most of these places were laid out similarly, and Ellery found what she wanted quickly. She was choosing the last items when she saw something move out of the corner of her eye. The familiar sensation of being watched prickled her skin and sent a flutter of fear into her belly. It was here. Shit. Shit, shit, shit.

She was in the middle of the store, near the tills. She could drop the stuff and make a run for it. Stop somewhere else. Somewhere smaller.

Something scraped then thunked onto the floor the next aisle over.

A tin being pushed off a shelf. Then it happened again. And again. Scrape, thunk, roll. Scrape, thunk, roll. Getting closer. Ellery forced down the panic that rose up inside her. Her muscles ached to move, to flee.

"Ellery. Jackson." The voice sounded rusty, and the words were spongy and soft. "I can hear you breathing." Scrape, thunk, roll.

Ellery took two steps towards the tills. She strained her ears to listen for its footsteps, to try to place where it was.

"I can smell your fear." Scrape, thunk, roll.

Closer. It was definitely coming closer.

Ellery took another step. The exit looked tantalizingly close.

"I can hear your primitive little brain straining." Scrape, thunk, roll.

Ellery bolted.

She pumped her legs.

She pistoned her arms.

Something gave chase, and it was gaining.

She slammed through the exit and vaulted the car blocking her way like an Olympic athlete. Her lungs burned, but she managed to shout a warning to Loveday.

"Run. It's coming. Run."

Loveday grabbed Rocky, piled him in the pushchair with Claude, and was already on the move when Ellery reached her. They had to leave their packs, but it couldn't be helped.

Ellery was painfully aware the pushchair was slowing them down, but what could they do?

Something hit her from behind, and the breath went out of her lungs. She dropped to her knees, and pain seared her kidneys as it struck her again. She heard rather than felt the blow which landed against the back of her head. She tried to look up, to see if Loveday got away, but couldn't raise her head. The words *Loveday, run*, died on her lips as the world lost focus and the lights went out.

Chapter Thirty-Four

Terry wasn't in the mood for this shit. They'd walked for hours, it seemed, with no breaks. If he didn't know better, he'd think Dani was trying to finish him off. She strode on ahead, always keeping enough distance that she'd be able to bolt from him. The girl wasn't as stupid as she looked.

Not that Terry planned on doing anything to her. For one thing, that fucking devil who sucker-punched him like a cowardly bastard would probably kill him. Terry didn't mind admitting he was wary of it. He'd be a fool not to be wary of the devil. Because that's what it was, wasn't it? He'd made a fucking deal with the devil to get his son back. But the devil lied, and part of Terry knew his son was gone forever. Gone like most of the fucking country.

He had to try, though. It wasn't completely out of the realm of possibility that somehow this girl was the key to getting back Little Terry. If the devil walked the earth and people had vanished, then it wasn't unlikely, was it?

"Mr. Pratt, we should get some more food and water. We'll hit the motorway proper soon, and there aren't any services for over twenty miles," Dani said.

He stopped and looked around. They were by a petrol station. A couple of cars sat uselessly by the dead pumps. Over by the entrance to the shop, the newspaper stands still held papers from before. Terry picked one up. "You go ahead, love. I'm going to sit out here in one of them cars and have a rest."

Terry picked the red car because it was new and looked comfortable. The door was unlocked which was handy. When he lowered himself into the front passenger seat, his knees popped and cracked, and he sighed with the pleasure of being off his feet. He shouldn't be this unfit for a man of his age, but it was what you got from too much beer and too many kebabs. And Shirl's shitty cooking.

Terry scanned the front page. It was all about the storm. They hadn't got it too bad in London. Apart from everyone fucking disappearing. He turned a few pages until he came to a story that caught his eye. It was about Rosemary Decker. Well that was interesting, wasn't it?

Apparently she was some religious nut who was convinced the storm was going to bring about the end of the world. Terry laughed. Not such a nutter after all. Why did she want Dani, though? Did she even know about Dani, or was he going to turn up with the girl and she'd have vanished like the others?

Behind him the rear door opened and the car dipped slightly as someone climbed in.

"Hello, Terry."

Terry's balls climbed into his throat, and he hated himself for his fear of this fucking thing. Terry started to sweat. "What now?" he asked and tried to keep the tremor from his voice. He couldn't bring himself to turn around and look at it. He thought it might send him mad.

"I wanted to make sure you were staying on track. Think of me as your supervisor."

Terry couldn't place its accent. It spoke normally enough, but something about its voice was off. Most likely because the devil wasn't used to speaking English.

"It's amusing to me how you humans assign religion to the things you do not understand. Even if you are not religious."

"I'm a Catholic," Terry said.

"You beat your wife and you drink too much. Not a very good Catholic."

Terry sucked in a breath. "I don't—"

"Oh, don't waste my time with denial, Terry. It's no concern of mine who you beat. My concern is that you get the girl to Rosemary Decker."

"Unharmed?"

He didn't know how, but Terry felt it shrug.

"Doesn't matter to me what state she's in, as long as she's alive."

"Why?"

"Information above your pay grade, I'm afraid."

Terry bristled. No one fucking spoke to him like that. No one treated him like that. Not even this fucking devil thing—or whatever it was. "Fuck you, mate. No one tells me what to do." Stupid thing to say, maybe, but fuck it.

"I thought you wanted to see your son again."

"He's gone. Just like the rest of them. You lie. It's what you do."

"Are you sure?"

The seat creaked behind Terry, and he felt it lean close, felt its breath on his neck. And there was that weird Plasticine smell again.

"What if I'm not lying, Terry? And even if I am, what have you got to lose?"

And that was the crux of it. What did he have to lose? Nothing at all. Terry had already lost everything that mattered to him. He'd feel some guilt, of course, leading the girl to her death like that, but really, she probably would have died out here on her own anyway. And it wasn't like he kidnapped her—she wanted him to go with her.

And there was a chance. A chance he'd see his boy again. Wasn't it worth it for that? Even the smallest chance?

"Very good, Terry," the thing said, and Terry felt it move away from him. Felt the car dip again as it climbed out.

Still, Terry didn't turn around. Didn't want to see it, even if it did have to get in and out of cars like a normal man instead of teleporting or whatever the fuck devils did.

Terry picked up the paper with shaking hands and tried to concentrate on the article about Rosemary Decker. The Plasticine smell lingered.

CHAPTER THIRTY-FIVE

Loveday leaned against the side of the van. Her arms ached from dragging Ellery. She thought she might be able to get her up and inside, but Ellery was too heavy. She made do with laying her by the back doors, with Loveday's jacket under her head.

Loveday hadn't seen what hit Ellery. She heard a grunt, and when she looked behind her, Ellery was sprawled on the ground. Whatever hit her was long gone. Loveday should have listened to her gut back at the superstore. She knew something was off. Instead, she let Ellery go inside because Loveday was selfish. Catering to her own needs, as usual.

Now, here they were with Ellery lying unconscious and all their stuff at the superstore. Loveday could go back and get it, but until Ellery woke and told her what happened, she didn't want to risk it. But it was getting colder, especially at night. The van wouldn't offer them much protection from the weather. It hadn't rained yet, but Loveday could tell from the heavy grey sky it was only a matter of time. She hoped Ellery woke up soon.

But what if she didn't? It wasn't like Loveday could call an ambulance. There was only the two of them. She couldn't think about it. Ellery had to wake up.

Loveday sighed. The wheel had come off the pushchair too. She'd driven it over a rock as she ran, and the bloody thing went spinning off under a car and tipped poor old Claude out. He was inside the van now, mainly sleeping, but occasionally waking up to give Loveday a dirty look. She'd apologized, but apparently he wasn't ready to forgive and forget. She could go and get the wheel, try to put it back on. It wasn't like she had anything else to do. They were stuck here until Ellery woke up. Loveday watched her. The steady rise and fall of her chest. It looked like she was dreaming. Her eyes were moving back and forth under her eyelids, and Loveday thought that must be a good sign.

Although what Loveday knew about head injuries wouldn't fill the back of a postage stamp. Ellery could be in a coma for all she knew. Shit. She shouldn't think that way. Ellery would be fine.

Loveday inspected her head again, felt the bump, no bigger than a marble. She would be fine. Loveday stroked her temple, ran her fingers through Ellery's hair. She couldn't lose her. And not just because Loveday knew she wouldn't survive the journey alone. Not even because they had come to be friends. Some part of Loveday recognized some part of Ellery, and they'd slotted into place like a dovetail joint.

She'd felt it that day on the bench where Ellery found her crying. She felt it when they lay beside each other each night. Even if they never acted on it, there was something powerful between them, and they would always fit together. Loveday knew that if she lost Ellery, she would lose some part of herself. The part that gave her the courage to walk up to the man with the knife, the part that desperately wanted to save Dani. Perhaps the last part of her that wasn't jaded and tarnished and scared and selfish.

She rocked back on her heels, tucked her hands under her armpits, and looked up at the sky.

If it was possible, the clouds were greyer and heavier. The temperature had dropped. It would be dark soon. How would she keep them both warm? She supposed she might be forced to go back to the superstore after all.

Loveday looked over at the cars abandoned like a giant child's toys on the road. She had an idea.

The first car she tried was locked. She considered smashing the window but decided to try a few more first. She couldn't feel anything watching her, but better safe than sorry, and there was no point making noise unless she had to.

Loveday was luckier with the next few. One had a couple of

fleece-lined blankets inside. They smelled of dog, but beggars couldn't be choosers. She also found a wind-up torch, first aid kit, a family bag of salt-and-vinegar crisps, two bottles of water, and an unauthorized Britney Spears biography.

CHAPTER THIRTY-SIX

Rosemary looked at the three women and two men. She'd decided to send a group off to look for the girl. She was getting impatient. They were running out of time. The people in front of her had volunteered, and they looked healthy and strong.

After the unfortunate incident with that woman, lots of people left the hangar. She'd briefly considered refusing to allow it. But as quickly as they left, more people arrived, and the numbers were improving again. It was good, though. This way, only the most devoted would be part of her new world. The Judases who snuck out in the middle of the night would be judged by the storm that was coming. A storm bigger than the one before, which would change the shape of the world. All human accomplishment would be rubble at the bottom of oceans.

The people standing in front of her were the ones she wanted by her side when that time came. Obedient and unquestioning, they accepted what she told them about the girl. They were true believers, good Christians who trusted Rosemary as God's representative on earth and believed fully in the teachings of the Bible.

She told them to stick to the main roads and motorways in the hope they would intercept the girl somewhere in the Midlands, depending on how quickly she was walking.

Rosemary hadn't had any visions for a while. She took it to mean she was on the right path. It troubled her she couldn't mark the progress of the girl, though. But Rosemary felt her. Felt the foul sickness of that creature in her bones, getting closer all the time. God trusted Rosemary to destroy the girl, and Rosemary would not fail.

❖

Ellery floated above everything. She saw towns and cities and the networks of roads that connected them all snaking across the landscape. She was too high and it shouldn't be possible, but she saw clusters of people below, all moving in the same direction. North. They looked like ants.

A huge body of water raced inland from the east. It gained speed and height until it crashed onto the shore and then kept going, obliterating everything. Buildings, trees, pylons were torn up from their foundations and propelled along in the swirling mass of water.

The ants began to run, but they had no chance. The water scooped them up like unruly children. Smashed them against the floating debris and held them under.

The water kept coming. Wave after wave after wave. And now it came from the south and the west, flooding the land and destroying everything in its path. The mark of mankind had been slapped down and torn apart in minutes.

This is how it ends, Ellery thought. *Thousands of years and this is how it ends. Not in days, not even in hours but in minutes. As if we never were.* She felt numb. Couldn't quite comprehend it.

She looked to the north. The water hadn't reached all the way there. Spots of green were visible, poking above the water. Enough to live on? Maybe. If they could get there in time.

What did the girl Dani have to do with it? Why was she so important?

Ellery's stomach dropped in time with her descent. She was rushing downward. She flew in an arc, and then she was flying over the water, heading north.

On the small area of land, people milled about, but none of them saw her. They were gathering around a pile of rocks, picking them up. Some tested a stone's weight and either put it back and chose another or, seemingly satisfied, walked away. Ellery decided to follow them.

"Well, what was the alternative?" one woman asked another. Both were in their thirties.

"I don't know, but it seems wrong," the other woman said.

The first woman looked scared, leaned in close to the other. "Don't say that sort of thing. You'll get in trouble—and me with you."

"Me and John, we're leaving," the second woman said. "Soon. The water's receded a fair bit already."

The first woman looked panicked. "Don't tell me. I don't want to know. I don't want any part of it."

"You could come with us—"

A horn blared and both women flinched.

"Come on. It's time. We shouldn't be late."

Ellery followed the women behind a row of tents to a strip of land where more people stood around, all holding rocks. Some looked excited and others like they might be sick.

Slowly, they turned to face the same direction. Ellery looked and saw a woman standing, head down, flanked by two men who each held one of her arms. They forced her to her knees and she knelt as if in prayer. The men moved away.

Suddenly Ellery knew what was about to happen with a sick certainty. They were going to stone her to death. People moved into a circle around her, and Ellery with them. Finally the woman looked up, straight at Ellery, and she saw it wasn't a woman at all. It was a girl. Dani. This was Dani.

Ellery pushed through the crowd to get to her, but something held her back. She struggled but couldn't get free. She turned to see who was holding her, but no one was there. No one was paying any attention to her. Except Dani, who still held her eyes.

Until the first rock hit her.

There was a crunch and she fell sideways.

More rocks rained down, and Ellery still struggled. She screamed at them to stop, but no one paid any attention. Dani was lost in a cloud of blood and dust.

A woman walked into view. Impossibly tall, she used her foot to prod Dani's body onto its back.

Ellery saw her nod, smile, and look up to the sky, hands clasped together in prayer.

The woman turned back to the crowd. Her cold eyes scanned them, and Ellery watched people shrink back when her gaze fell on them. The name *Rosemary Decker* was whispered among the crowd. That must be her.

When she saw Ellery, she frowned.

"Who are you?" Her voice was loud, commanding in the quiet crowd. "You aren't supposed to be here."

Ellery felt rage burn in her throat. "My name is Ellery Jackson.

And I'm coming for you." Her voice sounded stronger and more confident than she felt. Especially when Rosemary Decker recoiled.

"You aren't supposed to be here. You won't be. I've sent my people out to look, and they will find you." Rosemary Decker smiled now, full of confidence.

"No, they won't. I know your name now, and I'm coming for you."

"I'll see you soon, then," she said.

Suddenly, Ellery was propelled backward. It was like she was on a bungee cord. And then she was falling through space, between the planets and the stars, and Earth was below her, coming closer. She rocketed forward, through the atmosphere, and saw the landscape she remembered—probably for the last time. She thought how beautiful the planet was.

She saw herself, lying on the ground with her head on Loveday's jacket. Loveday sat off to the side, Rocky in her lap. Ellery thought she was beautiful too.

Loveday looked up, right at Ellery, and frowned. "What the fu—"

CHAPTER THIRTY-SEVEN

"—ck?" Loveday couldn't believe what she was seeing. She rubbed her eyes as Rocky jumped off her lap and started barking madly. He ran to Ellery and licked her face.

What was that? It looked like something fell from the sky and into Ellery's body. Something bright but solid. It must be her imagination. Brought on by stress or something.

Rocky continued to lick Ellery, and Loveday had to pull him off her. He'd slobbered all over Ellery's face, and Loveday used her sleeve to wipe it away. She almost fell over backward when Ellery's eyes snapped open.

"Shit." Loveday was relieved to see Ellery's eyes looked clear and alert. "Welcome back." She shuffled away so Ellery could sit up.

"How long was I out?"

"About two hours—wait, what are you doing?"

Ellery wobbled to her feet and looked around. "We should go. Where's our stuff?"

"Back at the superstore, and I think we should wait until tomorrow. It's getting dark."

"Why didn't you go back for it?"

Loveday narrowed her eyes and her shoulders tensed. "You came out of there like a bat out of hell and screamed at me to run. Before I could ask you what happened, you were out cold. What was I supposed to do?"

Ellery touched the back of her head and winced. "You're right. Sorry."

"Does your head hurt? I checked when you were out, and you seemed okay apart from a bump."

"I'm fine. Just sore. Something was in the superstore. It chased me out, and then knocked me down. The thing from before." Ellery sat back down.

"I didn't see it."

"I'm not making it up."

"I know, I know," Loveday soothed. She looked at Ellery properly. She had dark circles under her eyes, and she looked exhausted. "I think we should stay in the back of the van tonight. We can pick up our stuff tomorrow."

Ellery nodded. "You're probably right. I can't feel that thing around any more. Can you?"

Loveday shook her head. "No."

They got in the van. Loveday held Ellery's arm to help her. It took Ellery several tries to get her foot up. Loveday supported Ellery with a hand on her back as she climbed in.

Loveday didn't want to think too much about how unsteady Ellery was. Or about the blow to her head, or how long she'd been unconscious. There was no doctor to take her to, and nothing she could do to help. Loveday pushed down the feeling of helplessness and settled Ellery in the van.

She arranged the blanket over her, tried to make her comfortable. Ellery gave her a weak smile.

"You don't need to fuss. I'm okay."

Loveday noticed she was wringing her hands. She quickly unclasped them and left them dangling uselessly by her sides. "I'm more Nurse Ratched than Florence Nightingale."

Ellery laughed. "It's okay. I'm okay."

Ellery's calm voice soothed her. Shouldn't they be doing this the other way around? Wasn't Ellery supposed to be the awkward one?

"I found a torch. And a book." Loveday rummaged in the corner of the van, relieved to have something to do.

"Loveday, I'm fine. Seriously, come and sit under the blanket with me. It's cold." Ellery lifted one corner in invitation.

Loveday thought about it. It *was* cold. But it would also mean snuggling up with Ellery. Under the blanket. Touching her. Loveday's stomach lurched in a not unpleasant way.

"Please," Ellery said softly.

Loveday bit her lip, nodded. She got in beside Ellery, who was warm and soft beside her.

Rocky and Claude cuddled up with them under the blankets. It was sort of nice. Probably too nice. Something was beginning to give way around her heart and it made her nervous. No—that was a lie. It terrified her.

"I'd kill for a cup of coffee," Loveday said into the dark. They sat with their shoulders, hips, thighs pressed tightly against each other.

"I'd kill for some chocolate," Ellery replied.

"What kind?"

"One with peanut butter in. What about you? What's your favourite chocolate?" Ellery asked.

"Caramel. I can't believe you like peanut butter in your chocolate."

"Why not? It's delicious."

"No, it isn't. It's gross. If I'd known your chocolate preferences before, well, I'm not sure I would have come with you."

"You hate it that much? I never would have guessed. When you used to bring Claude into the surgery, I thought to myself, now there's a woman who doesn't judge people on their chocolate choices. How wrong I was."

"You remembered me?" Loveday tried to keep the pleasure out of her voice. Ellery shifted beside her.

"Well, yes. I mean, I knew of you from your books."

Loveday smiled into the dark. "Is that the reason?"

Ellery sighed. "And from around town?"

"Is that a question?" Loveday knew she should stop, but she was having fun. Teasing Ellery made her forget her nervousness. Her sense something was about to happen.

"I don't think I should say any more," Ellery whispered.

Loveday turned her head to Ellery's ear and felt her shiver. "I remember you too."

"Do you?"

"Yes."

Loveday felt Ellery's head turn towards her and knew their lips were inches apart. The rational, logical part of her was shouting *stop*. No good could come of this. But she was tired and scared and cold, and she wanted to feel something else for a while. She hadn't felt anything for a long time. Finally, here with Ellery, she thought she might be close to the old her. Before Grace, before the fire, before she'd hurt and been hurt in return. Ellery made her feel hopeful.

Loveday closed the distance. Brushed her lips gently over Ellery's. Her lips were soft, hesitant. Loveday reached up and found the back of Ellery's head, stroked her neck, her hair. She was surprised but pleased when Ellery's mouth became more forceful, demanding.

Loveday gave over control of the kiss to Ellery. Ellery's hands framed her face, and then her thumb brushed Loveday's chin, down her throat, and her fingers came to rest at her collarbone.

Loveday pulled back, felt Ellery's hands drop away. She continued to stroke the back of Ellery's neck. She didn't want to stop—didn't want Ellery to think she was rejecting her—but she had to stop, for both their sakes. If their brief kiss was anything to go by, Loveday was already in much further than she'd ever intended to be, and it wouldn't take much more to send her completely over. The kiss was everything she knew it would be. Gentle and loving and sweet—just like Ellery. Loveday could kiss her forever.

How did she let it get so far? How had it gone from attraction to this need inside that threatened to drown her? As she stared into Ellery's beautiful eyes, she knew how. It was impossible not to care for Ellery. She would be so easy to fall in love with. That was why she had to stop things now.

Loveday stroked Ellery's cheek and smiled.

"That was nice," Ellery whispered.

Loveday rested her forehead against Ellery's. "It was. Very nice."

"We should stop before we do something you'll regret."

Loveday sighed, nodded. She didn't miss the *you'll* in Ellery's sentence. It made her happy Ellery wouldn't regret it, but sad she would never be able to give Ellery what she wanted. What she deserved. Loveday moved her head away from Ellery's.

"We should get some sleep," she said.

"Yeah."

They burrowed down under the blankets still pressed against each other. Loveday closed her eyes and tried not to think about the kiss and how it had been more than nice, and what that meant.

CHAPTER THIRTY-EIGHT

Terry stood outside Dani's tent. He wiped his sweaty palms on his jeans, now crusted with dirt and his own blood. He was nervous, and Terry never got nervous. That nasty fucking devil in the petrol station had thrown him off. And Terry couldn't get what it had told him out of his head. *As long as she's alive.* That's what it told him. Terry had to wonder, what did this woman plan to do with Dani if the only rule was she wasn't dead?

Couldn't be anything good. Not if what he read about her in the newspaper was true. Proper bloody nutter. Going on about the end of the world and new dawn in God's light or some load of old bollocks like that. And what did that make him? At least the mad old bag believed what she was peddling. Terry, on the other hand, was standing outside a young girl's tent because some fucking creature out of a nightmare told him she only had to be alive.

He sighed and pulled his hand, which had moved to the tent flap without him noticing, away.

"Mr. Pratt?"

Terry almost jumped out of his skin. He turned around. "Bloody hell, love."

"Sorry. What are you doing by my tent?"

Terry almost squirmed under her knowing gaze. She didn't say much, but he'd learned it was all going on under the surface with this one.

"Was going to see if you wanted a cup of tea. I didn't realize you were already up."

"I went for a wash."

And now he saw her hair was damp. A towel slung over her shoulder. What he wouldn't give for a bath.

"Is there a stream or something?" he asked.

"Yeah. Down there through the trees. It looked pretty clean." She shrugged. "But how would I know?"

"I'll pop down, then."

Terry noticed she didn't move from where she was. She did that all the time now. Stayed away from him. Their time on the road and him needing to ration his beer had improved his fitness, but he doubted he could catch her.

Not that he wanted to. As long as she played nice, there was no reason she couldn't enjoy her last few days before they got where they were going. If, along the way, she wanted to take care of any needs they might share, well, that would be okay too.

Terry gathered up this things and headed in the direction she'd come. He pretended not to notice the wide berth she gave him. Or the shifty fucking look in her eye that told him something was up. He'd seen it a few times on Shirl after they'd fallen out. Like she was hiding something, mulling over something. Like she wanted to leave him.

A couple of years ago, he'd been in the shed. Usually he never went in there, but he needed something—he couldn't remember what it was. He found a bag. A black nylon holdall. It looked new. Terry opened it. Inside were some of Shirl's clothes and a leaflet for a women's shelter.

At first he was angry. If she hadn't been out shopping, he probably would have clumped her one. Apart from that first time, she'd never tried to leave him. Now it seemed like she was planning it again. After his rage burned out, Terry decided he had a better plan than laying into her when she got home.

He put all her clothes back in her wardrobe. Nice and neat, like she would have done. He put his work stuff in the holdall and threw out his old one and left it by the stairs where he usually did. Where she would see it. The leaflet he burned.

For weeks, he never said a word to her, but every time she went near that holdall she flinched, and he'd smile at her. A smile that said, *I know, Shirl. I know all about it because you can't hide anything from me.* He watched as she waited for her punishment. For him to say something. Day by day she got a bit more confident, a bit more like her old self. Then, one day, wham. He let her have it.

Terry walked off a little ways into the trees where Dani wouldn't see him. When he judged enough time had passed and she wouldn't be looking out for him, he started to walk back.

❖

Loveday woke up as middle spoon. Ellery was at her back and Rocky was tucked against her stomach. Both of them were giving off a nice amount of heat. Their night in the van hadn't been as awful as she was expecting. And that kiss. It was a good kiss. It promised a lot. Loveday still wasn't sure if she wanted to find out exactly what that was.

Telling Ellery about her past was cathartic. She hadn't realized how much of a weight she'd carried over it. The guilt was eased but still there, at the edges of her conscience. Poking holes in any idea she might have of pursuing something more with Ellery.

Loveday slipped out from between the sleeping beauties and felt her way over to the doors. After a couple of fumbles, she managed to open them and let the light in. She squinted against it. Another bright and beautiful day. Cold, though. She shivered and pulled on her coat.

Loveday glanced back at the still sleeping Ellery and smiled when she saw Claude wrapped around her head. He'd taken to her too.

She decided to let them sleep. It wouldn't take long to go back to the superstore and get their stuff. Hopefully, it would still be there. It was unlikely anyone would take it. There wasn't anyone around to take anything any more. She climbed out of the van.

"Where are you going?"

Loveday jumped. "Jesus, Ellery." She turned to see Ellery sitting up in the van, bleary-eyed and with her hair sticking up at odd angles.

"Sorry. Where are you going?"

"Back to the superstore to get our stuff," Loveday said.

"Hang on, I'll come with you."

"No, stay there. Try to get some more sleep. You took a nasty bang to the head yesterday."

"I'm fine."

Loveday blew out a breath and counted to five. "So am I. I'm not—"

"I know, I know. You aren't a fragile doll or something." Ellery rolled her eyes. "I'm still coming."

"Why?"

"Safety in numbers."

"You're a pain in the arse. Stay there. I mean it."

"No."

"Ellery. I'm perfectly capable of getting our stuff by myself."

"There's something I didn't tell you yesterday. I was going to but...well, I didn't know how to."

Loveday narrowed her eyes. "What?"

"Let me come with you, and I'll explain afterwards." Ellery untangled herself from the blankets and scrambled over.

"Explain now."

"There are people out looking for us. I had a dream yesterday when I was unconscious and I saw it—most of it, anyway. Why we have to help the girl."

Loveday fought against being pissed off Ellery hadn't told her this before.

"Go on."

Chapter Thirty-Nine

Carly Wilson was the most popular girl in Rosemary's school. For her tenth birthday, her parents rented a hall, hired a bouncy castle and a magician. Rosemary really wanted to see the magician. Carly was given permission to hand out invites to the party just before playtime. Rosemary watched as she made her way between the desks, bestowing small pink glittery invitations on everyone. Listened to them shriek with delight as they were chosen.

When Carly paused briefly at Rosemary's desk, Rosemary's heart swelled with excitement, anticipation. Then Carly moved on. Rosemary felt her cheeks burn. She remembered gripping the edges of her desk, feeling the grain of the wood. She squeezed hard and willed herself not to cry.

It shouldn't have come as a surprise. The other children hadn't wanted to play with Rosemary. She was too tall, too strange, too serious. She got used to being alone, to enjoying her own company or the company of adults, whom she had more in common with anyway. Popularity wasn't important to her, and it continued to elude her into adulthood.

Until now. When she walked through the hangar, conversation stopped. People wanted to talk to her, to listen to her. They hung on her every word, and God help her, it was addicting. She wondered if this was how Jesus felt.

Rosemary knew she was no Jesus. But scared people, confused people were desperate for guidance. Rosemary's time had come. Now *she* was Carly. Bestowing invitations on the chosen few. The old ways had let these people down, and they were looking for a saviour. Someone to lead them out of the darkness.

Of the initial investors, two had survived the vanishing. They waited for her now in a makeshift meeting room. They had demanded to speak with her after the incident with the woman. They didn't understand their money and influence had disappeared along with the old world. Now, they were just like everyone else.

She sat down.

"We're concerned, Rosemary." One of them leaned back in his chair and steepled his fingers in front of him, gazed down at her over his nose. A feat she admired, considering he was only five feet four inches.

"Very concerned," the second one echoed, taller but still not important.

Rosemary nodded as she gripped the armrests of her chair.

"We understand things have changed. New rules, et cetera. But really, you can't just go around murdering anyone who doesn't agree with you," the short one said.

"As much as you might want to—would have made shareholder meetings a damn sight easier though," the taller one said.

The two men shared a laugh. Rosemary ran her palms over the rough material of the armrests, the coarse fabric tickling her skin in an unpleasant way.

"What we're trying to say," the short one continued, "is you need to show a bit of restraint. We simply can't have this sort of thing going on."

Rosemary looked at each man, so pleased with himself in his handmade suit. The master of his universe. No doubt in his mind he was someone important.

The shorter one had missed a patch on his neck shaving. Right where the collar of his shirt dug in. Five black hairs sprouted proudly.

"You will not summon me again. I am not an unruly employee. I am not your subordinate." Rosemary stood, and the chair squealed as it scraped on the concrete floor. "I am the truth and the light and I will not be reprimanded by you."

"Now, hang on just a min—"

"Your way is finished. Over. You led us down this path, and God saw fit to punish us all."

"Rosemary—"

"You'll keep quiet. You'll do as you're told. God willing you'll spend the rest of your days begging for forgiveness from the people you sold down the river, and for what? What do you have to show for it? You pathetic little men."

The short one opened his mouth, closed it again. His face was blotchy, shiny. Rosemary turned, walked out. To Chloe-Claire, as she passed her on the way out, she said, "Don't you ever let them summon me again."

❖

Dani worked quick, Terry would give her that. He'd only been gone ten minutes at most, and she'd already gotten her tent down. Now she was stuffing things in her bag. Her back was to him and she was crouched down.

He was careful to move quietly, didn't want her legging it, or he'd never get hold of her. Terry's blood boiled. How dare she. Who did she think she was, thinking she could leave him?

"Going somewhere?"

The look of shock on her face almost made him laugh as she spun round so fast she'd probably given herself whiplash.

"Thought I'd get a start on packing up."

"Yeah? You sure that's what you were doing, love?"

He watched her eyes dart to the left seconds before she jumped up and tried to run. She was fast, but Terry wasn't that slow. And he was bigger, stronger. He reached out and grabbed her arm, squeezed until she gasped.

"Let go of me."

It was a demand, and Terry didn't like it. He yanked her towards him, got her in a sort of bear hug, and held her close.

"I'm not a fucking mug. I know exactly what you were up to." He whispered it in her ear and felt her shudder, try to pull away.

"I was just packing up our stuff."

"Lying bitch." Terry pushed her away from him and backhanded her. She fell, sprawled on the ground, and held her cheek. She looked up at him, confusion and fear in her face. Just like Shirl in the early days.

"Is there even a stream down there?" He inclined his head.

Dani nodded. "I wasn't lying."

"Maybe not about that."

"Mr. Pratt—"

"Save it. I'm not interested in any more of your crap. Now I'm going to tie you up, and we're going to go down to that stream together." He laughed at the look of horror that crossed her face. "Don't worry. I'm not after any funny business. Just want to keep you where I can see you." It wasn't a total lie. For the moment, he wasn't interested in anything other than a wash.

Terry pulled her up by the same arm he'd grabbed the first time and dragged her over to her disassembled tent. She was a right bony little thing. Wouldn't take much to snap her in half.

"Don't fucking move, or I'll kick your head in."

Terry picked up a couple of the guide ropes from Dani's tent. He pulled her hands behind her back and trussed her up. The second one he tied around her neck and to her hands and left a longer bit to lead her by.

"Giddy-up," he said and tugged on the guide rope.

"Fuck off."

Terry smacked her on the back of the head and she stumbled. "That's not very nice. I'll let it go this time because of the circumstances, but you say anything like that to me again and I'll knock you the fuck out."

He tugged again, then pushed her in the back. "Let's go. You lead the way."

She was silent as she led him through the trees, head down and shoulders slumped. She wasn't stupid. She knew she wasn't going anywhere.

Terry heard the stream before he saw it. Something about the sound of running water had always appealed to him. He had a little pond in the garden with a small fountain. Sometimes he'd go out there with a paper and listen to it. He always found it peaceful. It calmed him. If he was in one of his black moods, it helped. He wasn't entirely sure why but thought it might have something to do with the Saturdays he'd spent fishing with his dad.

His dad was always patient with him by the water. He never shouted or got angry, and they would sit for hours, sometimes not saying anything at all.

Terry tied Dani to a tree with the end of the guide rope from her neck. He did it tight. Tight enough that he'd probably have to cut it away when he was ready to leave.

"You might want to avert your eyes now, love. Or not. Up to you."

Terry stripped and stepped into the water. It only came up to just below his knees, and it was freezing bloody cold. All the same, it was nice. He sat down and dipped his head into the water. The cut on his head stung, but it was good all the same. He looked up to see Dani sitting in the same place with her head down.

For the first time since he woke up to find everyone gone, Terry was finally starting to feel in control. Dani wasn't going to be a problem now. All he had to do was get her up north, and he'd see his son again. Maybe. If that thing wasn't lying to him.

He ignored the twinge of guilt in his gut for Dani. Desperate times called for desperate measures, and he needed to look out for himself in this.

CHAPTER FORTY

Ellery braced herself for the torrent of questions Loveday would shortly unleash. Ellery wondered if it was a writer thing.

"So let me get this right, the girl Dani, who we're supposed to save or whatever, is going to be stoned to death by the Children of the Ark woman?" Loveday asked.

"If we don't find her first."

Loveday and Ellery sat side by side on the edge of the van. It was still early enough that the air smelled fresh and new. Earthy. Ellery loved it.

"Why? I mean, why does Rosemary Decker want to kill her?"

"I don't know. She's mental? I wasn't shown that."

"And she saw you? She knows you—we—exist. That we're trying to find Dani as well?"

"Yes. And she's sending a scouting party to intercept us."

Ellery could still remember how Rosemary Decker's eyes looked, full of fury and madness. Arrogance. She didn't fear them at all. Why would she? It sounded like she had everything set up for a takeover while they were scrambling around trying to figure out what the bloody hell was going on.

"Why didn't you tell me all this yesterday?" Loveday asked.

"I was going to. Inside the van. But, well." Ellery shifted uncomfortably. She hadn't planned on bringing up the kiss. Wasn't sure if Loveday would want her to—probably not, if their almost kiss had sent her into such a tailspin.

"We kissed. And then it all just flew out of your mind?"

Ellery was relieved to hear Loveday's words laced with humour.

"Something like that. Why did you kiss me?" She hadn't meant to ask that either. Her tongue was a traitorous thing.

"I wanted to."

Ellery turned to face Loveday. "You know, that's not actually an answer."

"It's the only one I can give you at the moment. I like you, Ellery, but I don't think—"

Ellery silenced her with another kiss. At first Loveday didn't respond and Ellery panicked. She started to pull away, but then Loveday put her hand on the back of Ellery's head and brought her closer. Like last night. Loveday's lips moved against hers, gently at first and then more forcefully.

Loveday broke the kiss. "As I was saying, I can't offer you anything close to what you deserve. I don't think I have it in me any more. And I can't tell you why I wanted to kiss you. Beyond the obvious, I mean."

"What's the obvious?"

"I'm attracted to you. Only, I don't think it's enough."

Ellery was confused and slightly wounded. "You don't know if you're attracted to me enough?"

Loveday laughed and bumped her shoulder. "No, I mean I don't know if attraction is enough. To risk what we have. Things are different now, and we need each other. I'm not sure if it's a good idea to complicate things. Plus, I make bad decisions when it comes to my love life."

Ellery nodded as her heart sank. Of course, Loveday was right. It didn't matter that she was the first woman Ellery had been interested in in ages. The timing was bad, and they had a lot to lose if things didn't work out. They were all they had, and if the dreams were right, they had not too much longer to get to high ground. In the grand scheme of things, a relationship wasn't worth the risk. It didn't stop the heavy, disappointed feeling from settling in her belly. For someone who made her living writing romances, Loveday didn't seem to hold much store by them in her own life.

"Are you okay?" Loveday asked.

"Yeah, of course. You're right. I wouldn't want to jeopardize what we have. There's bigger things for us to worry about."

Loveday squeezed her hand. "Okay. Good. Shall we go and get our stuff, then?"

They walked in amiable silence back to the superstore. Ellery kept her ears open for the sound of people. She couldn't shake the look in Rosemary's eyes. Pure hate. Ellery didn't doubt that she'd sent a search party out to look for them or what would happen if they caught her and Loveday. Once she got her map back she'd plot a route that didn't take them along the motorway because surely that's where the search party would be looking for them.

At least on back roads there were more places to duck out of sight. But what about the girl? Was she on a motorway? After seeing her stoned to death in the dream, there was no way Ellery was leaving her to be picked up by Rosemary Decker's people.

"You look deep in thought," Loveday said.

"Sorry, I was just deciding whether we should hit the back roads or stay on the motorways."

"This search party will probably be on the motorway. But Dani might be too. She probably will be."

Ellery liked how Loveday just knew. For the first time in her life, she didn't feel the need to constantly explain herself. They were in sync in a way she'd never experienced before. But she mustn't think like that. Loveday had made her feelings clear. Just friends. Who sometimes kissed. That wasn't fucked up at all.

"Now you're smiling." Loveday bumped her shoulder.

"Sorry. I was still thinking about what to do."

"Such a liar." Loveday laughed.

"What was I thinking about, then? You're the psychic after all." Shit, had she gone too far? Was that below the belt?

"Well…"

To Ellery's relief, Loveday put her hands out as though she held a crystal ball and looked into the space between.

"You were thinking about our kiss."

"Bit full of yourself."

Loveday shrugged and grinned. "Am I wrong, though?"

"Which one?" Ellery ignored the question.

"Both of them. I'm a good kisser, and I've no doubt I blew your socks off."

Ellery couldn't help but laugh. She liked this side of Loveday. "You're arrogant, but you're right."

"It's not arrogance, it's confidence."

"Right."

"What? I—"

Ellery cut her off with a squeeze to her arm. "We're here."

Up ahead was the looming superstore. Still some distance away, it towered over the landscape. A great shiny square box against green fields. Fields that were usually teeming with rabbits. She was struck again by the absence of anything with four legs. The animals seemed to have totally vanished off the face of the earth.

Ellery took a deep breath. She could do this. They weren't going inside, just to the car park where they'd left their stuff. She could do this.

CHAPTER FORTY-ONE

They were making even worse time than usual. Terry was convinced Dani was dragging her feet to slow them down. He'd considered untying her hands and putting her rucksack on her back but decided against it. He didn't want to chance her getting the upper hand and running off.

In the end he'd sorted through their stuff and only kept the essentials—he threw most of her gear away—and now carried it in his own rucksack. It was fucking heavy even though they'd pretty much run out of water and food. He could take out his beers, but they were one of the small pleasures he had left in life.

He tugged hard on the rope around her neck. She made a choking noise and stumbled. Never said a word. Stupid little bitch. None of this would have happened if she hadn't tried to run.

"This is your own fault." Terry felt the blackness rise up inside him like a wave. He struggled to control it—he really didn't want to hurt Dani. For one thing, he needed her alive, and for another, he didn't want her slowing him down any more than she already was.

Instead, he placated himself by giving another vicious tug on the rope. This time she fell to her knees. She hissed through her teeth but still didn't speak.

"I said, *this is your fault*. You shouldn't have tried to run away."

She wouldn't even look at him.

"Get up. Get the fuck up. Stupid bitch."

Dani struggled to her feet and he saw her knees were bloody. It gave him some satisfaction. Appeased that blackness and pushed it back down a little.

Terry dragged her along again, tugging on the rope every now and again to make her stumble and choke. Her neck would probably be red-raw by now. Lucky that devil said she only had to be alive.

In the distance, Terry saw a shape. Big and square. His eyes weren't great without the glasses he refused to wear, but he thought it might be one of those big supermarkets they had on the edge of towns.

He tugged Dani over to him and gripped the back of her head.

"What's that?"

"Looks like a superstore."

"How far?"

"Half a mile?"

"Come on, then."

He gave a jerk on her rope to get her moving. It was almost like having a dog but not as good company.

"Do you ever fucking say anything?" Terry asked.

"What do you want me to say?"

"Don't get bloody smart with me."

"I'm not, Mr. Pratt."

"You just don't, I don't know, ever make any conversation."

"I'm not a big talker."

"Not like your old man, then." Terry snorted. That bloke could talk the hind legs off a donkey.

"Not much, no."

"You miss him?"

"Yes."

"It's like pulling teeth with you. Never mind."

"I don't know—"

"Just shut your mouth."

The black mood had lifted slightly but left him a bit grumpy. The sooner they could stop and he could have a beer, the better.

Terry remembered that along with her other stuff, he'd also dumped her tent. They'd be sharing tonight. That might turn out to be fun. And it would be dark, so he wouldn't have to look at her miserable face.

The supermarket was closer now. Christ, it was big. Terry hated these bloody places, but it would have some decent food and clean clothes inside. Things were looking up.

❖

Loveday heard them first. Voices. They'd made their way carefully towards the superstore in case the thing that hurt Ellery was still here. They were crouched behind a car near the entrance to the car park.

"Do you hear that?" she whispered.

"Yeah. Voices."

"How far away?"

Ellery shrugged beside her. "Hard to tell. Sounds are carrying a lot better now the other noises have stopped."

That hadn't occurred to Loveday until now. No drone of cars or planes, no voices. Except for the birds who seemed to be doing all right for themselves.

"What should we do? Wait here? Leave?"

"Let's see who it is first. We should get on the other side of the car so they can't see us. We can peer round the sides."

Loveday nodded, and they scooted behind the car to face the road.

After what seemed like forever, but was probably only a few minutes, a man came walking into the car park with a young woman attached to a thin rope. He held the other end in his hand.

What the fuck?

Loveday looked at Ellery who seemed just as horrified as she was. Ellery held out her hand in a *just wait* gesture.

Loveday looked to the road again. The man wasn't old, maybe in his forties, but he didn't look particularly in shape. Could the two of them take him?

Every so often he tugged on the rope, causing the young woman to stumble and cough. Her hands were tied behind her back. Loveday wanted to kill him. When she looked at Ellery, she was sure she was thinking the same thing.

She was also sure that this was Dani. What the bloody hell were they going to do?

❖

Terry needed a nap. He'd been lugging their shit for ages, and he wanted a beer and a little sleep. He'd brought some more guide ropes so he could tie up her feet. Not much she could do trussed up like a turkey.

The supermarket might be good place to have his nap. He could shut her in the toilets and lie down in front of them. That way, if she somehow managed to get free, she'd still have to get past him in the doorway.

"Come on, good girl." The rope tugging was starting to get boring, so he didn't bother doing it this time.

"Are we going in there?" she asked. Her voice sounded scratchy. Maybe he'd been pulling a bit too much.

"Talk about stating the bloody obvious. What do you think?"

"I don't think it's a good idea."

"I don't give a shit what you think, love. It's where we're going. Come on. I need a nap and some clean clothes."

"We still have a few hours of daylight left. We could walk some more."

Annoyed at being questioned, Terry pulled hard on the rope again. She stumbled but didn't fall.

"Shut up. I didn't ask for your opinion. This isn't a committee. We're going inside."

He tried to pull her forward, but she dug her heels in. What was she playing at?

"No."

"No? What do you mean *no*?"

"I'm not going in there."

"Why not?"

"I don't think it'd be very good for me."

"What the fuck are you talking about? I've got the rope, remember? You'll go where I tell you to, young lady."

"Mr. Pratt."

Okay, now he was pissed off. It wasn't the black mood, not really. He was tired and hungry but it wasn't the black mood. It could be, though, if she kept pushing.

"I'm going to say this once—"

"Let her go."

Terry spun around to face the new voice. Dani was pulled round with him.

"Who the fuck are you?" he asked. It was two women. One of

them was pretty tasty. The other one was clearly a dyke. Dani would be in good company.

"None of your business. Let her go," said the dykey looking one.

"Listen, love, you might look like a man but—"

"Oh, shut up, you horrible little psychopath," the other one—the pretty one—said.

"Little?" Terry was five foot ten.

The bitch dropped her eyes to the front of his trousers. "I wasn't talking about your height."

Next thing he knew, the blokey one had pulled a knife. Wicked sharp looking thing. Shit.

"Untie her. Now," she said.

Her voice was shaky, high-pitched, and nervous. Terry might have thought she was bluffing, but there was something in her eyes. Something he recognized. Something that told Terry she just might stab him if he gave her reason to. Maybe she was even looking for a reason.

"All right. Let's not get carried away," he said.

He thought furiously. There was no way he was giving up Dani. She was the link to his son. He'd die before he let these two take her. But it was two against one, and one of them had a knife. Once Dani was free, it would be three against one, and he really didn't fancy his chances then. Even if it was only three women.

"I won't tell you again," the one with the knife said.

Terry had an idea. "Okay, okay. I'll untie her. I need to use my knife, though, because I did it really tight."

"I don't think so," she said.

Could he take these two? Even if one of them did have a knife? If he could get it off her, maybe.

"He's got more rope in his bag. Tie him up first," Dani piped up. Bitch.

"Ellery?" The pretty one looked at the one with the knife.

"Go ahead." She didn't take her eyes off him.

"There's no need for that, love. I'm not going to do anything."

"Liar," Dani said.

"I agree," said the pretty one.

All of them were bitches.

The pretty one started snooping in his rucksack and pulled out beer bottle after beer bottle. "Got a bit of a problem, have you?"

Terry clenched his fists and swallowed the angry words perched on his tongue. He needed to play nice.

The pretty one stood, came towards him with a length of guide rope. Terry waited. He needed to time this right. As she reached out to tie his hands, he pivoted, grabbed her with one hand around her waist, spun her away from him, and put his other arm around her neck. He pulled her close.

"Go on," he whispered in her ear, "keep struggling. I like the way it makes you rub against my cock."

She stopped struggling and held herself stiff.

"Right, now we've got that sorted, you"—he nodded at the dykey one—"chuck the knife away. Far enough so you can't reach it."

She hesitated, so he squeezed the pretty one's neck with his forearm. She choked and tried to claw him off. "Pack that in. Don't fucking scratch me." The pretty one stopped, and he let up on her neck.

"I'll throw the knife. Just stop doing that to her." She flung the knife, and it skidded away and under a car.

Now what? Dani was already tied up, so she wasn't a problem. But these two, he wasn't sure how to proceed. The sensible thing to do was strangle the one he had hold of. It was a shame because she was a looker, but needs must. He was doing it for Little Terry.

"Right, me and the girls are going inside, and you are going to piss off. Got it?"

"No way. I'm not leaving them alone with you."

"It's either that or I'll snap this one's neck. It'll be over before you can get near us." He didn't know if that was true. He'd never snapped a human being's neck before, but he assumed it was the same principle. And dykey didn't know, did she?

"Fine, fine." She held her hands out in front of her, palms up. "I'll go."

"No! Ellery, take Dani with you. He can't stop all three of us. Take her."

Terry tightened his grip on her neck again, cut off her air. "Shut the fuck up." He squeezed and squeezed and squeezed, and for a moment he wondered if he was going to stop. He didn't want to, but he needed to. She was his leverage.

"Jesus, stop! Stop! I'll go. Please!" The dykey one—Ellery—was walking backward, away from them. The pretty one was coughing and spluttering, and Dani was crying. Fuck's sake. Bloody women.

And what was that other noise? Sounded like a fucking earthquake. A deep rolling rumble that shook the ground and almost made him lose his footing.

"What is that?" he heard Ellery say as she twisted around to look.

Out of nowhere a great herd of animals, all shapes and sizes, came thundering past. Cows, deer, dogs, sheep, and horses. Pigs, donkeys, ponies, and—he swore—a kangaroo.

What the fuck was going on? In the next instant, searing, agonizing pain between his legs. He dropped to his knees, thought he might throw up, wanted to scream. Oh, the fucking pain. He clutched himself, doubled over. Tears poured down his cheeks and he could barely breathe.

Now his hands were being pulled behind his back. He was weak as a baby, and he couldn't stop them. What did they do? What had they done to him *down there*? Sweat and snot mingled with his tears and he was really crying now. Fucking rotten bitches.

Chapter Forty-Two

Ellery wiped at the raw skin on Dani's neck. She struggled to tamp down her rage. How dare he. The wickedness of people sometimes left her speechless. This was why she spent all her time with animals. They were never cruel on purpose. How could anyone lead another person around on a piece of rope?

The light in the superstore wasn't great, but it was enough to see by. She was reluctant to come back after yesterday, but whatever chased her seemed to be gone.

She really wanted to talk to Dani about the dreams and the weird stampede outside but decided to wait until they were away from Terry Pratt. He hadn't said much at all. She could tell he was still in pain from the kick to the balls Loveday had dealt him. Ellery smiled just thinking about it. While the rest of them had been mesmerized by the animals, Loveday was saving the day. Ellery thought she was incredible.

The stampede was something she'd have to think about later. All her training told her it was almost an impossibility to have such a strange variety of animals running together—working together. It just shouldn't happen. Same species, yes. Or if there was a bush fire. But the fire they'd seen didn't seem to be heading this way, and Ellery had seen nothing else that would explain such a large herd of animals moving together like this. But now wasn't the time to get into it, even though her brain itched to come up with a logical reason for it happening.

None of them bothered to wipe the dried snot off Terry's face. The general consensus was he was a piece of shit and no one wanted to touch him.

Ellery looked up at the sound of squeaky wheels. Loveday was back with her shopping trolley.

"Okay, I've got a bit of everything. And more food for the pets," Loveday said. "I'll start putting it in the rucksacks in a minute."

They'd left Rocky and Claude at the van and Ellery wanted to get back to them as soon as possible. They'd already been away too long.

Loveday crouched beside Ellery and inspected Dani's neck. "That looks sore."

Ellery briefly closed her eyes as Loveday's warm breath washed over her cheek. Relished the warm hand on the shoulder Loveday used to steady herself.

"It's okay. Just stings," Dani said.

The girl wasn't much for talking. Or maybe it was the fact Terry was sitting close by, watching their every move. Ellery used the ropes from Dani to tie him up further then added some duct tape and more rope she found down one of the aisles.

Ellery wasn't sure what to do with him. She couldn't let him go, but she didn't want to leave him to starve to death either. Despite what he'd done and what he was planning to do, Ellery wasn't without mercy. She wouldn't stoop to his level. Convincing Loveday of that was another story. Maybe she could loosen a few of the ropes so he could eventually free himself? It was risky, but she couldn't think of a better solution.

"So what happens now?" he asked.

Ellery looked up from cleaning Dani's neck. Despite being out of shape, he was powerful. Big hands. Dark eyes that didn't stop moving, watching, assessing.

"We leave. You stay here," she replied.

"You're going to just leave me to die?"

"You don't deserve any better," Loveday cut in.

Ellery watched him swallow whatever words were about to come out of his mouth. She got the impression he wasn't used to women like Loveday.

"We can't do that, Loveday," Dani said. "It's not right."

Nor was putting a rope around a human being's neck until her skin was rubbed raw, but Ellery wasn't going to argue the point. She agreed with her.

"I'll loosen the ropes a bit. It'll take you a while to get them undone. Too long for you to be able to catch up with us," Ellery said.

"Is that a good idea?" Loveday stopped filling the rucksacks and looked at Terry with total loathing. "I say let him rot."

"You're a right little charmer." Terry smiled at Loveday and Ellery shivered. Too many teeth and his eyes were cruel.

"Ellery, I think letting him go is a mistake." Loveday ignored him and looked hard at Ellery.

"We can't just leave him to starve."

"Why not?"

"It's wrong," Dani said.

Loveday spun to face her. "What do you think he was going to do to you? Do you know? Do you have any idea?"

"Loveday," Ellery warned.

"I wasn't going to do anything to her. She was trying to run away from me."

Except that was a lie. Ellery was certain they'd got to Dani just in time.

"I know what he was going to do, Loveday. I'm not stupid. He's also planning to hand me over to that woman, Rosemary Decker. He thinks it'll help him get his son back," Dani said. It was the most she'd spoken. "Even so, we can't leave him to die. It's wrong."

"She's lying. I was just helping her get north, like she asked me to," Terry cut in.

"Will you shut up. No one's talking to you," Loveday said.

"Now listen, love—"

"Everyone be quiet." Ellery was surprised at the sharpness in her own voice. "I'm going to loosen the ropes. We're going to leave. That's the end of it."

Loveday huffed and silently went back to stuffing items in their rucksacks. Ellery would speak to her later. Right now, she wanted to get done in here and get back to the pets.

CHAPTER FORTY-THREE

Rosemary dug her fingernails into her palms to keep from screaming. She felt them break the skin.

"We should have it fixed within a week," Gordon said. "The damage isn't too bad. Should T-Cut right out."

Rosemary looked at the words someone had scratched into the side of the *Ark 2*. She reached out and touched them, felt where they scarred her beautiful boat. She traced their outline, leaving a thin smear of blood, bright red against the clean white.

"Who did this?" She turned to Chloe-Claire. "Who did this?"

"We don't know. We're looking into it," Chloe-Claire said.

"How can you not know? How can no one have seen anything at all?"

"I don't know, Ms. Decker."

"Find out. Find out. Find out." Rosemary was aware she was spraying spittle into Chloe-Claire's face but couldn't seem to stop herself. Someone had dared to deface her boat, her dream, her life's work. And no one cared. No one seemed to care at all.

"Ms. Decker—" Gordon said, and she rounded on him, pushed him against the side of *Ark 2*, balling her fist into his shirt.

"You fix it. Fix it now."

His eyes were wide and his face had gone red and she couldn't stop herself, couldn't calm down. She clutched at him tighter, twisted the rough fabric in her fist and pulled, so his sour breath washed over her face, their mouths inches apart in some sick parody of lovers. Someone had defaced the *Ark 2*. Scratched vile blasphemous words into its flank, and she was the only one who cared.

Who would do such a thing? She knew. Oh, she knew. Those one-percenters from the other day, that's who. Who else would scratch *Burn in hell murdering bitch* into her pride and joy?

A hand touched her shoulder, and she whirled around, grabbed the hand, wrenched it away from her, and heard a snap. Chloe-Claire screamed. Rosemary pushed her away. She fell hard, clutching her arm.

Around them, people had begun to gather. She looked at their faces, wide-eyed and afraid as though she was some kind of lunatic.

She wiped at her chin, at the saliva which coated it. She looked down at Chloe-Claire, cowering like a beaten dog, her screams now soft sobs. Rosemary looked behind her at Gordon, standing against the *Ark 2*, his shirt bunched up and his hands spread out in supplication.

The crowd moved closer to her, and several peeled away as if to come towards her. Rosemary fled.

❖

Terry worked at the knots on his left wrist. His fingers were greasy with sweat, and his nails too short to pick at the knots effectively. It looked like he might die in here after all.

Fuck.

His balls ached. He wiped at his brow with his inner wrist, the rough rope scratching his forehead and making him itch. Loveday—nothing lovable about that cunt—got more rope from somewhere. It wasn't smooth like the guide ropes from the tent. He reckoned she probably shopped around to find the most uncomfortable. Seemed like something the bitch would do.

Terry gave up. There was no way he was getting these knots undone. Maybe he'd try again later. The miserable cows left him some food and water so he'd be okay for a few days yet. Of course, the longer he sat here, the further away they got, and the less likely he'd be able to catch them.

Terry really wanted to catch them. If only to choke the life out of Loveday with the rope he was now bound with. She'd made an enemy out of him, and if he ever got out of here, she'd regret it. The other one—Ellery—he'd kill her quick. She hadn't been too bad beyond the knife business.

Dani was a means to an end. He'd get her to Rosemary Decker, then get his son back.

"Here we are again, Terry. Not very good at this, are you?"

Terry groaned. This was all he fucking needed. That creepy little devil was back.

"Leave me alone," Terry said.

The devil thing stepped out from an aisle, eating a packet of crisps. Cheese and onion. Terry looked away before he saw its face.

"You can look at me, Terry. You won't turn to stone." It sounded amused.

"I'd rather not. What do you want?"

"I believe it's more about what you might want."

He listened as the thing sucked on a crisp. It made horrible slurping noises. Probably didn't have teeth.

"I don't need anything from you."

"You've been tied up by two women, and it seems you can't undo the knots they loosened for you."

Terry's head shot up and at the last minute he averted his gaze so he wouldn't have to look at its face.

"How do you know about that? Were you here this whole time?"

"In a manner of speaking."

"What does that mean?"

"I saw what happened."

"So why didn't you stop them? Why didn't you help me?"

The thing slurped on another crisp. "Not in the rules, I'm afraid."

"What? What fucking rules? You know what, I don't care. Just piss off. Leave me alone. Or kill me. I've had enough."

"Now, now, Terry. There's no need to be dramatic. I'm not going to kill you. I'm going to untie you. And then you're going to go after the girl and get her back."

"What if I don't want to? What if I'm sick of all this?"

"If you don't, you'll never see your son again."

Terry heard the thing get up, heard joints pop, and was surprised to discover it must have bones. Maybe blood and flesh and somewhere a beating heart.

It came close to him, and Terry squeezed his eyes shut. He didn't want to look at it. He sucked in a breath as the thing touched him. It tugged at the rope around his wrists and he found its fingers were warm.

"What are you?" he asked, afraid of the answer.

"I'm the Bringer of Chaos. I've been around a long time, Terry. I'll still be here after you've rotted away and your bones are nothing but dust. Find the girl. Head north."

Terry tugged his wrists apart and the rope fell away. He opened his eyes and got to work on his ankles. He tried not to feel the panic which had set in when the thing came back and was still not gone. He pushed it down somewhere and thought instead about his son. All he had to do was get the girl back. That, and teach Loveday a lesson. It wouldn't be long before it was all over.

CHAPTER FORTY-FOUR

It was full dark by the time they pitched their tents. Ellery wanted to get as much distance between them and the superstore as possible. Loveday agreed. She understood why Ellery hadn't wanted to leave Terry there to rot, but Ellery didn't feel what she did. It was the wrong decision.

He was coming after them. She knew that like she knew other things. She couldn't keep forcing Ellery to go against her morals, though. They would just have to be ready for him again.

"You should come and eat," Ellery said.

Loveday looked over to where she sat with Dani. "We should keep watch tonight. In case he shows up."

"Okay." Ellery nodded. "But still, you should eat."

Loveday wasn't hungry. There was a churning in her gut which pushed out all need of food. She wanted to run, to get away from here. Where would she go? She couldn't leave Ellery and Dani. Not this time, no matter how much her intuition told her to.

"Ellery." She sat down. "You know he's coming for us?"

Ellery reached over and squeezed her hand. She squeezed back. "Yes, I know. But not tonight."

"You don't know that." Loveday shook off her hand.

"He's slow. And unfit. And I don't think he can see so well in the dark," Dani said, then shoved a spoonful of food into her mouth.

"All the same, we should take it in turns to keep watch. I wrote a book once where the baddie turned up unexpectedly. We can be caught unawares—we need to keep watch," Loveday said.

"*Heartbeat.* I read that. It's one of my favourites. And we will. Please eat." Ellery passed over a bowl of the nasty pasta concoction.

Loveday took it. "Thanks." She was somewhat mollified by the compliment. It was one of her favourites too.

"Are we going to talk about the animals?" Dani slurped up the last of her food. "Is there any more?"

"There's a lot we need to talk about." Loveday handed over her pasta. "Have this. I'm not hungry."

"Loveday—"

"Ellery, you aren't my mother, so give it a bloody rest."

Dani looked between the two of them, unsure. Hunger won out and she took Loveday's mess tin.

"The animals are obviously heading north too. I think that's pretty clear. Maybe they had dreams. Do animals dream, Ellery?" Loveday asked.

Ellery paused in her cleaning-up activities. "Yes. They do. We should be careful. Getting caught in a stampede would not be good."

"Dani, you should know, this woman Rosemary Decker has sent out a scouting party to find you. Ellery wants to stick to the back roads as much as possible."

Dani scraped the bottom of her tin and nodded. "Yeah, I know. Mr. Pratt was supposed to deliver me to her."

"How much do you know? About your purpose?" Loveday asked.

Dani shrugged in that teenage way, and Loveday had trouble reconciling her with the girl from their dreams. "I'm supposed to head north. You two were meant to come and get me, or I'd be, like, stoned to death or something."

Loveday caught Ellery's eye and they shared a smile. "Right, so you know about as much as us. Not why we had to get you away from him or anything."

"My dreams are hazy. I think I'm some big deal, but I don't know why. Or what I'm supposed to do." Dani shrugged again and stood. She brushed the leaves and dirt off her jeans. "I'm going to turn in. Wake me up when it's my turn to keep watch."

With that, she headed into her tent and zipped it up. Loveday noticed Rocky rushed in with her. Little traitor.

Loveday leaned close to Ellery, who was rinsing out their mess tins. "Do you believe her?"

"That she doesn't know any more than us? No."

Loveday glanced at Dani's tent. "She's lying through her bloody teeth."

"She doesn't know us. Look who she's been travelling with for the past week. Can't blame her for being wary." Ellery leaned the tins upside down against a log to dry off.

"Well, she needs to tell us soon. Besides, her dreams must have told her we're the good guys."

"Give her a chance, Loveday. Let her get her bearings before you bamboozle her." Ellery laughed.

"Fine. You're right." Loveday grinned. "And you've changed your tune. All you ever do is moan about how obscure the dreams are."

Ellery stood. "She's a teenager. She'll tell us in her own time. If it looks like it's taking too long, we'll hurry her along. Look, I'll take the first watch. You get some sleep."

"No, I'll go first," Loveday said.

"You almost had the life choked out of you today. Get a bit of rest."

Loveday was about to argue, but the shadow which passed over Ellery's face stopped her. She looked haunted. Before she could think about what she was doing, Loveday kissed her gently on the lips. "I'm okay." She kissed her again, longer this time.

"I know you are. But before, I thought he was really going to kill you." Ellery toed something on the ground.

"I'm fine. But I'll go and get some rest if it'll make you feel better."

"It will."

Loveday rolled her eyes. "Night, then. Wake me in a few hours."

On her way to the tent, she turned back to see Ellery settling back down in front of the fire they made. She really needed to stop sending her such mixed messages. The truth was she liked Ellery, really liked her. It was ironic really. After a lifetime of bad decisions, she finally met a woman who would be good for her. Only she couldn't risk it. If her past form was anything to go by, she'd fuck it all up anyway, and there was too much to lose.

Loveday climbed into her sleeping bag and was immediately joined by Claude. "At least you didn't abandon me for the new girl." She pressed her face against his soft fur and let herself be lulled to sleep by his contented purring.

❖

Ellery tried not to panic. Beyond the fire it was pitch black. She tried not to hear the sounds of the night and imagine the worst.

She didn't have Loveday's intuition, but she knew Terry Pratt was coming for them. She was banking on them being able to put too much distance between them for him to ever be able to catch them up. Maybe it was foolish, and maybe she was too soft, too weak, but she could never have left him to die. Loveday had something inside her that Ellery lacked. A streak of something cold and totally geared towards self-preservation.

Something crunched, rustled behind her. Ellery swung her torch in the direction but saw nothing. Probably just an animal.

She held the torch in place for a moment longer, the light trained on the scraggly bushes. Not big enough for a man to hide in.

Ellery knew she should get up and check, make sure, but she couldn't. It was too dark. She wiped a trembling hand across her mouth. Sweat had gathered on her top lip. She was too warm. *Get a grip. Grow up.* It was probably a rat or a mouse. It wasn't a monster, a bogeyman, or Terry Pratt.

She clicked off the torch, turned back to the fire. It started to rain. Spitting at first and then harder. Ellery drew her coat around her and pushed up her hood. She waited and watched and tried not to panic.

❖

Terry tripped over something in the dark and came down heavy on his knees. Loose gravel tore into his palms.

His night vision was shit, and he was exhausted, but he kept moving. He had to close the distance. They would walk faster than him, so he had to use the night to make up the difference.

Terry picked himself up off the ground, and he stumbled, his legs nearly gave out. An image of his son flashed across his mind's eye, and his legs straightened, strengthened, and he moved on.

❖

Ellery jerked awake. Something clamped on to her shoulder and she screamed.

"It's only me," Loveday said from behind her.

"Fuck. You scared me." Ellery's heart started to beat at a more normal rhythm. "What's up? It's still the middle of the night."

"We need to leave. Now," Loveday said.

"Why?"

"He's coming. He's close."

Ellery's skin prickled and her scalp went tight. "Are you sure?"

Loveday nodded. She picked up mess tins and mugs. "Yes. Come on."

"Can you tell how far away he is?" Ellery stayed sitting.

Loveday sighed, dropped the mess tins and mugs, and turned to her, hands on hips. "No. But he's close enough. I can feel him getting nearer."

Ellery nodded. "I'll wake Dani."

❖

Fuck. Terry looked around the hastily vacated campsite. Boot prints in the spongy damp earth, grass still flattened from their tents. He must have just missed them. He couldn't walk any more tonight. In the dark, he doubted they'd get too much further. Terry hadn't bothered with a tent or much besides beer. He laid out a sleeping bag and got inside it. It would be damp in a few minutes, but he didn't care. He opened a beer, drank half in one go, and ran the back of his hand over his mouth.

The torch wound down, and he couldn't be bothered to wind it back up again. Terry downed the rest of his beer, threw the empty bottle in the bushes, and opened another.

His stomach rumbled. He couldn't remember the last time he'd eaten. He didn't care. He downed the beer and opened another.

❖

Rosemary sat in a leather swivel chair. She was on the *Ark 2*. It was beautiful. Out of the windows she could see only water. It was flat and delicate and looked like glass.

"Things aren't going to plan, Rosemary."

There it was, that voice again. She hadn't heard it in weeks. It wasn't how she expected the voice of God to sound. Wet, spongy, foreign.

He was behind her and she didn't dare turn around. "There have been some hiccups, I agree."

"Hiccups? They're saying you've lost your mind. They're planning to move against you."

Rosemary almost turned around. "Who?"

"The instigators are the two investors. They've gathered some willing people to them."

"How dare they?" Rage burned in Rosemary's chest, her palms itched. "I'll stop them."

"How many are still loyal to you? Do you know?"

Rosemary thought. She was preparing another group to go in search of the girl and her protectors. Perhaps she could hold them back for a time. "About six I trust to carry out anything serious." God moved closer to her, and Rosemary closed her eyes. She daren't look at Him.

"Good. You need to mobilize them. Remove the threat. Kill them all."

"The investors, you mean?"

"Kill them all. Kill them all. Kill them all."

❖

Rosemary closed her door when the screaming started. She gave the order in the early morning, her breath visible in the frigid air as they clustered outside. It seemed to take her words and carry them away. There wasn't much privacy in the hangar, and when she gave the order, it would need to be carried out quickly. The others nodded, said little. They understood what was at stake. They were glad to do God's work.

She ordered them to split into two groups. Each would neutralize one of the investors. At the same time, so one could not warn the other. She had the names of the people who had colluded with them. They would be next, and it would be done publicly. That was the screaming she heard now. She'd opened her door briefly to watch one man being chased down. He tripped, dropped to the ground. She watched as one of her disciples fell on him and stuck the knife in, arm moving in an arc, over and over again. It was mesmerizing.

She told herself she didn't enjoy it, that it was necessary to pave the way for a new world. Civilizations throughout history were built on the spilt blood of traitors. This one would be no different.

Soon the screaming stopped. It was done. Rosemary got on her knees and began to pray.

Chapter Forty-Five

L oveday was exhausted. She stumbled again and would have fallen if Dani hadn't grabbed her arm. They walked through the rest of the night and into the morning. The feeling of dread had receded, and she thought it would be safe to stop for a few hours. They had to. She was about to fall down.

"Let's stop."

Dani sighed next to her. "Thank God. I'm knackered."

"I think we all are." Ellery maneuvered the pram off the road and onto a patch of scraggly grass. "If we rest for a bit, then walk another five miles or so, there's a motorway services with a hotel."

"Are you serious?" Loveday thought about sleeping in a proper bed and almost wanted to keep walking. Her legs had other ideas, though.

"Yes." Ellery laughed.

Loveday sat beside her. "You look exhausted too. Don't take this the wrong way, but I'm glad."

"Thanks a lot."

"I just mean, I'm about ready to fall down. I feel better knowing you feel the same."

Ellery rolled her eyes and bumped Loveday's shoulder. "It's not a competition. How are you doing, Dani?"

Dani was lying flat on her back despite the damp, dewy ground. "I want to run the next few miles to get to that bed, but my legs are jelly."

Loveday laughed and poked Dani's leg with her boot. "You're a million years younger than us. No excuse not to charge ahead and make up the beds for us."

Dani grunted. The walk through the night had the benefit of bringing them closer together. Dani didn't seem so guarded and actually had a pretty good sense of humour. Loveday liked her.

"If I'd realized I'd have to look out for you two old dears, I would have gone it alone," Dani joked. She sat up and pulled Rocky to her. He submitted graciously to ear and back scratches.

"Shut up and make this old dear some coffee." Loveday poked her again and Dani laughed.

"Fine. But only because your arthritis is probably playing up with the damp weather."

"Cheeky little shit."

Loveday sneezed. Dani probably wasn't far off with her assessment. All the walking had made Loveday's bones ache.

Ellery looked up from her map and smiled. "This is nice." Her brow creased. "I mean, even though we're running from one psychopath. Possibly straight to another. And, you know, the world is about to have the fuck flooded out of it. Possibly."

Dani looked at Loveday who shook her head.

"Yeah. Wonderful," Dani said.

"Shit. Sorry. That was insensitive. And weird," Ellery said. She rubbed the back of her neck.

Loveday burst out laughing. She wanted to hug poor Ellery, so she did. "We know what you meant."

"Yeah. Even if it was totally weird." Dani nudged her shoulder.

"How long can we rest here, do you think?" Ellery asked Loveday, obviously wanting to change the subject.

Dani went back to the coffee.

"I don't feel him as strongly as last night. It's hard to say. I don't see things, only feel them. I feel like he's a good day's walk away from us."

"So we can rest tonight?" Ellery asked.

"Yes. I think so." Loveday took a crumpled tissue from her pocket and blew her nose.

"He won't stop." Dani didn't look up from the coffee pot.

Loveday glanced at Ellery who shrugged.

"As long as we can get far enough away from him—"

"He won't stop. He thinks handing me over to Rosemary Decker will bring back his son."

"He told you that?" Ellery asked. She folded the map and stuffed it in her pocket.

"No. I saw it in the dream. We'd left by then, and I was waiting for the right time to ditch him." Dani poured out coffee into three tin mugs. Loveday took hers gratefully.

"What else did you see in the dreams?" Loveday asked gently.

Dani sighed, sipped her coffee. "I'm supposed to save the world or some bullshit like that. You two were going to come and help me get north."

"Do you know how you're going to save the world? I mean, are you going to bring people back? The ones who vanished?" Ellery asked.

"No. Not like that. I don't really understand it. But I know a storm is coming. Worse than before. And if we don't get to high ground in time, then we'll die."

"So you don't know much more than us." Loveday sipped her coffee. It tasted good and warmed her insides. She was freezing cold. "Then we just keeping moving. Try to stay ahead of Terry Pratt, and avoid this death squad or whatever it is that's coming for us. Easy."

No one answered her. They drank their coffee in silence. It started to rain.

CHAPTER FORTY-SIX

The hangar was quiet. Most people avoided Rosemary like the plague. She didn't mind. It was better to be feared and have no more opposition. They'd come around. Once they realized everything she did was for their own good and the glory of God. If not, well, she'd shown what would happen. Rosemary didn't expect any more dissent.

"Any news?" she asked Chloe-Claire, who was back to work and sporting a splint on her arm. She didn't appear to hold a grudge against Rosemary.

"They've almost repaired the *Ark 2*. The graffiti is almost invisible."

Except Rosemary knew it was there. Knew that someone had dared to carve an obscenity into her beloved boat. It didn't matter that those responsible were lying in a ditch outside the hangar—injustice burned in her stomach.

And where was the girl? Why hadn't the scouting party she'd sent out found her yet? Rosemary was growing impatient. The storm was almost upon them, and she wanted the girl dead before they got on the boat. Her and the ones with her. Rosemary had seen one of them in a dream. Something about her tugged at Rosemary unpleasantly. Did she know her? Had they met before? Fear settled around her.

She stood up quickly, keen to shake it off. She would go and see the *Ark 2*. In the past it had always made her feel better. She forced thoughts of the woman in the dream from her mind.

❖

By the time they reached the hotel at the services, the rain was coming down in sheets and it was clear Loveday was sick.

Really sick.

They helped her strip out of her wet clothes—even waterproofs couldn't repel the quantity of rain which lashed down—and get under the covers in one of the rooms on the first floor. The hotel was one of those generic flat boxes that squatted by the side of main roads or at motorway services. Every room looked the same, and every piece of furniture was square and made from laminate.

But it was better than camping, and some of the rooms were unoccupied, so they didn't have to deal with vanished people's suitcases and dirty sheets.

Ellery hung out their wet things in the bathroom, hoping they might dry overnight but not holding out much hope. Loveday let out a machine gun of sneezes in the other room, and Ellery thought they might be here for a few days yet.

"Shall I go over to the services and pick up some cold medicine?" Dani asked from the doorway.

"No, I'll go. You stay here with Loveday."

Dani hesitated, nodded.

"What?" Ellery asked.

"Be careful. I know Loveday said he was a way behind us, but if we have to stay here for a while, he'll catch us up."

Ellery rubbed the back of her head. Her hair was longer now, and she could get her fingers through it. "I know."

She didn't know what else to say. Loveday was sick and they couldn't move her. Terry would catch them up.

Loveday began coughing. It sounded phlegmy and rough. Ellery wasn't a human doctor, but she knew an infection when she heard one. If they could find a chemist, she'd probably be able to find the correct antibiotics if the cough didn't clear up on its own.

Ellery tried not to worry, but it was pointless. She worried about Loveday when she wasn't sick. Pretty much all she thought about was Loveday. Well, that and the kiss they'd shared. She played that one over and over in her head on a continuous loop. She thought about the way Loveday pursed her lips and got a little line on her brow when Ellery had done something to piss her off. Ellery loved that line. She loved those lips. She was pathetic. She'd fall apart without Loveday. Loveday had to be okay.

Ellery sighed and stood. "I won't be long. Maybe get another duvet from one of the other rooms. In case she's cold."

The benefit of everything electrical not working was the mechanisms for the bedroom doors were disabled. The downside was it was bloody cold in here.

❖

Terry was drenched but didn't care. He wiped the rain from his eyes every few feet and stopped pulling his hood back up. The wind kept whipping it off his head anyway.

His thighs burned and his feet ached but he pushed on. When he thought he might fall down with exhaustion, he thought of his son and kept going.

He was so close now. Finally in the north of the country. Terry had never been further than Essex, and looking around he thought he probably hadn't been missing much. Fields and trees and low hedges everywhere. A motorway sign told him some services were fifteen miles up ahead. He'd probably get there by tomorrow.

Water ran like a river across the tarmac and over his boots, soaking them. His wet socks rubbed his feet and squelched between his toes. He was freezing. His teeth chattered and his hands were red with the cold.

Still, Terry walked on. He thought about his son and how close he was to the end of all this. He thought about Loveday and how he would teach her a lesson. He thought about Dani and her young, firm body. Mostly he thought about his son. He didn't think hardly at all about that fucking devil and if he was a liar and if this was all for nothing.

❖

Ellery directed her torch over the shelves. The shop in the services only stocked a basic assortment of cold medicine. She picked up cough mixture, cold tablets, tissues, paracetamol, and cough drops. She hesitated over the chocolate. But when she heard a noise from somewhere in the building and remembered her visit to the superstore, she grabbed a handful of bars, stuffed them in her bag, and hurried out.

The rain hadn't let up, and water streamed across the car park. Like before, cars squatted, abandoned, some parked up, and some had coasted into walls and into each other. It was eerie. The sun was setting, but it had been dark most of the afternoon because of the weather. The air was cold and crisp and clean. She wondered if this was the beginning of the end.

Ellery jogged across the car park and into the hotel. She shook the water from her hair and headed for the stairs. Just as empty and gloomy as the services, it would soon be pitch black inside.

"It's me," she called out as she walked down the hall towards their room.

Inside, Loveday lay beneath a pile of bedclothes, only the top of her auburn head visible. Dani sat in a chair by the window reading. She looked up. "She's been asleep since you left. Coughing and sneezing and stuff."

Ellery went to the bed and sat down. She pulled the duvet down slightly and felt Loveday's head. Clammy but not hot. A bad cold but not flu. Thank God.

"Loveday." She shook her gently.

Loveday cracked open one eye. "Did you bring drugs?" Her voice was scratchy and she sounded bunged up.

"Yeah. And tissues."

Ellery gave her the medicine and a small bottle of orange juice. She noticed Loveday's hand shake as she drank.

"Loveday, can you feel him? I mean, do you know where he is?"

Loveday swallowed the pills, winced, and wiped her hand across her forehead. "I don't. I'm sorry. My head is so stuffy."

"It's okay. Don't worry. Just sleep," Ellery said.

"For a little while. I'll be ready to go tomorrow. I promise."

Ellery glanced at Dani who was biting her lip. "We'll see. For now, just concentrate on getting better."

Loveday grunted, lay back down, and burrowed under the duvet. She turned on her side, away from Ellery.

Ellery tried to ignore the sick feeling in her stomach. It was just a cold—the flu, at worst. People got over it all the time. Loveday was young and healthy, and there was no reason to worry. She would be up and about in no time. Ellery knew all this, but still the sick feeling remained—a sense of dread. It nagged and pawed at her even though she knew she was being irrational. But she couldn't lose Loveday. She just couldn't.

"It'll be dark soon," Dani said. She turned in the chair and looked outside.

"Yes. Leave the curtains open. We shouldn't put our torches on."

"I'll watch out the window. Just in case."

The rain beat in a steady rhythm against the glass and Ellery wondered if he would come tonight.

CHAPTER FORTY-SEVEN

Terry squeezed out his socks and watched the water pour. He'd finally taken refuge in an abandoned car. The rain hadn't let up, and it had become too dark to carry on walking. He dumped his backpack after it became so waterlogged he could barely carry it. Of course he'd taken out the beers first and put them in his coat pockets.

He drank one now and watched a raindrop trail jerkily down the windowpane. He downed the beer. Opened another. He tried to remember the last time he'd eaten and couldn't. He was tired.

Terry struggled out of his coat. His jumper was soaked, so he took that off as well. The car was cold. He downed the beer, then drew his knees up to his chest. He felt around in his pocket for his lighter and cigarettes. The cigarettes were damp, so he ran the flame from his lighter along one to dry it out.

Terry took a deep drag and leaned his head back against the seat. Better. He opened another beer—his last one—and took a sip. He would make this one last.

Terry took another drag, and the cigarette crackled, the tip glowed red hot. The car quickly filled with smoke, the smell burning his eyes and tickling his nose.

If the women were on the same road as him, and if he could catch them tomorrow close to the services, then he might have an idea. Terry smiled to himself.

❖

Loveday couldn't breathe. She sat up in bed and tried to blow her nose. Her ears popped. Her head felt like it was stuffed with cotton wool, and even as she reached out to find Terry, she knew it was no good. Too foggy and heavy inside her head.

Across the room, Dani was curled up in a chair, fast asleep. Ellery was on the bed with her but right over on the edge. Loveday guessed it was so she wouldn't disturb her. Ellery was sweet like that. Loveday didn't think she'd ever met anyone as sweet as Ellery. The warm feeling lapped at her insides, and she smiled. Then she sneezed.

God, she felt like crap. Rocky raised his head off his paws, and his eyes shone in the dark. He and Claude were at the end of the bed. Their pram had been soaked through in the rain.

It was still coming down now, a thick wall of water which didn't seem inclined to stop. Loveday guessed this was the start of it. The big flood. Before she'd gotten sick, Ellery thought they probably had another four or five days' travel. She would have to be ready to go tomorrow because she couldn't afford to slow them down.

"How are you feeling?" Ellery asked.

Loveday felt her turn in the bed.

"I'm okay," she said before a coughing fit betrayed her.

She felt the bed dip as Ellery stood, rustled around, then handed her a small plastic cup.

"Here, you can take some more cough mixture now."

Loveday took it gratefully, then lay back down.

"Let's try again. How are you feeling?"

Loveday sighed. "Like dogshit. But I'll be ready to go tomorrow."

"No. We'll stay here until you're better. We don't have doctors any more, Loveday. If you get sicker, there's nothing anyone can do."

Loveday reached out and squeezed Ellery's hand. "We also don't have the luxury of hanging around."

"Let's see how you feel in the morning, okay?" Ellery shifted and lay beside her.

Loveday moved in close, and Ellery's arms came around her. She should tell her not to, she might get sick, but it felt good. Comforting. And Loveday was selfish, after all.

❖

As soon as the sun began to rise, Terry started walking.

❖

Ellery splashed her face with water from the sink. Dani sat on the edge of the bathtub, eating cold custard from a can.

"You know, maybe we could find something to, like, pull her along in?" In the mirror she watched Dani lick her spoon.

"Like what? A giant pram?" Ellery towelled off. Her eyes felt less grainy now.

"No."

"Wheelbarrow?"

Dani laughed. "Shut up, Ellery. I'm being serious."

Ellery turned. "She needs to rest and stay warm and dry."

"I know. But Terry is…I mean, he wasn't nice to start with, but as we'd been going along he got worse. I think he's completely mental now, instead of just a bit."

"We stopped him before."

"Yeah, because a massive herd of animals turned up and distracted him. We should at least, like, get some knives or something."

Ellery looked at the Dani, watched her scrape around the can with her index finger, not a line on her painfully young face and certainly nothing about her to indicate she was the saviour of mankind.

"What?" Dani paused with her finger in front of her mouth, a blob of yellow custard balanced precariously on the end of it.

"I'm struggling to see you as the leader of our new world," Ellery said.

Dani shrugged. "Yeah, me too. It's fucked up."

Ellery sighed. "You really have no more idea than me and Loveday?"

"I swear." Dani crossed her heart. "I'd tell you if I did. I trust you now."

"Okay, then. I'm going to head over to the services and get some more food. I'll take Rocky."

"Get knives," Dani called after her.

❖

Ellery pulled a few tins off the shelves and stuffed them in a little bag. The rain was still going full steam ahead and drummed on the roof in a steady roar. It was hard to hear anything inside the building. Any noise would be muffled.

She moved down the aisle and picked up a paperback, then put it down and took another. It was gloomy in here and hard to see much of anything.

Finally, she was satisfied with what she had, and she went back around to the entrance. She paused by a rack selling phone chargers, earphones, batteries and cocked her head to the side, waited. She shook her head slightly, glanced around, and walked to the exit.

Terry knew it was now or never. He shot out from behind the newspaper stand and thrust the knife into her back.

She made a *hmpff* sound, probably expelling air from her lungs, and swung around. Terry caught her again in the stomach.

He slashed at her, felt the knife bury itself in her to the hilt. He pulled it out and stabbed again.

He stabbed again and again and again.

She fell to the ground, let go of her bag, and a can of something spilled out and rolled across the floor.

Terry fell upon her.

❖

Loveday sat up, looked around the room until she saw Dani, back in the chair by the window.

Oh no. "Run," she said. "He's here."

❖

Terry filled a plastic jerrycan with petrol from the pump. Blood ran down his free hand and mixed with the rain. It was probably worse than it looked. No one told you you could cut yourself when you stabbed someone.

When the can was full he carried it with his good hand into the hotel and set it by the front doors. He turned and went back for another.

❖

Loveday shut Claude and Rocky in the bathroom. She wouldn't think about Ellery.

She'd told Dani to run and hide somewhere upstairs. Surely Terry would work his way up the building, bottom to top. If she could intercept him at this level, maybe Dani would be okay. Maybe Ellery would turn up and hit him over the head with another brick.

Loveday crouched by the door with the knife and waited. She coughed, sniffed. She tried not to think about Ellery.

Terry poured petrol along the corridor of the ground floor. He poured it over the seating area, the rack of magazines and newspapers. He poured it over the reception desk and the curtains in the front window.

He picked up the second can and took it with him up to the first floor. His hand dripped blood on the carpet. He was making a mess, but that didn't matter now.

CHAPTER FORTY-EIGHT

Rosemary was impatient. Still no news from the search party which left days ago. She looked over the platform at the ants scurrying around below. Fewer than before. Some executed and many had left after.

Not so many people coming in now. Either they were bypassing her altogether, or most of the survivors were accounted for.

Still, she had a decent number of dedicated followers. Good, strong people. It wouldn't be long now. She was almost ready. She'd cleaned house and removed the troublemakers and Judases. All that was left to do was kill the girl. Kill the girl and start a brand new world.

❖

Loveday heard him call out. She didn't dare peek around the corner. It was gloomy enough and she had a chance of taking him by surprise.

"Hello? Anyone here? Where are you, you bitches?"

She stayed quiet. Felt a tickle in her throat, and she desperately tried not to cough. She wiped her hands on her knees, raised herself into a crouch behind the door, and ignored the pounding in her head. She felt like shit but would feel even worse if Terry got hold of her, she was sure.

"Come out, come out, wherever you are," he crooned, getting closer.

She heard sloshing and wondered what he was doing. Drinking? No, it was too loud to be from one of his bottles.

"Room service," he screamed.

Then a bang. He must have kicked a door open. Bang. Slosh. Bang.

What was he doing? Then she smelled it. Petrol. Her legs twitched. She wanted to run and keep running and get away from here. She wouldn't. She couldn't. For once, she would stay and fight. Whatever happened, she wouldn't be a coward again.

Bang. Slosh. Bang. "Where are you?" He was right outside. "Ah. What have we got here?"

She saw his shadow in the doorway. The smell of petrol burned her nostrils and lodged in the back of her throat.

Loveday waited, the knife heavy in her hand. She gripped it tighter, squeezed her eyes shut, and prayed for the courage to do what she had to next.

Terry stepped into the room, and Loveday lunged at him.

❖

Terry caught her, dropped the jerrycan, and spun her around and into the door.

A blinding pain in his side and he looked down. Saw where her knife stuck out of him.

"Bitch," he said and slammed her into the door.

He glanced over his shoulder where petrol was leaking all over the floor. Oh, well. Terry used one arm to hold Loveday against the door by her throat. He took his lighter out of his pocket, flicked it, and held it up in front of her.

"Where is she?" he asked.

"Fuck off."

Terry smiled, shoved her hard against the door. "I'm going to kill you, but it's up to you how quick I do it. Where is she?"

"She's gone. I told her to run and she's gone."

"Liar. I would have seen her. Probably about the time I finished killing your little mate."

Terry felt her sag against the door. Her head dropped slightly. "No," she whispered.

"Tell me where Dani is, or I swear to God, I'll burn you alive." The lighter was getting hot in his hand.

She looked up, met his eyes, and nodded. "Okay," she said and leaned her head in close to his.

Then the bitch headbutted him.

His nose crunched, burst, and the pain was excruciating. Terry fell to his knees clutching at his face. Oh, the pain. Then she kicked him. Right in the ribs. Bitch. He rolled over. The flame from his lighter burned his hand, and he dropped it. Right by the jerrycan.

The whole place went up. Flames rushed up his arm where he'd spilt petrol on it. They licked over his body in a wave of heat and pain. He tried to scream, but they leapt into his mouth and nose, and then he was consumed by fire.

❖

Loveday ran to the bathroom and grabbed the pets. With one tucked under each arm, she dashed past Terry, who was writhing on the floor, and out of the room. The fire was already spreading, chasing a path into the corridor. She had to get out. She had to find Dani. She could not think about Ellery.

"Dani!" she shouted. "Dani!" Again.

Loveday ran to the stairwell. "Dani!"

Shit. What should she do? She glanced behind her to see the fire engulfing most of the first floor. She couldn't leave Dani here. Claude was starting to wriggle in her arms. He'd starfish any minute, and she'd lose hold of him.

Loveday looked down the stairs. Then back up. "Dani!" She tried one more time.

Then, feet pounding on the stairs. Thank God.

"What's happening. Is he gone?" Dani bolted down the stairs and skidded to a stop in front of her.

"Yes, he's gone." Loveday glanced behind her. "We have to get out of here—he's set the place on fire."

They hurried down the stairs and outside into the rain. They found a car unlocked and put the pets inside.

"Where's Ellery?" Dani asked.

The look in her eyes told Loveday she had guessed already. "I don't know. He said…he said he killed her." Loveday forced the words out. She couldn't believe them.

"The services," Dani said. "That's where she'll be."

They jogged across the car park. Somewhere in the hotel a window shattered.

Ellery was lying in the entrance to the services. It looked like she had tried to crawl outside, probably to warn them, a trail of blood marking her progress. She'd managed to crawl ten feet before she died.

Loveday dropped to her knees. She reached out and touched Ellery. She had been such a fool. Such a fool. And now Ellery was dead, and she could never tell her.

Someone wailed. Oh God, it was her. She gripped Ellery, held on to her. Buried her face in her hair, sticky with blood, but Loveday didn't care. Ellery was gone, and now she could never tell her what a fool she'd been.

Dani knelt beside her. She was crying. "We have to go. The fire might jump, and we have to go."

"I can't leave her." The knowledge hit Loveday like a brick. "I can't. I just can't."

Dani tugged on her arm. "We have to go now."

"No. You do something." Loveday sat up, grabbed the front of Dani's shirt. "You're the saviour of mankind—*you do something.*" Now she was shouting, screaming in Dani's face. "Do something. What's the point of you if you won't *do* something."

Dani's arms came around her and held her. She whispered that it would be all right into Loveday's hair, but it wouldn't. How could it ever be all right? She'd just realized she loved Ellery, and now she could never tell her.

CHAPTER FORTY-NINE

Rosemary sat in the chair on her boat. She was calm.
"One of them is dead," the voice behind her said.
"There's been a lot of killing lately," she replied.
"Yes, but all in the name of God, so hardly a sin." A creak as He sat down.
"In your name, you mean?" Rosemary said. She looked out the window. The seas were grey and choppy.
"Yes, yes." He drummed his fingers. "The man I sent to bring her to you is also dead. A setback but not a calamity. They will still come."
"And the search party? Are they near?" Rosemary asked.
"They are closing in. It's possible they might miss each other, but even if that's so, they are heading straight towards you. I made sure."
Rosemary felt the sway of the boat as it rode the choppy sea. "So we are set. It's almost over."
"Almost. The beginning will start soon."

Rosemary opened her eyes. She sat up in her bed. She was well-rested and the sense of urgency was gone. The stress was gone. She had trusted in God, and He had delivered, and now a new world was beginning. She would have the girl and kill the girl and anyone else who got in the way.
She had an idea. She would take a group with her and set out to meet the girl. Maybe only a few miles, but she wanted to see her face when she realized she had lost and Rosemary had won.

❖

They wrapped Ellery in blankets and dragged her body with them, back to the motorway. Loveday didn't want to leave her there, in that place. They would bury her somewhere nice, somewhere she would have liked.

Fresh tears streamed down her face but were lost in the rain that battered them. Together they heaved her into the back of a lorry they found unlocked and climbed in after her.

"I'll go back to the services soon. Find us some food and blankets." Dani said.

Loveday nodded. She was numb and didn't really care. She knew she was cold, and she knew she was sick, but she couldn't feel it. Couldn't feel anything except numbness, like she'd been anaesthetized.

Dani shrugged off her jumper. "You should take yours off too. It's soaked and your teeth are chattering."

Loveday pulled her knees up to her chest and closed her eyes.

Sometime later, the doors to the lorry opened. It was Dani. Loveday must have fallen asleep.

"Here." She draped a blanket over Loveday. "I got some clothes too. Only fleeces, but they're dry."

Loveday closed her eyes again.

"Loveday, please. Ellery wouldn't want to see you like this."

Loveday bolted up. "How do you know? You barely knew her at all."

Dani recoiled like she'd slapped her. Loveday felt bad. "I'm sorry. I didn't mean that."

"It's okay," Dani said. She shuffled back towards the lorry doors.

"No, it isn't. It's not okay. I'm sorry." Loveday pulled off her wet things and put on the dry fleece.

"I brought some medicine too. Cold stuff. Are you hungry?" Dani shuffled closer.

"Sure," Loveday said. She wasn't, but Dani was right. Ellery wouldn't want to see her like this. She'd been determined to help Dani. Right from the start but especially after the dream, Ellery wanted to save her. To get her to safety. Even when she was dying—and she would have known she was dying—she'd tried to get to them, to warn them.

They ate in the semi-darkness, cold ravioli from a can and custard for afters. Loveday took more cold medicine and tried to sleep. Rocky and Claude curled up with her, and she was grateful for that at least, but she missed Ellery so much the force of it threatened to pull her under and drown her.

❖

Sometime later the door to the lorry opened. At first Loveday thought it was Dani, then realized she was lying beside her. A torch shone its light inside, and the lorry swayed as someone climbed in.

Loveday sat up and tried her best to shield Dani. "Who are you?"

"Don't be afraid." The voice sounded strange. Deep, with a foreign tinge. It was without inflection.

"Who are you?" she repeated. Dani shifted behind her, and she put her hand on her and squeezed. It was dark. Maybe he wouldn't see her if she kept quiet and kept still.

"In your language I would be called a Keeper of the Balance."

Great, a random nutter had found his way inside the lorry. Why couldn't they catch a break?

"Okay, then." Loveday had got the better of Terry, and he was much bigger than this guy, so she wasn't worried. It was dark in the lorry, but she got the sense of someone thin and frail. There was something familiar about him.

"Loveday, I'm not here to hurt you," he said and moved closer still.

How did he know her name?

"He's telling the truth," Dani said and moved out from behind her. "I've seen him in my dreams."

Loveday looked from one to the other. "I'm really not in the mood for all this. I'm sick. Ellery is dead. I've just fought off a total psychopath and escaped a fire. Can I not just have one night that's drama free?"

"I'm afraid not." She couldn't see his face but she felt the smile in his words. "I'm sorry about the…drama? And I'm sorry about your friend."

"What exactly does a Keeper of the Balance do, then?" she asked.

Loveday rubbed her eyes and coughed. "Are you the one who's been making us have all these dreams? Who caused the white light?"

"Yes."

Loveday laughed but not because it was funny. "You drove Ellery mad. She's so—was so—logical, and she just hated all the cryptic crap. She would have really wanted to talk to you." A sob escaped her, and she was mortified. She didn't want to cry in front of him.

"You may ask me anything you want," he said.

"Was it you? Back in town? In Libby Lee's bedroom? In Ellery's garden?"

"I was in Ellery's garden. There is another. The Bringer of Chaos. He was there too. His agenda is different from ours. His kind want to see the end of humanity. He wants you all dead."

"Ours? There's more of you?" Dani asked.

Loveday had forgotten she was there. She was consumed with the conflicting desires to find out what was going on and to strangle him. He was the reason Ellery was dead. He had started all this in the first place.

"We have existed since before. At different points, when it became clear that your kind would destroy the world, we were forced to step in."

"Kill us all, you mean?" Loveday said.

"Not all of you but most, yes."

"That's despicable," Loveday said.

"Hey, was it you that started the Dark Ages?" Dani asked.

"Yes. But each time we make sure there are enough of you to start again, to continue your species. And there is always one who will lead you in the right direction. Show you a way to live that is…good. Most of the time you kill them."

"Why bother with us? It sounds like we're beyond redemption if you have to keep sorting us out." Bitterness welled up inside Loveday, and she struggled to swallow it back down. How dare he cull human beings like deer?

"Your species is capable of the most beautiful things. Your art is something we could never achieve." He looked at Ellery's body. "The sacrifices you make for each other out of love. We prefer you alive. Except now. This time you have taken things to the brink. This is your last chance, and so it is imperative Dani survives. This time, there will be no more beginnings. We are hoping your love for each other will be enough."

"Love?" Loveday sneered. "What do you know about love? What does anyone? Ellery did. Ellery knew about love, and look what happened," Loveday shouted. "Look what she got for her trouble."

"Loveday..." Dani said.

"No." Loveday stood, fisted her hands at her sides. Tears streamed down her cheeks. "She didn't deserve this. She was good and she was kind and she didn't deserve this."

"So bring her back," he said. Loveday realized he was looking at Dani. "Bring her back."

"What do you mean?" Dani asked.

"You know."

"I don't."

"Yes. You do."

Dani shook her head. Loveday looked at her, and even in the dark she could tell Dani knew something.

"Dani," he said. Not unkindly.

"I'm scared."

"What exactly can she do?" Loveday asked.

"Great things. She can lead you to the light. But she must be brave."

"What...how do I bring her back?" Dani had drawn up her knees. She was so young. She looked between them.

"You know," he said again.

Loveday went to her. "Please, Dani. If there's something you can do."

Dani nodded. "I'll try." She stood up and went to Ellery's body. Knelt down and moved the blanket away from her face. She let out a sob. She held her hands out over Ellery, palms flat and fingers stretched.

Then her hands began to glow. They lit up the interior of the lorry. And then Ellery began to glow. The light from Dani's hands spread out and filled the lorry. It settled over Loveday like a warm blanket, and she pulled it around her, breathed it in. For the first time in years she felt happy. Truly happy.

"Oh," she said. "The light is love."

Over in the corner, Ellery sat up.

Chapter Fifty

Ellery looked around. It was bright in here, and both Loveday and Dani were looking at her in wonder. To her right sat a tall thin pale man. No, he looked like a man, but that wasn't what he was.

Then she was hit full force by Rocky, Loveday, and Dani. Even Claude rubbed up against her. She fell backward but they didn't let up.

"What's going on? Hey, let me up." She laughed. She felt happy, light. They moved off her but didn't let go. "Why are you crying? Loveday? What's wrong?"

Loveday reached out and stroked her face. It was like she couldn't believe Ellery was really there. Then she kissed her full on the mouth. Ellery remembered. She had died. She remembered the feeling of failure which swamped her when she realized she wouldn't be able to save them. The way she gripped Terry's ankle as she lay dying, the material of his trousers rough against her fingers. He shook her off and walked away.

Ellery clung to Loveday, broke the kiss, and rested her forehead against hers. "I'm sorry. I didn't know—"

Loveday kissed her again. Beside them, Dani cleared her throat. "It's getting a bit awkward now."

Ellery laughed, pulled away from Loveday, and pulled Dani to her. She kissed the top of her head and ruffled her hair. "I have no idea what you did, but thank you."

Dani leaned back and shrugged. "You're welcome. I would have done it sooner if I'd known."

"We still have things to talk about," the strange man who wasn't really a man said.

Loveday huffed. "Can you not just give us one minute of happiness? Haven't we earned it?"

"It's not about what you've earned. It's about what you must do now," he said.

"We already know. Head north, save Dani," Loveday mimicked.

"She's waiting for you up there. And she will kill you." He ignored her.

Ellery stroked her hand down Dani's back when she shivered. "How do we make sure that doesn't happen?" she asked.

❖

Loveday kicked away twigs and loose rocks. She started putting the tent up. Dani was helping Ellery take the cast off Rocky's leg. She'd already put her tent up.

They'd walked all of yesterday into a town. All their possessions had been lost in the fire. Rocky and Claude seemed to enjoy their new upgraded pram.

Loveday was nervous. She planned to tell Ellery tonight. She'd wanted to yesterday, but there was no privacy. Telling someone you loved them should be done in private. In case they don't feel the same, so they can let you down gently. And Ellery would let her down gently. She pegged the guide ropes on the tent and tightened them so they stretched taut. There.

Loveday had watched her carefully since her...resurrection she supposed it was. She was the same Ellery. Maybe a bit quieter. Maybe a little more serious. Loveday wanted to ask her if she'd felt anything, if she'd seen a white light. She wanted to know what happened when you died, but most of all she wanted to know if Ellery loved her back.

"Hey, look at Rocky," Dani called.

Loveday forced a smile as she watched him dart from Dani to Ellery, wagging his tail and trying to lick them.

"Good boy," she called, and he came bounding over. He jumped up on his back legs and she scratched behind his ears.

Claude sauntered past them all, completely uninterested in Rocky's recovery, and disappeared into the tent for his pre-dinner nap.

"How much longer, do you think, before we get there?" Dani asked around a mouthful of pasta.

Ellery had her mess tin balanced on her lap, spoon in one hand, map in the other, brow furrowed. "Because we're sticking to the B roads, probably another three or four days."

"Why?" Loveday asked Dani.

Dani shrugged and stuffed another spoonful of food in her mouth. "This is it. Isn't it? Our last few days before everything changes again."

No one answered her. The Keeper had told them the plan. It was up to them now. Them and their faith in each other. And Dani.

❖

Ellery opened her sleeping bag and climbed inside. Loveday had been quiet all evening. She'd refused to meet Ellery's eyes, and Ellery wondered if she was freaked out about the whole dying and coming back to life thing.

Should she ask? Or leave it alone? Loveday hated to be put on the spot or talk about things before she was ready.

"We need to talk," Loveday said.

"Okay." Ellery braced herself. She faced Loveday who was sitting in her own sleeping bag, picking at a loose thread in the stitching.

"I'm not sure how to start," Loveday said.

"Try starting from the beginning," Ellery said softly. Whatever came next she would be okay with.

Loveday looked up, then away. Took a deep breath. "I'm not good at this."

Ellery waited.

"You know I like you. It's just that…"

Ellery's heart sank. "Did the whole dying thing freak you out? Because I can sleep in Dani's tent—"

"No." Loveday reached across and clutched Ellery's hand. Then, softer, "No, that's not it."

"You're regretting the whole kissing thing? Because—"

"Ellery, shut up." Loveday squeezed her hand.

"Sorry. Serious conversations make me nervous."

Loveday laughed. "Me too. Look, what I'm trying to say, and it's probably not the right time—God, you probably aren't even interested, or you aren't any more. I mean, you've been through a lot and—"

"Jesus Christ, Loveday, will you just spit it out."

"I'm pretty sure I love you. I'm in love with you, I mean. Which is mad because we've only known each other a short time. But it feels real."

Ellery sat in stunned silence. She willed her mouth to move, form words, anything. She did not expect this.

"Oh, shit, I've ruined everything, haven't I? Look, we can just forget it if you want." Loveday tried to pull her hand away. It brought Ellery to her senses. She tugged Loveday closer.

"Is this because I died? Like, some kind of reaction to it?"

Loveday's eyes narrowed and Ellery realized she'd said the wrong thing. "Ellery. I don't go around telling people I love them as a *reaction* to them dying. Well...you know what I mean."

"Loveday, after we kissed, you told me you didn't feel that way about me."

"I lied," Loveday said and tugged her hand away. "I was scared and I lied. I tried not to love you, I really tried. I didn't want to love you, and I tried so hard not to."

"What changed?" Ellery's head was spinning.

"When you died, I realized I was lost without you. When I thought I wouldn't see you again, I understood. And I was so angry with myself." Loveday looked up, met Ellery's eyes. "Because I would never be able to tell you."

Ellery didn't speak. She didn't know what to say.

"I understand if you don't feel the same way. Or if I pushed you away. I know I'm hard work. I'm guarded. I'm closed off. I just wanted you to know. I wanted—"

Ellery had heard enough. She leaned forward, took Loveday's face between her hands, and kissed her. Loveday's arms came around her shoulders, held on.

Ellery broke the kiss. "For the avoidance of doubt, I love you too. It probably is way too soon, but it's how I feel, all the same. One thing I've learned recently is that life is short. Why waste time?"

Loveday stroked Ellery's neck, smiled, and rested her forehead against Ellery's. "Agreed."

"Also—"

Loveday put her fingers against Ellery's lips. "No more talking. Time to be shush."

Ellery laughed. She kissed Loveday again. She pushed against her until Loveday was on her back and Ellery hovered over her. She leaned back slightly to take in the sight of her. She was beautiful.

Ellery stroked Loveday's cheek, brushed her thumb over Loveday's bottom lip. This was everything she needed.

She lowered herself onto Loveday, kissed her again. Felt Loveday's thighs come around her and squeeze her hips. Ellery started to rock into her, and Loveday sighed and reached for her shoulders to pull her closer. She gripped hard as Ellery ran her lips over Loveday's collarbone, over the soft skin behind her ear.

Ellery slipped her hand under Loveday's jumper and cupped her breast. She stroked her nipple over the fabric of her bra. Loveday groaned and arched into the touch. "Please," she whispered, and something came loose inside Ellery. Roughly, she pulled Loveday's jumper over her head and threw it aside. She was desperate to feel skin on skin.

Loveday took off her bra while Ellery struggled out of her jumper, T-shirt, jeans, and underwear. When they came together again it was in a crush of lips, hands squeezing, stroking, rubbing, and gripping. Finally Ellery couldn't stand it any more. She slid down Loveday's body, taking Loveday's jeans and underwear with her. In a moment, her mouth was on Loveday. She buried her face in her, breathed in the delicate scent, and groaned. Her head spun and her hands shook. She was really here. Loveday was really here. And they were doing this.

Ellery started to lick her. She explored every fold and dip. She ran her tongue over Loveday's opening, and Loveday bucked, gripped Ellery's head, and pushed against her. Hard. Ellery took Loveday's clit into her mouth and began to suck gently. It wasn't enough. She needed to be closer. Ellery slid two fingers inside Loveday, and Loveday began to move. With hard thrusts and deep moans she pushed herself onto Ellery's fingers, took her deep, and then expelled her again. Over and over and over again until she stopped, stiffened, and cried out. Ellery bore down on her clit and sucked it hard. Loveday cried out again, then went still.

"Fucking hell," Loveday said.

Ellery gave her one last kiss, which made Loveday flinch, then crawled up to lie beside her.

Loveday turned towards Ellery so she was pressed against her side. She trailed her hand from her chest down to her belly button, then ran her fingers over the soft hair at the juncture of her thighs. Ellery groaned and Loveday smiled.

Loveday traced Ellery's outer lips with one finger. Ellery parted her legs, and Loveday took the hint. She used two fingers to massage Ellery's clit. Ellery was so wet, and Loveday groaned when Ellery grabbed her hand and pressed Loveday's fingers harder against her. Ellery began to move her hips and her breathing became heavy. Loveday could tell she was on the edge, but she didn't want Ellery to come before she could taste her. Who knew if they'd get this chance again?

Loveday slid down on the sleeping bag and took Ellery into her mouth. Ellery clutched Loveday's head and ground herself against Loveday. Loveday could tell she was losing control. She remembered thinking about how it might feel to make the vet snap—it seemed like an age ago now—and she was about to find out.

Ellery came hard and without warning. She gripped Loveday's head and held it against her as she thrust against Loveday's mouth. Then she was still. The only sound was Ellery's laboured breathing.

"Fucking hell," Ellery said, echoing Loveday's earlier statement.

Loveday laughed. "I know."

Ellery pulled Loveday up and into her arms, and Loveday snuggled in. She tucked her head beneath Ellery's chin and smiled into her neck. Whatever happened next, at least they'd had this. And if they were lucky, they'd have it again. Forever.

Ellery whistled a made-up tune as she balanced a pan of water over the fire. The rain had finally let up, and the sun was shining. She could almost imagine she was on a camping trip. Almost. If she ignored the eyes that watched her from the trees, cold and calculating. They'd been on her when she woke up this morning with Loveday in her arms. They'd been on her when she got the fire going, tidied the camp, and washed.

They weren't far now. Maybe only a few more days until they

reached the base of Ben Nevis. Where they would have to face Rosemary Decker and the Children of the Ark. Ellery rubbed the back of her neck and shook off the feeling of dread. She would enjoy these last few days. None of them knew what would happen next. They had to have faith, and that was easier for her than for Loveday, she knew.

"Gross. You had sex, didn't you?"

Ellery jumped at the sound of Dani's voice and nearly kicked over the pan of water. "Bloody hell, Dani. It's rude to sneak up on people." She held her hand to her heart.

"Sorry."

Except she didn't look sorry, she looked smug in the way only teenagers could.

"You did, though, didn't you?"

"Did what?" Ellery busied herself making coffee.

Dani huffed and sat on a tarp she'd laid out. "Why are you being so difficult? You and Loveday had sex last night. Didn't you?"

Shit, had Dani heard them? That would be mortifying.

"Don't worry, I didn't hear anything. You've been whistling for ages, and you look really pleased with yourself."

Dani grinned and Ellery struggled not to match it. "I don't know what you're talking about. But you can make yourself useful and fill up that pan again for porridge."

With a theatrical sigh, Dani dragged herself up and did as she was asked. "You can tell me, you know. I'm the saviour of mankind, after all."

"Then I shouldn't have to. You should already know, O omnipotent one." Ellery nudged Dani's hip with hers as she carried a mug of coffee back to the tent. Dani's giggle followed her inside.

She put the coffee down near the entrance and held the flap as Claude sauntered out. She stretched out alongside Loveday and watched her for a moment.

"What?" Loveday cracked an eye open.

"Nothing. I just wanted to look at you." Ellery placed a kiss on Loveday's forehead.

"Soppy git." Loveday reached up and pulled Ellery's face towards her. "My breath is horrible, but I want to kiss you."

"I don't care," Ellery replied and gave Loveday a long slow kiss.

She loved exploring Loveday's mouth. It was warm and soft and pretty much the best thing. "I also brought you coffee." Ellery pulled back slightly.

"You're an angel."

"Pretty much."

"Give it." Loveday pushed Ellery away and she laughed.

Outside, a loud rumble started, shaking the ground beneath them. "Dani," they both said at the same time.

CHAPTER FIFTY-ONE

Rosemary watched as crates of food, water, medicine, and weapons were loaded onto the *Ark 2*. This was the last of it. The hangar roof had been opened that morning and the scaffolding was being dismantled. Not long now.

The idea was that as the water level rose, so would the *Ark 2*, until all land was completely submerged. They would sail to where the land sat higher than in the UK and make their new home there. It might take a while to find the perfect place, but the *Ark 2* would more than meet their needs for a long time to come.

Things had settled down. Everyone who wanted to leave had left, and only the core faithful remained. *Let the rest drown.* She didn't want them in her new world anyway. The girl would be here any day. She was walking with her friends—a slow march to death. Rosemary would kill them all. They would either be captured by the scouting party or walk straight to her. Either way the outcome would be the same.

She would leave shortly to meet them. Not too far, she wanted to be able to get back in case the storm came early. But far enough that she would be the first to greet them. To see the looks on their faces when they realized everything was lost, and they'd chosen the wrong side. Them and everyone who had left or been neutralized. She'd shown time and again that she was stronger than all of them, smarter than all of them. She was a servant of God, His chosen one, and the new world was just around the corner.

❖

The animals were far enough away from them that it was safe to watch, though Loveday was still a little nervous. They were used to the occasional stampedes now, as animals of all shapes and sizes made their way north. This, though, this was something else. More like the first time outside the supermarket. There had to be over a thousand of them. They moved too quickly to count and with one purpose. Survival.

Time was running out. She felt it just as the animals did. They were running from certain destruction but was it to something much worse? She didn't know. None of them did. It was almost laughable. They were outnumbered, and this Rosemary Decker was prepared and ready for them.

Loveday sighed. The stampede was thinning out. Some of the slower, smaller animals ambled past. Loveday stood with Ellery and Dani, and they watched until the last animal was out of sight.

"We'd better make a move, then," Ellery said and turned to start packing their stuff away.

"Tell me why we have to walk straight to her. Why can't we sneak past and get to the top of the mountain?" Loveday asked.

"You know why, Loveday," Ellery replied as she clicked the clasps on her rucksack into place. "This is how it has to be. Have a little faith." And then Ellery winked at her.

Loveday shook her head, smiled. "A little faith? You'll forgive me for not being as on board as you with this stupid plan."

"It's not stupid," Dani piped up. "There's no real way past her, and we have to get to the top of the mountain to avoid the floods."

"I know, but relying on—" Loveday's mouth snapped shut. She cocked her head and listened. Were those voices or just her imagination? She looked at Ellery who seemed to be listening too. Loveday strained her ears.

Ellery held her fingers to her lips and gestured for Loveday and Dani to follow her deeper into the trees behind them. Loveday went to pick up her pack and Ellery shook her head.

She heard voices again, carried on the wind. The scuffle of boots on loose ground. Lots of them. The rucksacks would only slow them down. Loveday followed Ellery and Dani into the woods. The pets followed silently, but Loveday grabbed up Rocky anyway to pre-empt any heroics on his part.

After five minutes or so Ellery stopped. They had travelled quite far into what was quite a thick woods.

"I think we should keep going. I brought the map, and the trees should open out onto what looks like a track that joins up with a road heading north. Straight to the base of Ben Nevis," Ellery said.

"What about our stuff? That's a long walk, and with no food or water it's going to be hard," Loveday said.

"If we go back that way, we risk running into an ambush. They'll expect us to go back for our stuff. They might be waiting," Ellery said.

"Loveday, are they waiting? Can you tell?" Dani asked her.

She shook her head. "That other thing is blocking everything. I can feel it. It's been watching us, and that's all I can sense."

Dani nodded. "It's been doing it on purpose."

"I think so," Loveday said.

"So we keep walking. Going back is too risky," Ellery said. "We have our coats and that's the main thing. We might be lucky and find another camping shop along the way."

Loveday peered over her shoulder at the map. A great expanse of nothingness awaited them for the next fifty miles at least. The chances of finding a camping shop were remote. And they were still likely to run into Rosemary Decker before they even got the full fifty miles anyway.

But Ellery was right. They couldn't chance going back. "Can we maybe pick up a B road or something into a town?" she asked.

"No, they'll be tracking us once they find our stuff. They know where we're going. I don't think we should risk a main road," Ellery said.

Loveday blew out a breath and struggled to keep her cool. "Ellery, we are not going to be able to walk fifty miles without food or water or shelter. Nor will the pets. We'll all die."

"We won't make it that far anyway. I think Rosemary Decker will be waiting for us before we make it too much further," Dani said.

Loveday looked at her. She didn't seem scared or worried. She looked calm. Like Ellery, she trusted the Keeper—she had faith. Loveday wasn't sure she felt so confident. Still, what could she do? Not much. Her fate was very much out of her own hands, so fuck it.

They began to walk.

CHAPTER FIFTY-TWO

The head of the search party looked around. The girl and the others must have heard them coming. She'd told her team to keep quiet, but that had been an exercise in futility. Unlike her, they weren't trained. They talked and joked and stomped about. The girl and her friends couldn't have got far, though. And without their kit they wouldn't last five minutes out here.

She ordered several of the others to look through the bags for any maps, for anything that might indicate which route they planned to take. Although, if it were her, she would change her plan.

"Diana?"

She turned to face one of the search party team. "Find something?"

"No. If they had maps, they took them. Everything else is here, though. Including dog food."

They had a dog. That wasn't great news. Dogs were dangerous, unpredictable. Of course it depended on the size of the dog.

"And a cat," he said.

"What?"

"They have a cat too. Looks like they push them around in the pram. We didn't find any sign of a baby."

She looked over at the pram, parked tidily against a tree. What kind of weirdos were they? Pushing animals around in prams? At least she knew the dog couldn't be very big. Assuming they only had one dog. But people who pushed their animals around in prams were not to be trusted, and she'd need to be careful.

"Right." She addressed the rest of the team. "Let's head through the woods. See if we can't catch them up."

One by one, the team made their way into the trees.

❖

Ellery, Loveday, and Dani walked for two more days, drinking from streams when they found them and hoping they wouldn't get sick. They found a few houses dotted about and scavenged what food they could, slept in the unmade beds. They were exhausted. Between them, they took it in turns carrying the pets when they became too tired to walk—Claude more than Rocky. Ellery thought some of that was due more to laziness than actual tiredness.

They walked until they couldn't walk any more, desperate to stay ahead of the search party who were sure to be tracking them. The thing was still with them, jamming Loveday's psychic signal so she couldn't get a bead on them. Instead, they endured the cold, hateful eyes, the freezing temperatures, and the blisters.

They weren't in good shape. They all knew it, but none of them said it out loud. They walked on. Towards what, they didn't know, but certainly something worse than the people who hunted them.

Ben Nevis towered over them, looking much closer than it was. The mountain seemed to stretch for miles. It was fucking huge. The trees and woods had given way to bright green rolling fields and lakes. The rain had come again on the second day and didn't stop. Ellery knew this was it. The end. They were almost at the start of the beginning.

"There hasn't been a stampede for ages," Dani said as they trudged along a dirt track of sucking mud.

"Maybe all the animals got north already," Ellery puffed out.

"Maybe," Dani replied.

"Just our luck," Loveday said.

That was how their conversations went now. Short and disjointed. No one had the energy for more. At night, they tumbled into any bed they could find and fell into exhausted sleep. Even Rocky seemed lethargic.

The thing that followed them had finally gone. Ellery suspected it knew things were coming to an end now, that they were headed straight to Rosemary Decker where matters would be decided once and for all. For all of them. She could see the hangar in the distance with the *Ark 2* inside, she guessed. A dot on the landscape at the moment. Ellery thought they were no more than two days away from it.

They walked on.

On the second day they met Rosemary.

❖

For a moment, Loveday considered running. Her legs twitched and her feet itched to rise on their balls and take off. Rosemary Decker hadn't seen them yet, and maybe they could get past her. In the distance, the hangar towered over them, sleek and covered in shiny metal. Loveday guessed the *Ark 2* was inside. Maybe they could commandeer it. Go on a round-the-world cruise. Anything would be better than staying here and facing this and trusting an alien to come through for them.

"It's okay," Ellery whispered in her ear, her hand warm and sure on the small of Loveday's back. And she guessed it *was* okay. Win or lose they would stand together. Somehow, she'd gone from untrusting loner to sidekick to the saviour of woman- and mankind. What they were about to do was lunacy, but fuck it. At least she'd go down fighting. At least she'd make a stand for once in her life.

She stood next to Ellery with Dani between them. Up ahead, Rosemary Decker looked up from her spot at a campfire. Loveday thought she was reading a book. Not that it mattered. The people Rosemary was with noticed them about the same time, and they all stood up. Loveday counted eight. They were outnumbered, but they already knew that. Rocky began to growl low in his throat.

"Rosemary Decker?" Dani called out.

"Yes. You finally arrived," Rosemary replied, and Loveday almost laughed at how polite everyone was being.

Dani went to step forward and Loveday held her arm. "Don't. Not yet. Let them come closer."

"As you can see, you're outnumbered. You..." Rosemary turned to Loveday, and Loveday shivered under her gaze.

"What?" Loveday said.

"I've got no quarrel with you—you can go. No one will stop you. Carry on north or head into the hangar, it's up to you."

Loveday felt Ellery's eyes on her. She turned to meet them, fully expecting to see uncertainty in them. She was a coward, after all. Had been since the vanishing. Had been since she could remember. Of course Ellery would expect her to leave them.

Loveday braced herself and met Ellery's eyes. What she saw took her breath away. Trust. There was nothing but trust. Something clicked inside her, the last piece she had been holding back. She wasn't a coward, she wasn't untrustworthy. They could rely on her. She wouldn't leave them.

"Stick it up your arse, Rosemary," Loveday called out in a pleasant tone, and Dani sniggered beside her.

"Very well, then. You'll die with your friends."

The group around Rosemary split in half, and Loveday could tell they would try to flank them.

"Ellery, we need to spread out. Stop them corralling us."

Ellery nodded and moved away. Loveday and Dani followed suit, made almost a semicircle.

"What's the point?" Rosemary asked. "You're just prolonging the inevitable."

Loveday ignored her and concentrated on keeping the others from flanking her. She dared a glance at Ellery and hoped for some sort of signal. Ellery wouldn't look at her. She had her head cocked to the side, and Loveday realized she was listening. Suddenly, she dropped to the ground.

"What are you doing?" Rosemary asked.

Loveday watched as Ellery ignored Rosemary and held her palm flat against the dirt. Then she looked up and smiled. "It's time."

A low rumbling started. The earth began to shake, and Loveday almost fell over. The rumbling became a ferocious thundering, and several of Rosemary's people fell to the ground. Loveday watched as they scrambled back up and hurried over to Rosemary.

"What's happening?" Rosemary demanded. "What are you doing? Stop this. I demand that you stop this immediately."

Loveday reached for Dani, grabbed her hand, and pulled her against her body. Loveday couldn't help but laugh. The look on Rosemary Decker's face was priceless. Shock, fear, and outrage appeared on her face in turn, like someone was cranking the handle on a one-armed bandit.

"You stop this now," she screamed, but the deafening thunder only got louder. It rolled across the valley and shook the ground so violently that Loveday wondered if the force of it would split the earth.

"What is that?" Rosemary screamed. "What on God's earth is *that*?"

Loveday didn't turn to look. She knew what it was, what was coming.

Rosemary turned and ran. Her people stood for a moment, looked around like lost sheep, and finally followed her. Loveday knew it was too late for any of them.

She turned in the direction Rosemary had been looking and saw it for herself. A huge cloud of dust—almost a fog—rolled towards them like a fist. It stretched to the horizon in every direction, and inside it she could just about make out the odd animal. Deer, horses, cows, and the odd dog. It was an army. Breathtaking. And they would never outrun it.

Loveday turned back again and saw Rosemary had come to the same conclusion. She pushed her people in front of her in an attempt to hide behind them as the stampede bore down.

Loveday held Dani tight, closed her eyes, and prayed.

❖

Ellery stood, wiped her palms on her trousers, and took a deep breath. She faced the stampede, widened her stance, and held her arms out in front of her, sweaty palms up, fingers spread. She'd already died once, and she didn't want to die again, but she had to trust that this would work. She had to.

The stampede bore down. Dust filled her mouth and stung her eyes and clogged her throat. She lost her footing and scrambled to regain it—she couldn't afford to fall. They were so close, and then a moment later they were upon her.

❖

Loveday shielded her eyes from the dust and managed to make out the animals parting like a sea around Ellery. She almost cried with relief and, at the same time, couldn't believe what she was seeing. They didn't even touch Ellery, just moved around her without losing speed or momentum. They kept the gap in place as they approached her and Dani and left them untouched too.

The Keeper was right. It had told the truth. Loveday turned to see whether Rosemary would be spared as well. As she did, she tripped and fell.

Her knees hit the ground and she gritted her teeth against the pain. She scrambled backward out of the path of the animals but too late. She felt a heavy thump to the side of her head and the world went dark.

❖

Ellery brushed back the hair from Loveday's head. "Loveday? Loveday, wake up."

Ellery was frantic. She couldn't lose Loveday. Not now. Not when it was all over. She could still hear the thundering of hooves as the stampede moved away. "Loveday? Loveday, it's me. Wake up." God, she had to wake up. She had to. Ellery couldn't go on without her.

"Please, Loveday. Please don't leave me," Ellery whispered.

Suddenly remembering her training, she felt for a pulse. She almost cried when she found it, strong and regular. Thank God, thank God. Tears blurred Ellery's eyes. Now if Loveday would only wake up.

Loveday groaned, opened her eyes. Relief washed over Ellery in a tidal wave.

"Thank God. Are you okay?" Ellery asked.

"Dani?" Loveday scrambled away from Ellery and sat up. "I lost her. Where is she?"

"I don't know." Fuck. Ellery looked around. She got up and ran to where bodies of Rosemary's people were scattered about, bloodied and trampled. Rosemary wasn't among them. Nor was Dani.

"I think Rosemary Decker has her," Ellery said. She felt sick. How could she have let Rosemary take her? What was wrong with her?

"It's not your fault," Loveday said and reached up to hold Ellery's hand. "It's not." She kissed Loveday's palm. "But we need to find her."

"Come on, I think I know where she's taken her." Ellery stood and helped Loveday to her feet.

"The hangar," Loveday said.

Ellery nodded and squeezed Loveday's hand. "Come on."

❖

Rosemary carried the girl up the scaffolding. She didn't have much time before the other two realized what had happened. She had to kill her quickly.

When the stampede came, Rosemary was buried beneath the bodies of her people. They were crushed to death, but she survived. It was another example of how God was protecting her, urging her onwards. Once she killed the girl and the girl's friends, the storm would come. All sin would be washed away. All sinners cast out. The righteous would inherit the ear—

She slipped on the ladder and almost fell. Sweat dripped into her eyes and maybe blood. Her head hurt and she was positive at least two of her ribs were broken. God would look after her.

She hefted the girl into a better position on her shoulders and continued climbing. It was slow and arduous work, but she needed to get all the way to the top. God had told her—get to the top, and throw the child off. It was simple work, but Rosemary's lungs ached and her throat was raw from the dust outside.

Inside the hangar, Ellery expected to be stopped. But there was hardly anyone there. Four or five people stood by the *Ark 2*, staring up. Ellery followed their gaze and her stomach lurched painfully when she saw what they were looking at.

Rosemary Decker was climbing the scaffolding, which wobbled and was detached in places. Shit. The thing looked like it would give way any minute. She had to get to Dani.

She hurried over to the small group gathered. "Excuse me, is there another way up?" she asked and pointed at the boat.

A woman turned to her. "There was a lift, but they've taken it away. I'd leave Rosemary to it if I were you, though—she's fucking mental. We were going to get out with most of the others, but we've left it too late."

Ellery ignored her and ran over to the scaffolding. She was running out of time. She had to get up there. She just hoped the scaffolding would hold her.

"I'm coming with you," Loveday said.

"Loveday, no. You've been through enough, and I think you're concussed."

"But—"

"The more time I stand down here and argue with you, the further away Rosemary's getting."

She almost laughed at the furrow in Loveday's brow.

"Fine. Go. Be careful."

"I will." Ellery planted a quick kiss on Loveday's mouth and began to climb.

Rosemary had a good lead on her. She wasn't far from the top. There wasn't much time left. Why wasn't there ever enough time?

The scaffolding was loose in places where it was being dismantled. Ellery tested the stairs as she made her way up. It felt like it was taking forever. But soon, she was running up them. They swayed and wobbled under her feet.

Sweat dripped into her eyes, and her legs burned. It was a long climb. How Rosemary was doing it carrying another person, she didn't know.

As Ellery's foot came down on a step, a piece of scaffolding came loose. She reached out, praying, and managed to grab hold of the next bit. Using all her strength she swung herself up and onto the next platform. There was a loud crash from below. Ellery didn't dare look down. She kept climbing.

When she was almost near the top, she heard a scream.

Ellery looked up.

Rosemary was trying to force Dani over the edge. Dani was fighting and kicking, but it was clear she was losing the battle.

"Leave her alone," Ellery shouted and sprinted the rest of the way up the stairs.

When she reached the top platform, she saw Rosemary had managed to get Dani over the other side and was trying to pry her fingers off the metal bar, the only thing stopping her from falling.

"Get away from her," Ellery shouted.

Rosemary barely glanced up. She lowered her head, and Ellery saw she meant to bite Dani's fingers.

Ellery moved quickly.

She gripped Rosemary around the neck from behind and tried to drag her backward.

Rosemary elbowed Ellery in the ribs, and she fought against the instinct to pull away. The pain was sharp.

Rosemary was strong, much stronger than she looked. She swung around and managed to land a punch on Ellery's chin.

Ellery lost her grip and dropped to her knees. Her head swam, and she fought to stay conscious. It took everything she had. Ellery got unsteadily to her feet and made a lunge for Rosemary, swinging her arms out in the hope of grabbing something.

Rosemary cried out and Ellery realized she had hold of her hair. She yanked hard and Rosemary fell backward into her. They crashed to the floor in a tangle of limbs. Rosemary was fast and focused. She jumped up and made straight for Dani. But Ellery was quick too. She reached for Rosemary again and grabbed her in a bear hug. She used all her strength to spin Rosemary around and push her to the floor.

Rosemary sprang up fast like a cage fighter and they circled each other.

"Give up and go away. I'll let you live. I only want her," Rosemary said.

"Never."

"Then you'll die too."

Suddenly, Rosemary lunged at her and Ellery knew she planned to bundle her over the edge of the scaffolding. At the last minute, Ellery moved to the side. She used all the strength she had to push Rosemary in the back and help her over the edge.

Rosemary screamed, an angry sound, full of hate and fury.

Then she was silent.

Ellery looked over the edge of the platform. Rosemary had fallen all the way to the ground where her broken body lay sprawled.

Ellery went to Dani who had managed to climb back over and onto the platform.

"Are you okay?" she asked.

Dani nodded. "I'm okay. We have to leave. We need to get to higher ground."

Ellery grimaced. She was tired and dirty and the thought of more climbing almost did her in. Swiftly on the heels of that was the knowledge she'd just killed someone. Her legs buckled and she gripped the rail tight. She'd done it to save Dani, but a life was a life, and she had just taken one.

Ellery felt a hand on the small of her back. "I'm sorry," Dani said. "Can't you bring her back? Like you did with me?" she asked.

Dani shook her head. "No. I'm sorry."

Ellery nodded. "I understand."

But did she? What made her life more valuable than Rosemary's? Who had the right to decide which life was worth saving and which was best left in a broken heap on a cold concrete floor?

"I'm sorry," Dani said again.

"I know you are. So am I," Ellery said and stood back from the rail. The thought of Loveday waiting for her saved her from complete despair.

"It's not long now. There's not much further to go." Dani put her hand on Ellery's arm and Ellery found the strength from somewhere to nod.

They would walk on. They'd keep going. They'd already won.

EPILOGUE

The storm came just as they reached a makeshift camp part way up Ben Nevis. A group of survivors—some from Rosemary's hangar but most from the rest of the country—had set up tents and campfires in a semi-sheltered part of the mountain.

The survivors, including Ellery, Loveday, and Dani, stayed there for several weeks. That was the time it took for the storm to eventually die down. Just like in their dreams, when they hiked down to look, they could see the water level had risen so high that it covered most of the lower land.

All in all there were probably a few hundred people in their camp, and they knew there were more scattered over Ben Nevis and the higher ground.

Rosemary's hangar and her boat had been swept away before the water receded again. Nothing of their old world was left.

Loveday sat outside the tent she shared with Ellery. Dani had the one next door, and the pets moved from one to the other depending on their moods.

"I found some mushrooms." Ellery sat down beside her and held out a fistful of them.

"No way am I eating those." Loveday shook her head.

"They're safe."

"Says who?"

"Nathan."

Loveday rolled her eyes. Nathan was Ellery's new friend and survival guru. He seemed nice enough, but one episode of Bear Grylls did not a survivalist make.

"I'm not touching them and neither are you. And if Nathan's got any sense he won't either."

"Fine," Ellery said and put them back in her pocket. "Where's Dani?"

"She made a new friend." Loveday grinned.

Although most people knew about Dani and that Rosemary had wanted to kill her, she'd asked Loveday and Ellery not to mention some of her more unusual talents. Though Loveday thought with idiots like Nathan eating random mushrooms, they'd need them soon.

"The Butterworth girl?" Ellery asked.

"The very one. They've been spending a lot of time together. It's sweet."

"Whatever you do, don't tell Dani you think it's sweet."

Loveday waved her hand. "Of course not. I'm not a total idiot."

"When did they head off?" Ellery asked.

Loveday squinted at the sun. She was still having trouble telling the time by it. "About an hour ago. Why?" She looked at Ellery.

Ellery waggled her eyebrows and nodded towards the tent.

Loveday's stomach flipped, and she grinned. Living in such close quarters with a teenager didn't leave much alone time. They had to take it where they could get it.

"Race you," Loveday said.

They zoomed into the tent, laughing.

About the Author

Eden lives in London with her rescue cat. When she's not working or writing, she can be found among the weeds in her allotment, trying to make vegetables grow.

Books Available From Bold Strokes Books

30 Dates in 30 Days by Elle Spencer. In this sophisticated contemporary romance, Veronica Welch is a busy lawyer who tries to find love the fast way—thirty dates in thirty days. (978-1-63555-498-4)

Finding Sky by Cass Sellars. Skylar Addison's search for a career intersects with her new boss's search for butterflies, but Skylar can't forgive Jess's intrusion into her life. Romance is the last thing they expect. (978-1-63555-521-9)

Hammers, Strings, and Beautiful Things by Morgan Lee Miller. While on tour with the biggest pop star in the world, rising musician Blair Bennett falls in love for the first time while coping with loss and depression. (978-1-63555-538-7)

Heart of a Killer by Yolanda Wallace. Contract killer Santana Masters's only interest is her next assignment—until a chance meeting with a beautiful stranger tempts her to change her ways. (978-1-63555-547-9)

Leading the Witness by Carsen Taite. When defense attorney Catherine Landauer reluctantly becomes the key witness in prosecutor Starr Rio's latest criminal trial, their hearts, careers, and lives may be at risk. (978-1-63555-512-7)

No Experience Required by Kimberly Cooper Griffin. Izzy Treadway has resigned herself to a life without romance because of her bipolar illness but wonders what she's gotten herself into when she agrees to write a book about love. (978-1-63555-561-5)

One Walk in Winter by Georgia Beers. Olivia Santini and Hayley Boyd Markham might be rivals at work, but they discover that lonely hearts often find company in the most unexpected of places. (978-1-63555-541-7)

The Inn at Netherfield Green by Aurora Rey. Advertising executive Lauren Montgomery and gin distiller Camden Crawley don't agree on anything except saving the Rose & Crown, the old English pub that's brought them together. (978-1-63555-445-8)

Top of Her Game by M. Ullrich. When it comes to life on the field and matters of the heart, losing isn't an option for pro athletes Kenzie Shaw and Sutton Flores. (978-1-63555-500-4)

Vanished by Eden Darry. First came the storm, and then the blinding white light that made everyone in town disappear. Another storm is coming, and Ellery and Loveday must find the chosen one or they won't survive. (978-1-63555-437-3)

All She Wants by Larkin Rose. Marci Jones and Tessa Dalton get more than they bargained for when their plans for a one-night stand turn into an opportunity for love. (978-1-63555-476-2)

Beautiful Accidents by Erin Zak. Stevie Adams doesn't believe in fate, not after losing her parents in a car crash. But she's about to discover that sometimes the best things in life happen purely by accident. (978-1-63555-497-7)

Before Now by Joy Argento. The instant Delaney Peyton and Jade Taylor meet, they sense a connection neither can explain. Can they overcome a betrayal that spans the centuries to reignite a love that can't be broken? (978-1-63555-525-7)

Breathe by Cari Hunter. Paramedic Jemima Pardon's chronic bad luck seems to be improving when she meets police officer Rosie Jones. But they face a battle to survive before they can find love. (978-1-63555-523-3)

Double-Crossed by Ali Vali. Hired thief and killer Reed Gable finds something in her scope that will change her life forever when she gets a contract to end casino accountant Brinley Myers's life. (978-1-63555-302-4)

False Horizons by CJ Birch. Jordan and Ash struggle with different views on the alien agenda and must find their way back to each other before they're swallowed up by a centuries-old war. Third in the New Horizons series. (978-1-63555-519-6)

Legacy by Charlotte Greene. In this paranormal mystery, five women hike to a remote cabin deep inside a national park—and unsettling events suggest that they should have stayed home. (978-1-63555-490-8)

Somewhere Along the Way by Kathleen Knowles. When Maxine Cooper moves to San Francisco during the summer of 1981, she learns that wherever you run, you cannot escape yourself. (978-1-63555-383-3)

Blood of the Pack by Jenny Frame. When Alpha of the Scottish pack Kenrick Wulver visits the Wolfgangs, she falls for Zaria Lupa, a wolf on the run. (978-1-63555-431-1)

Cause of Death by Sheri Lewis Wohl. Medical student Vi Akiak and K9 Search and Rescue officer Kate Renard must work together to find a killer before they end up the next targets. In the race for survival, they discover that love may be the biggest risk of all. (978-1-63555-441-0)

Chasing Sunset by Missouri Vaun. Hijinks and mishaps ensue as Iris and Finn set off on a road trip adventure, chasing the sunset, and falling in love along the way. (978-1-63555-454-0)

Double Down by MB Austin. When an unlikely friendship with Spanish pop star Erlea turns deeper, Celeste, in-house physician for the hotel hosting Erlea's show, has a choice to make—run or double down on love. (978-1-63555-423-6)

Party of Three by Sandy Lowe. Three friends are in for a wild night at billionaire heiress Eleanor McGregor's twenty-fifth birthday party. Love, lust, and doing the right thing, even when it hurts, turn the evening into one that will change their lives forever. (978-1-63555-246-1)

Sit. Stay. Love. by Karis Walsh. City girl Alana Brendt and country vet Tegan Evans both know they don't belong together. Only problem is, they're falling in love. (978-1-63555-439-7)

Where the Lies Hide by Renee Roman. As P.I. Camdyn Stark gets closer to solving the case, will her dark secrets and the lies she's buried jeopardize her future with the quietly beautiful Sarah Peters? (978-1-63555-371-0)

Beautiful Dreamer by Melissa Brayden. With love on the line, can Devyn Winters find it in her heart to stay in the small town of Dreamer's Bay, the one place she swore she'd never remain? (978-1-63555-305-5)

Create a Life to Love by Erin Zak. When sixteen-year-old Beth shows up at her birth mother's door, three lives will change forever. (978-1-63555-425-0)

Deadeye by Meredith Doench. Stranded while hunting the serial predator Deadeye, Special Agent Luce Hansen fights for survival while her lover, forensic pathologist Harper Bennett, hunts for clues to Hansen's disappearance along the killer's trail. (978-1-63555-253-9)

Endangered by Michelle Larkin. Shapeshifters Officer Aspen Wolfe and Dr. Tora Madigan fight their growing attraction as they work together to destroy a secret government agency that exterminates their kind. (978-1-63555-377-2)

Incognito by VK Powell. The only thing Evan Spears is focused on is capturing a fleeing murder suspect until wild card Frankie Strong is added to her team and causes chaos on and off the job. (978-1-63555-389-5)

Insult to Injury by Gun Brooke. After losing everything, Gail Owen withdraws to her old farmhouse and finds a destitute young woman, Romi Shepherd, living in a secret room. (978-1-63555-323-9)

Just One Moment by Dena Blake. If you were given the chance to have the love of your life back, could you ignore everything that went wrong and start over again? (978-1-63555-387-1)

Scene of the Crime by MJ Williamz. Cullen Mathew finds herself caught between the woman she thinks she loves but can no longer trust and a beautiful detective she can't stop thinking about who will stop at nothing to find the truth. (978-1-63555-405-2)

Fear of Falling by Georgia Beers. Singer Sophie James is ready to shake up her career, but her new manager, the gorgeous Dana Landon, has other ideas. (978-1-63555-443-4)

Daughter of No One by Sam Ledel. When their worlds are threatened, a princess and a village outcast must overcome their differences and embrace a budding attraction if they want to survive. (978-1-63555-427-4)